D1436484

He paused, trying to gauge her mood. 'Is there…anything else that's making you unhappy?'

Her sudden flush gave him his answer, but all she said was, 'No. Why should there be?'

He took a step closer. He couldn't go on pretending that he didn't care. 'Perhaps because you are not the only one forced to keep painful secrets.'

Her eyes widened. 'I don't know what you're talking about.'

'Don't you? You must know I'm drawn to you, Emma. That I think about you…far too much.'

He watched her eyes darken in pain. 'Lord Stewart, this is not a good idea.'

'Perhaps not,' he said quietly. 'My father asked me to counsel my brother as to the unsuitability of his relationship with your sister. I shudder to think what he would say if he knew I was also having to counsel myself against my feelings… for you.'

It had to happen. Perhaps it had been building to this right from the start. But the inevitability of the kiss still left Emma breathless. She watched Alex slowly take a step towards her, felt the warmth of his hands as they closed around her upper arms, and watched his head bend towards her with unmistakable intent.

AUTHOR NOTE

Longing. What a powerful emotion it is. The desire for something—or someone—you cannot have.

Today, there is very little stopping two people from being together, but in the Regency there were an endless number of obstacles standing in their way. Class distinction and the obligations owed to one's family. A gentleman's code of honour—for his promise, once given, was not lightly withdrawn. Not without incurring the wrath of his family and the condemnation of Society.

Such is the dilemma facing Alexander, Viscount Stewart, and Emma Darling, the woman with whom he falls in love. A woman he cannot have without losing the respect of his father, the affection of the woman he is promised to, and the good opinion of the Society in which he moves.

IMPROPER MISS DARLING is not a contemporary love story. It is a story about falling in love with the wrong person at the wrong time. It is a Regency love story. And it is about what two people desperately in love will risk to be together.

Enjoy!

IMPROPER MISS DARLING

Gail Whitiker

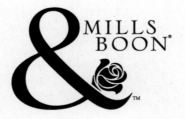

First published in Great Britain 2011
by Mills & Boon, an imprint of Harlequin (UK) Limited.
Large Print edition 2012
Harlequin (UK) Limited, Eton House, 18-24 Paradise Road,
Richmond, Surrey TW9 1SR

© Gail Whitiker 2011

ISBN: 978 0 263 22515 0

Harlequin (UK) policy is to use papers that are natural,
renewable and recyclable products and made from wood grown in
sustainable forests. The logging and manufacturing process conform
to the legal environmental regulations of the country of origin.

Printed and bound in Great Britain
by CPI Antony Rowe, Chippenham, Wiltshire

Gail Whitiker was born on the west coast of Wales and moved to Canada at an early age. Though she grew up reading everything from John Wyndham to Victoria Holt, frequent trips back to Wales inspired a fascination with castles and history, so it wasn't surprising that her first published book would be set in Regency England. Now an award-winning author of both historical and contemporary novels, Gail lives on Vancouver Island, where she continues to indulge her fascination with the past as well as enjoying travel, music, and spectacular scenery. Visit Gail at www.gailwhitiker.com

Previous novels by this author:

A MOST IMPROPER PROPOSAL*
THE GUARDIAN'S DILEMMA*
A SCANDALOUS COURTSHIP
A MOST UNSUITABLE BRIDE
A PROMISE TO RETURN
COURTING MISS VALLOIS
BRUSHED BY SCANDAL

*part of *The Steepwood Scandal* mini-series

**Did you know that some of these novels
are also available as eBooks?
Visit www.millsandboon.co.uk**

To Donna Baspaly.
A gifted artist, a wonderful friend,
and a truly remarkable woman.

Chapter One

The three letters arrived on Lord Stewart's desk within a few days of one another. Each had been written in the author's own distinct style and each was intended to sway the reader to the writer's assessment of a situation never before encountered: the unexpected engagement of Alex's younger brother, Peter, to a young lady unknown to his family or to society at large.

The letter from his father, the earl, had been typically bombastic—a strongly worded missive condemning his youngest son's behaviour, throwing out words like duty and obligation and saying that such conduct was not at all in keeping with what he expected from a member of his own family.

The letter from his mother had been more gently phrased, blaming the error of Peter's ways on the impulsiveness of his nature and pleading with Alex to intervene before it caused irreparable rifts within the family.

But the third and most heartwrenching letter had been written by Peter himself; a desperate outpouring of emotion inspired by his love for the lady to whom he had blithely pledged his troth, along with a request for Alex's support in light of his father's blatant disapproval and his mother's resultant unhappiness.

All Alex could think of as he reread the three letters was how remarkable it was that a single engagement could have spawned such a wide and diverse range of reactions.

Still, he supposed it was only to be expected. Peter might not be first in line for the title, but he was still the Earl of Widdicombe's son, and their father always had been a stickler for propriety. No episodes of drunkenness, excessive gambling, or contracting of unsuitable marriages had ever been permitted to tarnish the family name. Alex's ancestors prided themselves on their ability to rise above such weaknesses, eschewing the vices that had crippled so many other noble families. They had been responsible family men and landowners for centuries, and, in time, Alex would follow in their footsteps and take up the role he had been groomed for from birth. Peter would likely settle into religion or law, either being an acceptable occupation for the younger son of a peer, and both would marry ladies of high birth and exceptional breeding suitable to producing children worthy of carrying on the line.

At least, that *had* been the expectation until Peter had done the unthinkable by betrothing himself to an unknown girl from the country, who, in his father's words, *...while no doubt possessed of a pretty face, has absolutely nothing else to recommend her...*

Now it seemed the entire family was looking to Alex for a resolution, and time was of the essence since Peter was planning a family dinner for the coming week, followed by a grand ball and gathering two weeks after that at Ellingsworth Hall, his recently acquired country estate. And while Alex wasn't sure *anyone* was up to the task of smoothing an entire family's ruffled feathers in so short a time, he realised he was probably in the best position to try. If there was one thing at which he *did* excel, it was cutting through the layers of emotional chaos to get to the heart of the problem and resolve it before any lasting or serious damage could be done.

'Godfrey, have I anything of importance scheduled for the next few weeks?' he enquired of his steward.

That impeccably groomed gentleman turned the pages of a large leather-bound diary and scanned the entries. 'Nothing a few well-worded letters of regret won't take care of, my lord. Why?'

'It seems I am required in the country for a time.'

'In the *country?*' The steward looked at him askance. 'Now?'

'Unfortunately, my brother does not concern himself with the goings on in society. No doubt it slipped his mind that the Season would soon be underway.'

'No doubt,' Godfrey said, though his tone clearly indicated incredulity that anyone in the Earl of Widdicombe's family should be so negligent in their planning. 'I take it there is no chance he will change his mind?'

'None whatsoever.'

'Very well. I shall prepare the letters and have them ready for your signature by this evening.'

'Thank you.' Alex paused, frowning. 'When is Lady Glynnis due back?'

'The twenty-fourth, my lord. A week Friday.'

Friday. The day *after* his brother's dinner to introduce the members of his family to those of the young lady he intended to marry. Pity. Glynnis's presence would have gone a long way towards calming the troubled waters this first meeting was sure to stir up. His father *liked* Lady Glynnis Pettle. He heartily *approved* of Alex's plans to marry her. And he was far less likely to fly off the handle or to embarrass Peter in front of a houseful of guests if she was there lending her graceful manners and soothing influence to the proceedings.

Of course, there was always that *other* kind of

soothing influence, Alex reflected. One his father was known to be particularly fond of...

'Godfrey, have we any of the earl's favourite whisky tucked away in the cellar?'

'I believe so, my lord.'

'Good. Have a case of that put in the carriage as well.'

'I shall see to it at once.'

Might as well go in prepared for all eventualities, Alex thought as he slid the letters into his desk and locked the drawer. If it didn't help sweeten his father's mood, it would certainly improve his. He could sit back and watch as the rest of his family battled around him, all the while thanking the gods of fortune and fate that love had not chosen *him* to be the unfortunate recipient of Cupid's annoying little arrows.

If there was one thing Emma Darling longed for, it was harmony—the blissful absence of the emotional strife that turned one's life upside down and made rational people do completely irrational things. Witness her Aunt Augusta. For the last three weeks, Emma had been staying with her aunt in Bath, listening to her go on about her daughter's unhappy marriage and her son's unsuitable bride, about the loneliness of her life and the scandalous affair her husband was supposedly having with the widow next door. When she became too emotionally overwrought to function, Emma had made the tea and run errands, baked Chelsea buns and read poetry, all in an attempt to console her aunt in what was obviously a very trying time.

Then, without a word of explanation or thanks, Aunt Augusta had simply packed her bags and walked out, saying she was going to stay with a friend in Newport and that she wasn't coming back!

Not sure what else to do, Emma had hastily written letters to her cousins, explaining that their mother had gone to Newport and that it would be a good idea if one of them contacted her as soon as possible. Then she had written a note for her uncle with much the same message, adding that she would be leaving Bath the following day and returning home to Hampshire.

Emma doubted he would care. She had scarcely seen the man since her arrival in the spa town three weeks ago. And had she *known* the state of affairs in her aunt's house *before* boarding the coach, she would never have come in the first place. The only reason she had come to Bath was as a result of her father's other sister, Dorothy, suggesting upon her arrival at Dove's Hollow for her twice-annual visit, that Augusta 'wasn't well' and perhaps seeing Emma's smiling face would help lift her spirits.

Aware now that it would have taken a Belzonian

pulley to lift her aunt's spirits from the abyss into which they had fallen, Emma closed her eyes and breathed a sigh of relief that she was almost home— back at Dove's Hollow, where life was, for the most part, tranquil and uncomplicated. When she went downstairs in the morning, it would not be to find a middle-aged woman weeping into her tea, but her father, quietly perusing yesterday's copy of *The Times* as though there were nothing of greater importance that needed to be done. Rory and Ranger, their two ageing spaniels, would be lying at his feet and there would be pleasant conversation, perhaps something of interest to be shared, until her younger sister, Linette, came downstairs to fill the room with chatter about hairstyles and dress patterns and whatever gossip happened to be circulating in the local shops the previous day.

At that point, Mr Darling would pick up his paper and escape to his study for the rest of the morning, leaving his daughters to discuss the latest goings on in London and to speculate upon who was marrying for love and who was marrying to better their position in life.

Emma, who tended to believe that everyone wed for material gain, would eventually finish her tea, bid her sister good morning and then go about her day. If the summer months were upon them, she would head into the garden to cut fresh flowers for the various table arrangements, or take a book into the shady recesses of the garden to read. In autumn, she would don her riding habit and enjoy a brisk canter along the leaf-covered roads, or collect apples from the trees in the nearby orchard. Once winter fell and the air grew chill, she might harness Bess and take the trap down to the village to shop for fabric, or, if too cold to go out, gather up her embroidery and settle in front of the fireplace to sew.

But now in the spring, her days were devoted to painting, to capturing the myriad shades of the new season on canvas, from the pastel greens of the freshly burst buds to the delicate pink-and-white blossoms of apple and cherry trees. With brush in hand, she would venture into the garden and try to replicate the glorious panoply of colour all around her.

Having to spend three weeks with Aunt Augusta at such a time had been agony!

However, that was all behind her now, and with her brother away at Oxford and Linette in a lull between passionate storms, Emma had every expectation of life being uneventful. As the carriage finally rumbled to a halt in front of the old stone house, she found herself counting the minutes until she could escape into the peace and quiet of the garden with her easel and brushes—

'Emma, dear, welcome home,' Aunt Dorothy cried,

appearing in the courtyard as the carriage door swung open. 'Did you enjoy your stay in Bath?'

Emma frowned. Aunt Dorothy was still here? 'Not exactly, but I dare say you'll be hearing why from one of your nieces in the not-too-distant future. But what are *you* still doing here, Aunt?' she asked, climbing down from the carriage. 'I thought you were to have gone back to London weeks ago.'

'That was my intention, but there have been some interesting developments while you've been away and your father asked me if I would stay on a little longer.'

Developments? Emma wasn't sure she liked the sound of that. 'What kind of developments?'

'You'll see. Your father is waiting for you in his study.'

Emma paused, arrested by the expression on the older woman's face. 'Aunt Dorothy, you look like the cat that swallowed the canary. What *has* been going on?'

'I would love to tell you, my dear, but your father insists on giving you the news himself. But once he has, come to us in the drawing room and we will tell you all the things he has most likely forgotten.'

Emma didn't miss her aunt's use of the words *us* and *we*. 'Has this something to do with Linette?'

'It has, but more than that I dare not say.' She kissed Emma fondly on the cheek, smelling vaguely

of sherry and peppermint, and then turned to lead
the way into the house. Emma followed, wondering
what could have happened to warrant such an inex-
plicable turn of events. Aunt Dorothy was not fond
of country living. She only came to stay with them
twice a year, saying it was the least she could do for
her poor widowed brother and his three motherless
children, but Emma knew she counted the days until
she could return to London again.

What kind of 'development' could have prompted
her to stay on, *and* to look as though there was nowhere else she would rather be?

'Linette is *engaged?*' Emma repeated after her
father gave her the news. 'To whom?'

'Can you not guess?'

'In truth I cannot. The only gentleman of whom
she has spoken with any affection is Mr Taylor, but
I cannot imagine that he...' Emma stopped. 'Never
tell me *he* has proposed.'

'Yes, and very sweetly, according to your sister.'

'But...the youngest son of the Earl of Widdicombe?
Why on earth would he propose to Linette?'

'For all the usual reasons, I suppose. Apparently
he is head over heels in love with the girl and cannot
imagine life without her.'

'Good Lord.' Emma sat down in the nearest chair.
'Did he really say that?'

'He did, and naturally your sister is over the moon. There is to be a ball held in a few weeks' time to celebrate their betrothal.'

Emma's eyes widened. 'Not here!'

'Good Lord, no, we are not nearly grand enough. The festivities are to take place at Ellingsworth Hall. I believe Lady Widdicombe is coming down to oversee the arrangements. That's why I asked Dorothy to stay on. I thought it might be helpful for Linette to have an older woman to talk to. One who has... experience of marriage and would be able to offer advice in that regard. You understand.'

Oh, yes, Emma understood. Educating a young girl as to the 'expectations' of marriage was a job that usually fell to the mother or married older sister; but in the absence of both, her father had obviously decided that his widowed sister was the best person for the job.

Pity, Emma reflected drily. If her father had wanted his youngest daughter to learn about the expectations of marriage, he should have sent her to Bath. Linette would have learned a great deal more there than she had by staying here.

'When did all this happen?' Emma asked. 'I've only been gone three weeks.'

'The proposal was offered a few days after you left.'

'And no one wrote to tell me about it?'

Her father had the grace to look embarrassed. 'We thought it best not to. We knew you would wish to come home at once and Dorothy felt it better that you stayed with Gussie.' He tugged at his ear, a sure sign of his discomfort. 'I understand she is having some…family issues.'

'You could say that,' Emma muttered, not about to go into the details. 'Have you heard anything from Lord and Lady Widdicombe?'

'Not yet. They are in London and no doubt very busy with the Season. But I expect I will be hearing from his lordship quite soon.'

'I wonder what they think of this engagement,' Emma mused. 'Linette is the sweetest girl in the world, but the disparity between her social standing and Mr Taylor's cannot be denied. I would have thought it an insurmountable barrier to marriage.'

'As would I,' her father agreed. 'But young Mr Taylor doesn't seem to mind and there is nothing one can object to in Linette. She is as lovely as a spring day and as sweet as custard pie, although perhaps a trifle naïve.'

A great deal naïve, Emma was tempted to say. There was a world of difference between life at Dove's Hollow and the role she would be expected to fulfil as mistress of Ellingsworth Hall. Linette had never been exposed to society before. She had been to London once and had seemed happy enough to leave it. Her only social interactions since then had been at the local assemblies and dances that were held in the village of Little Moreton.

What a turnabout now to find her engaged to one of the most eligible bachelors in the county!

'I hope she knows what she is doing,' Emma murmured. 'I love Linette with all my heart, but she is a hopeless romantic and tends towards impulsive behaviour. What seems like a good idea one day is positively the worst the next, with scarcely a breath in between.'

'I know, and only time will tell how genuinely happy the two of them will be,' her father said. 'But you will have an opportunity to see for yourself tomorrow evening.'

'Tomorrow?'

'We have been invited to dine at Ellingsworth Hall. Just a small gathering of the immediate family. Your aunt will have all the details. In fact, you had best run along now, my dear, I'm sure she and your sister are at sixes and sevens waiting to tell you all about it.'

'Yes, I'm sure they are.' Emma managed a smile as she slowly got to her feet. 'Imagine, our little Linette engaged to the son of an earl. It is a tremendous match for her.'

'Yes, though considerably less so for him. But they are not wed yet.'

'Do you think one of them will cry off?'

'My dear, when it comes to matters of the heart, I have learned that nothing is impossible.' Her father retired to the comfort of his favourite chair beneath which Rory and Ranger slept and picked up one of his books. 'A burning passion can be doused with a few ill-chosen words and undying love can, in fact, die a quick and painful death. Nothing is as fickle as love. We would all do well to remember that.'

For the next hour, Emma was treated to a complete and extensive list of the Honourable Peter Taylor's qualities. According to Linette, he was the most handsome, the most charming, the most good-natured and the most patient of men. He was an accomplished rider, an excellent shot, spoke French like a native and even played the pianoforte.

By the time Emma reached her room, she was beginning to wonder whether her sister was marrying a saint rather than just a mere man. However, since Linette was also happier than Emma had ever seen her, establishing the difference seemed unimportant. She had found the man of her dreams and tomorrow evening they were to dine with Mr Taylor and his family at Ellingsworth Hall, a magnificent Elizabethan house nestled in over one hundred acres of rolling English countryside.

Not only that, two weeks later, friends and family

would be arriving for an extended house party. It would commence with a grand ball on the Friday evening, followed by a series of outdoor events on the Saturday afternoon and a formal dinner that evening. Guests would likely begin leaving Sunday morning, and by the time it was over, Emma was sure she would know everything there was to know about the illustrious Peter Taylor and his family. Even her brother, Ridley, had been sent a note, strongly suggesting that he make himself available for the festivities.

Emma thought longingly of her easel and brushes. It was a beautiful afternoon and she would have loved to spend some time enjoying the sights and sounds of nature, especially after the long, dreary hours she had been forced to spend with Aunt Augusta.

However, it was clear that artistic endeavours would have to wait. Her sister was to be married to the youngest son of the Earl of Widdicombe. There would be a hundred-and-one details to sort out, and, knowing Aunt Dorothy's tendency to tipple during times of high emotional stress, Emma suspected most of the decisions would have to be made by her. She would try to be as patient as possible, and make herself available for Linette in whatever capacity her sister required. Other than that, all she could do was offer up silent prayers that it wouldn't be too long before the whole dizzying affair was behind them.

* * *

Prior to leaving for the country, Alex stopped off in Mayfair to pay a call on his parents. He hadn't heard from either of them since making them aware of his intention to travel down to Ellingsworth and he was curious to know if they planned on attending the dinner Peter was giving to introduce his fiancée to whichever members of his family were present. Considering his father's sentiments about the match, Alex knew better than to consider his parent's attendance a foregone conclusion.

He found his mother seated at her desk in the Wedgwood Salon, going through a large pile of correspondence. Garbed in a morning gown of deep-turquoise silk, she looked the picture of serenity; but, upon closer inspection, Alex noticed that her complexion was pale and that she looked to have lost weight, something she could ill afford to do. He quietly crossed the room and bent to drop a kiss on the top of her dark, shining head. 'Good morning, Mother.'

'Alex!' Lady Widdicombe jumped. 'I'm sorry, darling, I was that caught up in my notes I didn't hear you come in. How are you?'

'Well. I'm on my way to Ellingsworth and thought I would stop by to find out if and when you and Father were driving down.'

His mother sighed. 'I shall be leaving tomorrow,

but your father won't be joining me. He's worked himself into such a state over this engagement, I've had to call in Dr Harrow.'

'Harrow? That can't have made Father happy. What did the doctor say?'

'That Richard could do with losing a little weight and have one less whisky before retiring. And that he was to rest for a few days.'

'Sage advice for any man, I suppose,' Alex said. 'Is he in his study?'

'No. He wasn't feeling quite the thing this morning so he decided to remain in his room.'

'Then I shall go and see him—'

'Alex, there's something I have to tell you,' his mother said abruptly. 'Something you need to know before you go upstairs...'

It was bad news. Alex knew it from the way she suddenly refused to meet his eyes. 'What's wrong?'

'It isn't just Peter's engagement that has upset your father. Last week he...collapsed, in his study,' she said slowly. 'Dr Harrow said it...could be his heart.'

His *heart?* Alex was stunned. His father was only fifty-nine years old and as fit as most men half his age. When had he suddenly developed problems of this nature? 'Has this happened before?'

'I don't know. He says it hasn't, but you know he doesn't like worrying us and he hates having to see the doctor.' His mother sighed. 'Naturally, he didn't want me to say anything to you at all. He said there was no point in upsetting you because in a matter of days it would all be fine. And maybe it will be. But I felt you had a right to know before you went down to see your brother.'

Alex walked slowly across the room, stopping by the long window. 'What did Harrow suggest?'

'That we restrict your father to a light diet. Boiled fish and broths, no rich desserts or sauces. And he must be kept as calm as possible.'

Calm. With his youngest son about to marry a woman of whom he heartily disapproved. It was like telling a starving fox to ignore the rabbit jumping up and down in front of his nose.

'On second thought, perhaps it's best Father not come down to Ellingsworth just yet,' Alex said. 'At least not until I've had a chance to see how things stand. With luck, I'll be able to rectify matters without Father ever having to be involved.'

'Oh, that *would* be wonderful, Alex,' his mother said. 'I do want Peter to be happy, but I would be lying if I said I wasn't concerned. We know absolutely nothing about this young woman. Who her people are, where she comes from, what her background is. And naturally that worries your father very much. He is afraid Peter has engaged himself to some fortune-hunting social climber.'

'We can't deny that the possibility exists,' Alex

acknowledged, 'but I'll find out what I can. And I understand if you would rather stay here with Father than travel all the way down to Hampshire.'

To his surprise, his mother shook her head. 'There's really nothing I can do here. Your father will be happier having Murdoch look after him. He thinks he's more likely to get that glass of whisky. But I've warned Murdoch not to indulge him and Dr Harrow did say he would look in while I was gone. Besides, I promised Peter I would take care of the arrangements for the ball. Being a man, he won't have a clue where to start. That's what I've been doing this morning,' she said, indicating the pile of papers on her desk. 'And to be honest, I do want to meet this young woman without your father being there to glower at her. If Peter cannot be dissuaded from going ahead with the marriage, I want to know what kind of person I am going to be welcoming into the family.' She sighed. 'I would like to feel there is at least *one* area of my life over which I have some control.'

The earl was dozing when Alex walked into his room, and though only a few weeks had passed since his last visit, Alex could definitely see a change in his father's appearance. His complexion was grey, his hands lay limp at his sides and there was a definite rattle in his chest when he breathed. Hard to equate the elderly-looking man slumped in his chair with the vital, powerful figure Alex had known all of his life. 'Father?' he ventured quietly.

'Hmm?' The earl's head moved, his eyes slowly opening. 'Oh, it's you, Alex. Didn't hear you come in.' He tried to sit up. 'Must be all this medication Harrow's been forcing down my throat. Told him I didn't want any of the damn stuff.'

'If he's giving you medication, it's because you *need* it,' Alex said, pulling up a chair next to his father's. 'And if you don't take it, I shall force it down your throat myself. We cannot have you messing about when it comes to your health.'

'Damnation! She told you, didn't she!' the earl railed. 'I knew she wouldn't be able to keep it to herself.'

'Yes, Mother told me and she was right to do so.'

'She was *not* right to do so and I'll tell you now, it is *not* my heart! It was indigestion. Brought on by a bit of bad pork.'

'A man does not collapse from indigestion,' Alex said calmly.

'Of course he does. I told Harrow as much too, the old quack! Said all I needed was a good glass of whisky!'

'I trust he didn't give you one.'

'He did not. Neither did Murdoch, damn his surly Scottish hide! I've a good mind to send him packing.'

Alex smiled. 'That would be a mistake, Father. Murdoch's been with you for nigh on forty years.'

'Yes, and he's getting far too uppity in his old age,' his father grumbled. He briefly closed his eyes, took a moment to catch his breath. 'So, what are you going to do about this situation with your brother?'

'Too early to say, but I'm on my way to Ellings-worth now.'

'Good, Alex, good, I have every confidence you'll be able to take care of it. And your timing couldn't be better. You know Peter's planned a dinner for the chit and her family on Thursday evening.'

'I heard.'

'Trumped-up little harpy,' the earl muttered. 'It was likely *her* idea that he hold a celebratory dinner in her honour so that she can get a taste of what her life is going to be like once she's lady of the manor. But we're not going to let that happen, are we, Alex? We're going to nip this in the bud long before it gets to that point.'

Unwilling to give his father false assurances, Alex merely said, 'I'll do what I can, sir. I take it you're not planning to be there.'

'Ha! I'd as soon spit in her eye as see her sit at my son's table. But Harrow has confined me to bed for a few days so I won't be able to go regardless. But *you* know what's what, Alex. You know we can't allow this marriage to take place.'

'It may be out of our hands. Have you spoken to Peter recently?'

'What's the point?' The earl's face twisted. 'He says he loves her and that's all there is to it. But we both know he's marrying beneath himself. And mark my words, he'll live to regret it.'

Alex decided not to address that for the moment. Marriages between mismatched social partners often did work out, but it wasn't easy and it usually required a considerable degree of sacrifice on one part or the other. 'Do you know anything about the girl?' he asked instead.

'Not yet, though I've engaged someone to make enquiries. And you needn't look at me like that,' he said when Alex raised an eyebrow in surprise. 'If there's bad blood in the family, I want to know about it *before* my son puts a ring on her finger!'

'It is possible you're exaggerating things, sir,' Alex said. 'She may be a perfectly charming young woman.'

'Really? Have you ever heard of the Darlings of Little Moreton? No, I thought not. Mark my words, she's after his money and an easy life. Peter won't believe that, of course. Reading his letter, you'd think she was an angel from heaven complete with fairy wings and a blasted halo! But I'll wager she's a common little chit with no breeding and bad manners. Pretty, but not at all suitable to being the wife of a Taylor.'

And that's really what it all came down to, Alex reflected drily. The appropriateness of the ladies his sons wished to marry. 'Well, I'll do what I can, but you should be prepared for the worst,' Alex said, getting to his feet. 'Peter's sensible enough to make up his own mind—'

'No man's sensible when it comes to women,' his father interrupted. 'That's why I'm so proud of you, Alex. You take your obligations seriously. Always have. Lady Glynnis Pettle is precisely the sort of woman your brother *should* be marrying. A woman who knows her place in society. One you'll never have to worry about. She's an earl's daughter, after all.'

Alex smiled. 'Yes, she is, but she's also a good friend and has been for a long time. As to the other matter, I'll do what I can, but I'm not making any promises.'

'I have faith in you, my boy,' his father said. 'You've been a good and dutiful son all your life. You've never once given me any reason to doubt you. If *anyone* is going to be able to resolve this mess and make Peter listen to sense, it's you.'

Chapter Two

Ellingsworth Hall was an exquisite Elizabethan house perched prettily on the edge of a vast wood. Unlike many such grand houses, it had not been ruined by tasteless additions thrust upon it by succeeding generations; but had retained the dignity of its origins, the mellow gold stone reflecting warmth and welcome to all who came near.

'The formal gardens in the back are exceptionally lovely,' Linette said as the carriage drew to a halt under the portico. 'Mr Taylor took me for a walk through them last week. He was remarkably knowledgeable about the names of the flowers. I just said they were all very pretty and that my sister would create the most beautiful arrangements if she had such a garden to draw upon.'

Emma smiled, silently adding botanist to the growing list of her future brother-in-law's accomplishments. 'I am content with the selection I have in our own gardens, Linette, but I suspect you will be grateful for the variety. The need for flower arrangements will be that much greater in a house the size of Ellingsworth.'

'Without question,' Aunt Dorothy said. 'Mrs Connelly told me the house has twenty-seven rooms, including twelve bedrooms.'

And Mrs Connelly would know, Emma thought drily. The wife of the local squire made it her business to know everything that went on in Little Moreton. In a bucolic village where the arrival of the post was the most exciting thing to happen in a day, the upcoming marriage of a peer's son to a local girl must have seemed like manna from heaven.

'Can this really be happening, Emma?' Linette asked in a voice of wonder. 'Or shall I wake up to find that it has all been a dream?'

'I certainly hope it is not a dream,' Emma said. 'Otherwise I shall have expended a great deal of time and effort getting dressed, and all for nothing.'

'It is never a waste of time to make oneself look pretty, Emma,' Aunt Dorothy chided. 'On such an auspicious occasion, we must all try to look our very best. Even your father has made more of an effort than usual.'

'I have made no more or less of an effort than I would have for any other occasion,' Mr Darling objected.

'Nonsense, Percy, you look quite the thing in your

new mulberry jacket. And I do like the way Jenks has tied your cravat. Simple, yet elegant. The hallmark of a gentleman.'

Emma smiled, aware that how they looked would likely be of secondary importance to how they behaved. They were about to meet the Earl and Countess of Widdicombe, two of society's most illustrious and influential members. Lord Widdicombe sat in the House of Lords and Lady Widdicombe was a close confidant of the patronesses of Almack's. They owned an elegant town house in London, a sprawling estate in Kent, and likely several other establishments with which Emma was not familiar.

By contrast, Emma's father was a former tutor and her late mother was the daughter of a well-to-do merchant. They had acquired Dove's Hollow upon the demise of Mr Darling's older brother, Cyril, who had apparently won the house and all its contents at the faro table. After Cyril's unfortunate death in a drunken brawl, the house had passed to Emma's father, who had been only too delighted to move his young family in and take up the life of a gentleman. They were not well travelled, did not go regularly to the theatre or museums, and though Emma had been to London once, she had not been formally presented at Court, having had no one to sponsor her or cover the costs of a Season.

Still, at least they made a presentable party as they

climbed the steps to the front door of the house her sister would soon be calling home. Aunt Dorothy was wearing a stylish new gown of *terre d'Eygpt* sarsenet, Linette was radiant in white muslin trimmed with double bands of gold embroidery and Emma's own gown was a shade of pale green she knew to be flattering to her dark hair and fair complexion.

Nevertheless, she was thankful she was not the one who would have to bear the brunt of the scrutiny tonight. This evening, she was simply a bystander. She would support her sister in every way she could, but if the earl and countess took it into their heads to be disdainful, she suspected there would be little any of them could do but smile as bravely as they could and count the minutes until it was all over.

They were greeted at the door by a tall and rather impressive-looking butler and shown into the elaborate Chinese drawing room. Linette had already informed them that Mr Taylor intended on having all of the reception rooms redone and that he had decided to start with this, the largest of the saloons. Emma, whose eye was always drawn to line and colour, paused on the threshold, impressed by the elegant proportions and by the deep crimson and gold colour scheme. Fire-breathing dragons and sword-wielding warriors were prominent throughout the room and the furnishings were Oriental in design. Two magnificent black-lacquer cabinets with ornate battle scenes hand painted in gold and crimson stood on either side of the long window.

The Countess of Widdicombe was seated on a red-velvet chair by the fireplace, hands folded calmly in her lap. She was a regal-looking woman, still relatively young, with a smooth, unlined complexion and glossy black hair artfully arranged in an elegant coiffure. Wearing a gown of rich crimson silk, she seemed almost an accessory to the room, her elegance and grace very much in keeping with her surroundings.

Emma thought she would have looked a great deal friendlier had she troubled herself to smile, but apparently smiles were not required of a countess when meeting a prospective daughter-in-law and her family for the first time.

Two other men occupied the room and stood on either side of the fireplace like mismatched bookends. Emma recognised Peter Taylor at once and, though he was not the kind of man that appealed to her, she could well understand Linette's attraction to him. He was not overly tall, but his slenderness conveyed the impression of height and the combined skills of his tailor and valet did the rest. His thick, nut-brown hair tapered neatly to his collar, and with quite the most charming smile Emma had ever seen and a demeanour that was totally without arrogance, he reminded her of an anxious puppy, desperate to be loved by one and all.

The other man, who was clearly too young to be the earl, was obviously the eldest son, Viscount Stewart. Lord Stewart towered over his younger brother by a good four inches and possessed the kind of looks that would invariably send young girls swooning. Thick black hair, luxurious as sable, was swept back from a broad forehead already tanned by the warm spring sun. His jaw was square, his mouth full lipped and sensual, his lashes dark under even darker brows.

Only his eyes were light, the clear, cornflower blue seemingly at odds with the rest of his appearance.

But where was Lord Widdicombe? Surely he should be here to greet his son's intended bride and her family?

'Mr Darling, I am so pleased you were able to come,' Peter Taylor said, quickly stepping forwards. 'Mother, may I present Mr Darling and his family.'

As Lady Widdicombe inclined her head, Emma studied her face for some indication as to what she was feeling. But apart from a slight stiffness of manner, there was nothing to indicate either pleasure or resentment. 'Good evening, Mr Darling. I do not believe you have met my eldest son, Lord Stewart?'

'I have not, Lady Widdicombe, but I am very pleased to do so.' Mr Darling bowed to both the countess and the heir, and then turned to introduce the members of his own family. 'May I present my sister, Mrs Grand, my eldest daughter, Emma, and, of course, my youngest daughter, Linette.'

'Mrs Grand, Miss Darling,' the countess said, her gaze resting on each of them for a moment. 'And Miss Linette Darling. Step forwards, child.'

Linette did, her cheeks taking on a deeper-pink hue as she moved closer to the countess's chair. Stopping a few feet in front of her, she executed a graceful curtsy.

The countess nodded her approval. 'How old are you, child?'

'Seventeen, your ladyship.'

'Seventeen. And you think you can make my son happy.'

'Of course she will make me happy, Mother,' Mr Taylor said, springing to Linette's defence. 'That is why—'

His mother's upraised hand silenced him. 'My question was addressed to Miss Linette, Peter. Kindly allow her to answer.'

All eyes swung back to Linette, who suddenly looked like the sacrificial lamb being led to the slaughter. 'I…I—'

'Speak up, child. I'm not going to eat you.'

'Of course not, Mother, but judging from the look of terror in Miss Linette's eyes, I'm not sure she believes you.'

It was Lord Stewart who spoke, the rich timbre of his voice drawing every eye in the room. He stepped away from the fireplace and offered Linette a surprisingly friendly smile. 'Good evening, Miss Linette. We are very pleased to welcome you and your family to Ellingsworth Hall.' His voice was low and deep, the tone undeniably reassuring.

Linette visibly relaxed. 'Th-thank you, Lord Stewart.'

'I regret that my father is not able to be with us this evening, but his health is not the best and it was necessary that he remain in London for a few days.'

'We are very sorry to hear that, my lord,' Mr Darling said in a tone of mingled relief and regret. Obviously, he too had been wondering at the reason behind the earl's absence. 'I hope he will be recovered in time for the coming festivities.'

'We certainly hope that will be the case,' Lord Stewart said. 'The doctor has advised a period of rest before resuming his social obligations. Especially one of this consequence.'

'Will there be...a lot of people in attendance?' Linette asked nervously.

'Indeed, most everyone has written to say they will be here,' Lady Widdicombe replied. 'I had my doubts about Lord and Lady Martindale, but their acceptance arrived yesterday, and even Lord and Lady Huffton said they would be willing to leave town for a weekend. Then there will be Sir George and Lady Monk, and of course, the Earl and Countess of Leyland and their daughter, Lady Glynnis Pettle, whom Alexander is soon to marry.'

'Marry?' Peter Taylor's eyebrows rose. 'I wasn't aware you'd proposed to Lady Glyn, Alex.'

'I haven't,' Lord Stewart said with a speaking glance at his mother.

'But we all know it is only a matter of time.' Lady Widdicombe turned to Emma's father with a complacent smile. 'There has been an understanding between the families for some time. Lady Glynnis's father is the Earl of Leyland and her mother the former Lady Georgiana Croft, daughter of the Marquis of Tunney. It is an excellent match.'

Mr Darling and Aunt Dorothy both offered dutiful murmurs of approval and Lady Widdicombe looked suitably appeased. Emma, who was not impressed by the countess's reluctance to appear as welcoming towards Linette as she was to this other unknown lady, rolled her eyes, only to flush when she caught Lord Stewart watching her.

'Miss Darling,' he said, his gaze moving over her so quickly she felt a draught. 'I would not have taken you for Miss Linette's sister. The resemblance between you is not immediately discernible.'

'Pray do not trouble yourself to be polite, Lord Stewart, the resemblance is not discernable after several hours of intense study. Linette has always been the beauty in the family,' Emma told him. 'I tend more towards the academic and the practical.'

'Oh, now, Emma, you are being far too critical of yourself,' Linette was quick to say. 'You play the piano, manage the household and paint the most wonderful landscapes.'

'All at the same time?' Lord Stewart favoured Emma with a brief smile. 'A remarkable talent indeed.'

Resisting the impulse to trade sarcasm for sarcasm, Emma said, 'It no doubt would be if I were able to do all three simultaneously, but I prefer to do them separately and I admit to painting with far more skill than I play.'

'How unfortunate,' Lady Widdicombe observed. 'A lady's talent on the pianoforte must always be deemed more valuable than her ability to paint. Painting is such a solitary occupation and one cannot socialise when one is alone.'

'True, but if a lady does not entertain well, surely it is kinder to her audience that she not make the attempt? I would far rather look at a well-executed painting than listen to a poorly played sonata.'

'Surely the answer is to practise more often, Miss Darling.'

'Only if there is something to be gained by the

effort.' Emma smiled. 'Apart from Linette, my family is not particularly gifted in the musical arena.'

The remark was followed by a rather startled silence, leaving Emma to conclude that speaking truthfully about one's abilities or lack thereof was probably not recommended. She couldn't be sure, but she thought her father was not the only one who breathed a sigh of relief when dinner was announced a short time later.

Dinner in the baronial dining room was exceptional, though Emma thought eating in the smaller, more intimate family dining room would have been far less intimidating. The great table, which could easily have sat forty, was set with crisp white linens, sparking crystal and the family silver. A magnificent silver epergne graced the centre of the table, while smaller flower arrangements at either end provided a welcome splash of colour against the backdrop of white and silver.

As host, Peter Taylor took his place at the head of the table, with his mother on his right and Linette on his left. Lord Stewart sat to Emma's right, while her father was on Lady Widdicombe's right with Aunt Dorothy beside him. And, as expected, the meal was outstanding. A variety of courses, each more tempting than the last, was served by liveried footmen while the butler poured the wine and kept a sharp eye on every servant in the room.

Emma couldn't help but smile as she thought of Jenks, their man of all trades. A country fellow at best, poor Jenks would have felt decidedly out of place here at Ellingsworth Hall. No doubt the servants below stairs were every bit as intimidating as the lofty family above.

'Something amuses you, Miss Darling?'

Emma looked up to find Lord Stewart's blue eyes fixed upon her. 'Yes, though I doubt anyone but myself would find it so.'

'How can you know if you do not give us an opportunity to hear it?'

'Because I learned long ago that while some things are amusing to all, others are not.' Emma's gaze moved around the room, touching on the elegant, the beautiful and the priceless. Somehow she knew her musings would definitely fall into the latter category. 'I am sorry to hear of your father's illness, Lord Stewart. I hope it is nothing serious.'

'I'm sure it is not.' Lord Stewart's practised smile moved easily into place. 'The doctor simply advised rest for a few days.'

'Still, such things are worrisome. While I'm sure the doctor is doing everything he can to speed Lord Widdicombe's recovery, it always weighs on one's mind.'

'As you say.' He raised his glass and glanced at her over the rim. 'Will your brother be joining us in two weeks' time? I understand he is presently studying law at Oxford.'

'Yes, but we sent word to let him know of the engagement and Ridley has assured us that he will be here in time.'

'As, hopefully, will Father,' Peter Taylor said, glancing at his mother. 'We must have *everyone* in attendance for such an important occasion. Isn't that right, Mother?'

Lady Widdicombe looked up and shared a brief glance with her eldest son. After a pause, Lord Stewart said, 'Of course everyone will be here, Peter. It is, after all, the celebration of your engagement. And, on that note, may I ask you to rise, raise your glasses and join me in a toast,' he said, getting to his feet. 'To my brother and his lady. May they experience good health, prosperity, and may they always be as happy as they are today.'

Emma dutifully raised her glass. It was not the most romantic of toasts, but perhaps Lord Stewart was not a romantic man. Just because he looked the part didn't mean he had the temperament to go along with it. She spared a quick glance for her sister, who was smiling blissfully into her fiancé's eyes and knew Linette didn't care a whit about flowery tributes or good wishes. She was in love and the man she loved, loved her in return.

Not even the most pedantic of toasts was going to rob her of the pleasure she found in that.

At the conclusion of meal, Lady Widdicombe led the ladies into the elegant Green Saloon, leaving the gentlemen free to enjoy their after-dinner indulgences. Emma, who was decidedly relieved to be away from the probing eyes of Lord Stewart, found the Green Saloon far more to her liking. It was peaceful after the dramatic Chinese room, due no doubt to the absence of snarling dragons and sabre-waving warriors everywhere she turned.

'Mrs Grand,' Lady Widdicombe said as she settled into an emerald-green wing chair. 'You are, I understand, a widow?'

'Yes. My husband died three years ago.'

'So you now live with your brother and take care of his family?'

'Oh, no, your ladyship. I live in London with a companion. I'm not one for country life,' Aunt Dorothy admitted. 'I prefer the hustle and bustle of town. Always something going on and plenty of shops to spend your time and your money in. But I try to come down at least twice a year to be with my brother and his family.'

'I see. Then I take it *you,* Miss Darling, have the

responsibility of running the house and looking after
your siblings,' the countess said.

Emma smiled. 'I look after the housekeeping and
the accounts, and I take care of Papa and Linette as
best I can, but my brother, Ridley, is presently away
at Oxford and quite able to look after himself.'

'And neither you nor your brother is married.'

'No.'

The countess turned to regard Aunt Dorothy again.
'Is it not unusual, Mrs Grand, for a younger daughter
to be settled in marriage before the older son and
daughter have made a suitable match?'

'I suppose it is, your ladyship.'

'Am I to assume, then, that Miss Darling has not
been to London?'

The older woman's cheeks coloured. 'I believe she
has.'

'But obviously met with no success.'

'On the contrary, I was most successful,' Emma
said, having had enough of people talking about her
as though she wasn't in the room. 'I spent a good
deal of time at the British Museum and, by the time
I left, I had sketched nearly the entire contents of the
Egyptian wing *and* made a decent start on ancient
Greece.'

The comment was clearly unexpected and the resultant look of surprise on Lady Widdicombe's face
prompted Aunt Dorothy to say, 'Emma is quite gifted

when it comes to drawing, Lady Widdicombe. Her sketches of the Elgin Marbles were really quite astonishing.'

'Indeed.' Lady Widdicombe turned her attention to Linette, obviously finding Emma's achievements less than noteworthy. 'Miss Linette, are you able to play the pianoforte?'

'I am, Lady Widdicombe.'

'Then pray be good enough to entertain us.'

'Yes, of course.' Linette quickly got up and moved to the instrument. 'Oh! A Broadwood grand piano.'

'Yes. Peter had it brought down from London.' Pride resonated in the countess's voice. 'He plays exquisitely.'

Linette ran her fingers lightly over the keys, picking out a simple tune. 'What a lovely sound. Emma, you must come and turn the pages for me.'

Dutifully, Emma got up and joined her sister.

'What shall I play?' Linette whispered. 'I am so nervous.'

'You have nothing to be nervous about.' Emma calmly flipped through the sheets of music on the platform and pulled one out. 'You play beautifully and your voice is that of an angel. And here is one of your favourite pieces.'

'"Greensleeves,"' Linette said, relieved. 'Yes, I shall be able to do justice to that.'

She began to play and though Emma dutifully

watched her progress so as not to miss turning the page at the appropriate time, she did risk an occasional glance at Lady Widdicombe to see if she was enjoying the performance. She hadn't missed the ambivalence in the countess's attitude towards Linette. While she wasn't precisely hostile, neither was she warmly welcoming. Fortunately, she seemed to appreciate Linette's skill on the pianoforte. She actually closed her eyes once or twice during the performance and was gracious in showing her appreciation at the end.

'Very nice, Miss Linette. You play tolerably well and have a very pleasant singing voice.'

'Thank you, Lady Widdicombe.'

'Of course, both would be improved by regular practice. I would advise you to take the required time during each day to do so.'

'Yes, Lady Widdicombe.'

'And now, it is Miss Darling's turn to entertain us,' the countess said. 'Unless she feels it will be too embarrassing for her.'

Emma smiled. Had Lady Widdicombe not tossed in that last line, she might have gracefully demurred. But never one to back away from a challenge, she sat down on the bench recently vacated by her sister and said, 'I do have one or two tolerable pieces in my repertoire. I simply shall not sing for that would be most humbling after Linette's performance. And

I doubt *that* would be improved if I were to practise every hour of every day from now until I died.'

Lady Widdicombe said nothing, allowing Emma a brief moment of victory. The countess might be able to tell Linette what she should and should not do, but she certainly wasn't going to exert the same influence over her. One had to draw the line somewhere.

It would have been a great deal better, Emma reflected later, had *she* been the first to perform and Linette the second. Because by the time Linette had taken Emma's vacant seat next to Aunt Dorothy and Emma was ready to play, the door opened again and the gentlemen walked in. And it became immediately evident that no one had been expecting to see *her* seated at the pianoforte. Emma saw a look of startled pleasure on her father's face and a slightly more cautious one on Mr Taylor's.

Lord Stewart's expression was unreadable. Nor could she glean anything from the tone of his voice, when, moving to stand beside the fireplace, he said, 'I did not expect you to honour us with a performance, Miss Darling.'

'I did not say I was unable to play, my lord,' Emma said evenly. 'Only that I do not play as well as I paint. Nor do I sing as well as my sister, whose performance you just missed.'

'Then I hope we may prevail upon Miss Linette to

sing for us again. But we should regret not hearing you play first.'

Equally sure he wouldn't have cared had she left immediately after dinner, Emma turned her attention back to the piano. Normally, she would have quailed at having to perform in front of such dignified company, but having recently discovered a piece by Bach that she liked very much, and having spent more time than usual practising it while at Aunt Augusta's house, Emma had managed to imprint the score firmly in her mind. Now, after giving herself a few minutes to recall the intricate opening, she placed her fingers upon the keys and began to play.

Music rolled forth. Not sweet and sentimental like Linette's 'Greensleeves,' but strong and powerful, the melody filling the room. It was one of passion and unrequited love, and on the exquisite instrument the notes rang true and clear. For once, Emma forgot about her audience and lost herself in the music. She had never performed on such a marvellous instrument before and she was astonished at how well the piece sounded. As she brought her hands down on the final chords, her heart was beating hard, her exhilaration at having executed the complicated piece without a mistake bringing an unexpected glow of triumph to her cheeks.

There was a moment's stunned silence. Then, enthusiastic applause broke out as Emma rose to take her bows. She saw a variety of expressions on the faces turned towards her. On her father's, pride, pure and simple. On her aunt's, pride mingled with relief, and on Linette's, astonished admiration. Peter Taylor's mouth was open and Lady Widdicombe was staring at her in disbelief.

Only Lord Stewart's expression bore no indication of surprise. 'You did not tell us the truth of your ability, Miss Darling. Seldom have I heard that piece played better or with more emotion.'

'Indeed, I believe you were having sport with us, Miss Darling,' Peter said. 'I vow she would give Lady Glynnis a run for her money. What say you, Alex?'

'I'd say Miss Darling could hold her own with anyone,' he answered evenly. 'Well done, Miss Darling.'

'Indeed, Emma, well done!' Linette said with unconcealed joy.

Emma politely inclined her head, grateful for the praise, but more relieved that she hadn't made a fool of herself in front of everyone in the room. She'd told herself when she'd sat down at the piano that she had wanted to make a good showing for Linette's sake and that she hadn't played the piece to impress anyone, but that wasn't entirely true.

She *had* wanted to make a good impression. She had wanted to impress *him*.

'Thank you, but it is one of the few pieces I play

well,' she said. 'As indicated earlier, my repertoire
is extremely limited.'

'If you were only to play that one piece, you would
find yourself welcome in any drawing room,' Lord
Stewart said.

The subtle words of praise had Emma raising her
eyes to his; something she immediately came to
regret. She didn't want him thinking she cared, any
more than she was willing to admit she did.

'Play something else, Miss Darling,' Peter im-
plored. 'You must have at least one other song with
which to entertain us.'

'What about "The Merry Piper"?' Aunt Dorothy
suggested.

Emma nodded. 'Only if Linette will sing.'

Not surprisingly, Linette was delighted to sing and
because they had performed the duet so many times,
Emma knew they acquitted themselves well. The
music was lovely and Linette's sweet soprano voice
made easy work of the lyrics. At the conclusion, they
were again met with enthusiastic applause.

'I say, the two of you must perform for our guests
at the ball,' Peter said. 'I don't believe I have ever
heard a lovelier duet.'

'Nonsense, Peter, musicians have already been
engaged,' his mother said. 'It is hardly the thing for
your...fiancée and her sister to entertain.'

'In that case, I am delighted we were treated to

the performance tonight.' He moved to stand beside Linette and taking her hand, raised it to his lips. 'Did I not tell you she was the most beautiful, the most gifted, the most remarkable young lady of my acquaintance?'

Emma hastily averted her eyes from the lovestruck look on her future brother-in-law's face and promptly locked gazes with Lord Stewart—whose expression was anything *but* lovestruck. What was he thinking as he watched the pretty scene unfold? That it was hopelessly romantic? An emotional embarrassment? Was he counting the minutes until he could politely slip away? The half-smile on his lips might be one of amusement, but it could just as easily signify boredom or contempt. He didn't strike Emma as the type of man who would find pleasure in such simple drawing-room entertainments.

'Well done, dearest,' Aunt Dorothy whispered as Emma sat back down beside her. 'Your father and I could not be more proud.'

Emma managed a fleeting smile, aware of being able to breathe a little easier now that the performance was over. But she was far from happy with her silly need to impress Peter's brother. Of what concern was it to her what he thought of her? The man was attractive, wealthy and heir to an earldom. He was no doubt used to women falling at his feet and to singing his praises in the hopes of attracting his attention.

Emma had no intention of becoming one of those women. She was not some simple-minded female easily swayed by good looks and an impressive title. She judged a man on the strength of his convictions, on the fairness of his mind and on the kindness of his words. What she had seen of Lord Stewart tonight was a man assessing a situation. One who had likely been asked to pass judgement on Linette and possibly on the rest of her family as well. Because when a man married, his bride's family became *his* family. Her assets became *his* assets. And her liabilities became *his* liabilities.

Was that what Lord Stewart had been sent here to find out? Emma wondered. The extent of the liability his brother was really taking on?

Chapter Three

Not surprisingly, a great deal of speculation followed the dinner at Ellingsworth Hall. Linette suffered alternating bouts of exhilaration and despair over what Lady Widdicombe's and Lord Stewart's feelings about her might have been, for while she was encouraged by her performance on the piano, she was equally convinced that her conversation at dinner had fallen far short of what was expected and that their impressions of her had been tainted as a result.

Naturally, Aunt Dorothy was of the opinion that Linette had done splendidly and that, in her estimation, the evening had been an unmitigated success. She declared the countess to be far more gracious than expected, that Lord Stewart was an elegant and handsome gentleman, and that Mr Taylor was exactly the type of man one might wish to have as a son-in-law.

Mr Darling was more reserved in his comments. Though he didn't say as much, Emma knew he believed that the real test of Linette's suitability would come during the weekend house party when many of Mr Taylor's friends and family would be in attendance and far more judgmental eyes would be focused on Linette than had been thus far.

In that, Emma tended to agree. Though Lady Widdicombe had been intimidating at the onset, by the end of the evening she had mellowed enough to give Linette a nod of approval and to tell her that she had played the pianoforte very nicely. Society, however, would take a far more critical view of the engagement and Emma felt sure there would be people at the ball who would be of the opinion that Mr Taylor could have done better. She feared a combination of ill will and jealousy would come together in the form of spiteful remarks that were neither fair nor warranted being directed towards Linette.

All of that she kept to herself, of course. Linette was anxious enough about the upcoming ball; there was no point in making matters worse by pointing out things that *might* happen. Besides, Emma had concerns enough of her own—not the least of which was the fact that the upcoming house party would again place her in the company of Lord Stewart.

She wished she could have said the thought didn't bother her, but she knew it for the half-truth that it was. The man unsettled her, arousing emotions and feelings she was not at all comfortable with. Several times throughout the dinner, she had felt his eyes on her and had looked up to find him watching her, as though hoping to find something lacking in her make-up.

It must have been that because she refused to believe it had anything to do with his interest in her as a woman. Not when he was all but engaged to a lady whose blood was as blue as his. But was he wondering, perhaps, if she thought to gain notoriety from her sister's success? To use Linette's connection to Peter as a way to move into better society herself?

The unpleasant speculation no doubt accounted for the terseness of her reply when Linette chanced to ask her about the gentleman as they strolled through the garden a few days later. 'What did *I* think of Lord Stewart?' Emma said. 'Why would you ask?'

'No particular reason.' Linette bent down to lift a slow-moving caterpillar off the path and settled him gently in the grass. 'I simply noticed him watching you throughout the evening and wondered what your opinions of him were.'

Emma took a deep breath. So Linette had noticed it too. 'I thought him…pleasant.'

'Nothing more?'

'What else would you have me say?'

'That he was exactly what he seemed. Handsome, charming and highly intimidating.'

'You found him intimidating?'

'Never tell me you did not?'

'I thought him serious, but hardly intimidating.' Emma drew her shawl more closely about her shoulders. 'But he is very different from his brother. Your Mr Taylor is certainly the more light-hearted of the two.'

'Yes, thank goodness. And now that you have spent an evening with him, do you not agree that he is wonderful, Emma?' Linette said, her face alight with love and happiness. 'I am convinced I am marrying the perfect man.'

Equally convinced there was no such thing, Emma said, 'I think the two of you will be very happy together.'

After a pause, Linette said, 'I wonder what Lady Glynnis will be like.'

'Lady Glynnis?'

'The young woman Lord Stewart is going to marry. Don't you remember? The countess seemed very pleased about the match.'

'I expect she would, given Lady Glynnis's position in society,' Emma said. 'As Lord Widdicombe's heir, it is Lord Stewart's duty to marry well.'

'It sounds as though she is very accomplished on the pianoforte.'

'I suspect the lady is accomplished in all areas of feminine endeavour. He would not have chosen her otherwise.'

'Do you think he loves her?' Linette asked.

Emma laughed. 'Good Lord, Linette, how am I to know that?'

'Well, did he strike you as the type of man who would marry for love?'

'I've no idea. I spoke to him briefly and in no great depth. You were there the entire time.'

'I know, but you are so much more perceptive about people than I. You see things I do not.'

'That is not always a good thing.'

'Well, perhaps we will know when we see the two of them together.' Linette fell into step beside her. 'You can always tell when two people are in love.'

'Oh yes?' Emma said, chuckling. 'And how do you do that?'

'The lady blushes and the man looks as though his heart is lost to all but her. They stand close together, even when there is no reason to do so, and they frequently exchange glances. Especially when they think no one is watching.'

'Gudgeon. You are making all of this up.'

'No, it's true!' Linette said with feeling. 'I saw Penelope Faith and Sir Wensley Cottonwood acting like that at the Parthingers' ball and they were betrothed the following week!'

'I cannot imagine Lord Stewart looking at *any* lady with stars in his eyes,' Emma said. 'He doesn't strike me as the type. Mr Taylor looks at you that way, but his temperament is vastly different from his brother's.'

'Yes, thank goodness. I think I am a little frightened of Lord Stewart, for all his being so handsome and charming,' Linette admitted. 'Nevertheless, it will be interesting to see him with Lady Glynnis on Friday evening. After all, if she is to be my sister-in-law, I do want her to like me.'

Impulsively, Emma stopped and hugged her sister close. 'No one can help but like you, dearest. You are the sweetest, gentlest, most kind-hearted person I know. If Lady Glynnis does *not* like you, we shall simply not like *her.*'

'That will not make for very pleasant family gatherings,' Linette said unhappily.

'I shouldn't worry about it.' Emma slipped her arm through her sister's. 'I doubt Lord Stewart is all that fond of country living. Once he and Lady Glynnis are married, we likely won't see either of them around Little Moreton for quite some time.'

Emma was seated at the far end of the garden when she noticed the horse and rider approaching from the direction of Ellingsworth Hall later that same day. The horse did not look to be of local stock. Big boned and with long, delicate legs and a proud arch to its neck, it was clearly a thoroughbred and therefore well beyond the reach of most of the young men who resided in Little Moreton.

As to the rider, Emma suspected it was Peter Taylor come to pay a call on her sister. Linette had informed her that he often stopped by for afternoon visits now they were officially betrothed, and, unconcerned, Emma went back to her painting. The sun was creating a fascinating interplay of light and shadow on the lily pond, and the ever-shifting patterns of blue and green were far more interesting to her than the gentleman coming to call. And when a dragonfly landed on the edge of a lily pad, the insect's huge silver wings shimmering in the sunlight, Emma caught her breath.

How did one capture something so magical? What colours did one use to replicate the translucence of its wings and the iridescent shading of its body? She thought about that for a while, mixing colours in her mind, and reached down for her palette—only to see a pair of dark-brown boots standing in the grass a few feet away.

'Good afternoon, Miss Darling.'

Emma knew the voice. Having heard it at dinner, she would have recognised it anywhere. But it was the last one she had been expecting to hear in her garden today. 'Good afternoon, Lord Stewart.' She raised her head and peered at him from beneath the brim of her bonnet. 'If you are looking for my father, you will find him in the house, most likely in his study.'

'Thank you, but it was you I came to see.'

'Oh?'

'I wondered if we might have a chat. If you do not mind me singling you out.'

'That would depend on what you were singling me out for.'

'I wish to talk to you about a matter of considerable importance.'

'Oh dear, that does sound alarming.' Emma put down her brush. 'Pray, forgive my attire. I was not expecting visitors.'

'No apologies are necessary. You look charming.'

Emma was too much of a lady to roll her eyes, but she was sorely tempted to do so given how easily the lies fell from his tongue. She was wearing a wide-brimmed sunhat with ribbons tied loosely beneath her chin, a painter's smock liberally smudged with paint, and though her hair was pinned up, she could feel the breeze tugging at loose wisps. Charming was decidedly not how she would have described her appearance. Still, he hadn't come with a view to courting her.

'Very well, Lord Stewart, you have my undivided attention. What is this important matter you wish to talk to me about?'

'Your sister, my brother and the unfortunate inequity of the match.'

Emma's eyes widened in shock. Mercy! The man certainly didn't beat around the bush. 'You will forgive me if I say I am somewhat taken aback by the remark, my lord.'

'I would have been more surprised had you said you were expecting it,' Lord Stewart acknowledged. 'But it is a subject I believe warrants further discussion.'

'I fail to see why. The inequity of the match obviously wasn't of concern to your brother when he asked Linette to marry him.'

'Of course not. My brother is romantic by nature and more impulsive than is wise.'

'Attributes shared by my sister, I'm afraid.' Emma looked up, shading her eyes with her hand. 'But what's done is done, wouldn't you agree?'

'Forgive me,' he said, belatedly aware that his position was causing her to stare directly into the sun. 'Perhaps we could take a walk?'

'As you like.' Emma put her brushes into a pot of water, then stood up and removed her smock. 'You do not tether your horse?' she asked, looking past him to the elegant thoroughbred grazing freely beyond.

'There is no need. He never wanders.' Lord Stewart stared at the easel for a moment. 'Impressive. You have a knack for blending colours so that they seem to melt into one another.'

'It is an attribute of watercolours. If a line is drawn too harshly, you simply brush a wash over it and the line softens. It is a very forgiving medium.'

'Only to those who know how to use it.' Lord Stewart smiled. 'You obviously do.'

It was a new and unusual experience to be complimented by a gentleman. Emma was used to most of the flattery going to Linette, but she had to admit to a warm glow of pleasure at hearing Lord Stewart praise her work. 'Thank you, but I am an amateur at best. My brother is the true artist in the family.' She fell into step beside him. 'So, you wish to talk about the unsuitability of the match between Linette and your brother.'

'Please don't misunderstand, Miss Darling,' he said quickly. 'Your sister is a lovely young woman with pleasing manners and a charming personality. But you cannot deny the disparity in their social situations.'

'Of course not, but your brother obviously doesn't care and given that your parents have not forbidden the match, I don't see what business it is of ours.'

He stopped, frowning. 'May I speak honestly, Miss Darling?'

'I wish you would.'

'Then I will tell you that my parents are *not* pleased

with the engagement and that they would very much like to see it come to an end,' he said bluntly. 'Particularly my father.'

Emma turned to look at him. 'Is that why he was not at dinner the other night?'

'No. His doctor *has* restricted him to bed, but I am not entirely sure he would have come had he been feeling well enough to do so. He has very strong opinions about the obligations owed to one's family.'

Emma wished she could have said she was surprised, but how could she when Lord Stewart was echoing her own concerns about the inequality of the match? 'Why did your father not voice his concerns when your brother first made him aware of his intentions to approach my sister?'

'Because Peter didn't tell him of his intentions until it was too late,' Lord Stewart admitted. 'Now, relations between them are strained to the point where it is difficult for either of them to speak about the situation with any degree of rationality.'

'I am sorry to hear that,' Emma said slowly. 'Does the countess also object to the marriage?'

A pained expression flashed across Lord Stewart's face. 'That is not as simple a question to answer. My brother holds…a very special place in my mother's heart. Above all, she wants him to be happy.'

Emma supposed it was not an uncommon failing of mothers, to wish their children well, but it was obviously a feeling not shared by her husband. And their antipathy towards the marriage at so early a stage did not bode well for Linette's future relationship with her in-laws. 'What did you hope to achieve by mentioning this to me, Lord Stewart?'

'Before I answer that, I would ask you a question.' He stopped by the base of a large tree and crossed his arms over his chest. 'Is your sister marrying my brother for love or for what she stands to gain by becoming his wife?'

It was only because the nature of the question caught her so completely off guard that Emma did not immediately take offence to what was a highly impertinent enquiry. 'Of course she loves him. Linette is not in the least mercenary. She would never marry if her heart was not fully engaged. You cannot be expected to know this, of course, but she has spoken of nothing but your brother since the day the two of them met.'

'I feared as much,' he said. 'Love is always harder to discourage than gain.'

'But surely it is not your place to discourage the relationship,' Emma said. 'If they are truly in love—'

'Oh, I believe they both *think* themselves in love, Miss Darling, but will it last? You strike me as being a sensible young woman, one who knows what the world is all about. And it is not about kindness and love. It is about establishing one's place through the acquisition of power and wealth. Love plays very little part in that.'

Emma said nothing, not at all sure she liked being coupled with this man when it came to their feelings about matters of the heart. She might not dream about finding romantic love for herself, but that did not mean she belittled it when it came to others.

'Does that also apply to your forthcoming engagement to Lady Glynnis?' she asked boldly. 'Is that union also based on the premise of what each of you stands to gain, with no consideration for love or other feelings?'

He raised one dark eyebrow. 'I did not come here to discuss *my* relationship, Miss Darling.'

'No, but in being so cavalier about my sister's, it seems only fair that I should ask you about the basis for yours. I may be sensible, my lord, but if I were ever to marry, I would hope to do so for love rather than gain.'

'Very well. My betrothal to Lady Glynnis was arranged by our parents and accepted by the lady and myself as being eminently sensible. Our interests are similar, our natures compatible and our desires and goals identical. And we happen to like and respect one another.'

'So, all in all, a very convenient partnership,' Emma said.

'You could say that.'

'Do you love her?'

He clearly wasn't expecting the question and Emma knew from the look on his face that he wasn't pleased about being asked. 'You don't believe in mincing words.'

'Not when the issue concerns me as deeply as this one. Do you love the lady you are planning to marry, Lord Stewart?'

He took his time, suddenly more interested in the antics of a robin pulling a worm from the grass than he was in giving her an answer. Finally, 'If being comfortable with a lady and enjoying time spent in her company is an indication of love, then, yes, I suppose I do.'

'My, how passionately you speak.'

'Would you have me quote sonnets?' he retorted sarcastically. 'Proclaim my undying love in the manner of poets and kings?'

'I would have you speak of nothing you did not feel,' Emma said. 'But neither will I listen to you condemn two people who so obviously *are* in love simply because you put no stock in the emotion. Your brother has proposed to my sister and been accepted. Were he to break it off now, he would suffer the consequences of his actions and she would be left heartbroken.'

'Perhaps, but if your sister were to cry off, she would be thought flighty, but not socially irresponsible,' he countered. 'Indeed, proceeding with this marriage would be the more socially irresponsible of the two options.'

To a degree, he was correct, but Emma had no intention of letting him think she agreed with him on this or any other front. Or of letting the remark go unchallenged. 'Why do you dislike Linette so much, my lord? Apart from having spent a few hours in her company, you know absolutely nothing about her.'

'Whether I like her or not has nothing to do with it. My brother's birth is such that he should have done better.'

'Then your parents should have stopped him from proposing to her!'

'And I've already told you they had no idea he intended to do so. And even if they had, it would not have made any difference.' He turned away so she might not see his face. 'My mother can deny him nothing. Even when she should.'

They were past the point of polite discussion now. They were arguing—and as someone who disliked conflict intensely, Emma knew they would achieve nothing by it. 'Lord Stewart, you are the heir to your father's title and estates. As long as you marry well, what does it matter how your brother settles his affairs?'

'It matters a great deal. I do not wish to see Peter take stock of his life in ten years' time and come to regret what he did in a youthful burst of passion. I would rather see him suffer now than in the future.'

'*Suffer?* You think your brother will *suffer* from being married to Linette?'

'That's not what I said—'

'But it is what you meant.' Dear Lord, the arrogance of the man! Did he really expect her to ask Linette to reconsider her acceptance of Mr Taylor's offer? To throw over the man she loved for the sake of...what? Lord Stewart's misplaced notion that his brother might be happier for it in the long run? 'Lord Stewart, I...appreciate the concern you must feel for your brother, but you must also understand that the concern I feel for my sister is equally great,' Emma said, forcing herself to speak in a calm and rational manner. 'I believe her to be deeply in love with Mr Taylor and I could not counsel her against marrying him when I *know* how unhappy it would make her.'

'Then you will not encourage her to think on it again.'

'I will not.'

'You could be sparing them both a great deal of heartache and embarrassment.'

'Apart from the fact of Linette's birth not being as lofty as you might like, she will not embarrass you or your family. She is good and loving and I know she will make your brother an excellent wife. I cannot do what you ask, my lord, nor am I sure your brother would thank me for doing so,' Emma said quietly. 'You saw how they looked at one another the other night. You heard how he spoke to her.'

'Lies can be convincingly enacted, Miss Darling. So much so that, sometimes, we only see and hear what we wish to.'

Emma's mouth hardened. 'I like to think I see what's there, my lord.' How dare he suggest that Linette would *lie* about her feelings! Linette, who was no more capable of deceit than a child. 'Now if you don't mind—'

'Excuse me, Miss Darling?'

A man's voice interrupted, one Emma did not recognise. Until she looked up and saw the newly appointed vicar of the church in Little Moreton approaching. 'Mr Tufton?'

John Tufton was a handsome young man with a shock of light brown hair and warm brown eyes. He had come from a parish in Sussex to take over St David's and was at least thirty years younger than his predecessor—a fact that had not gone unnoticed by the single ladies in Little Moreton. 'Good afternoon.' His smile was somewhat hesitant as he glanced from Emma to her companion. 'I hope I haven't come at a bad time?'

Aware that he couldn't have come at a better one, Emma said, 'Not at all, Mr Tufton. Lord Stewart was just leaving.'

'Lord Stewart?' The vicar's eyes widened. 'I was not aware you resided in the parish, my lord.'

'I do not.' Lord Stewart's voice was less than conciliatory. 'I am here visiting my brother.'

'Ah, yes, Mr Taylor. A most excellent gentleman. I made his acquaintance last week. I, myself, am newly arrived in Little Moreton and so am calling upon all of my parishioners in an attempt to get to know them better,' Mr Tufton said. 'There is generally so little time after Sunday service.'

'Of course.' Lord Stewart's mouth lifted in a sardonic smile. 'Everyone rushing home to enjoy their dinners.' He turned to Emma, his expression growing even more cynical. 'Well, I shall take up no more of your time, Miss Darling. But I hope we may continue our conversation in the near future.'

'Only if the subject differs from what we spoke of today, Lord Stewart. Mr Tufton,' Emma said, turning to smile at the parson. 'Perhaps you would be good enough to make your way to the house. I know my father and my aunt will be pleased to see you. I shall collect my things and join you there.'

'Excellent. And I do hope we will see you and your family at church on Sunday, Lord Stewart?'

'I really couldn't say.' Lord Stewart's eyes briefly connected with Emma's. 'There are so many other things of importance to concern oneself with when in the country.'

With a brief nod, he whistled for his horse. Emma didn't say a word as the elegant creature trotted obediently to his side. It made no sense that she should be annoyed that even the horse seemed to fall under his spell. Instead, she turned her back on him and walked purposefully towards her easel, heavy in heart and low in spirit.

Poor Linette. What would she say if she knew what her future brother-in-law was saying about her? Linette had gone to Ellingsworth Hall in fear of Mr Taylor's parents, yet now it seemed it was his brother who offered the biggest threat to her happiness. *He* did not want the marriage to take place. And where his father did not have the courage to show his displeasure and his mother hadn't the heart to, it seemed Lord Stewart had more than enough of both. He intended to march in and destroy his brother's and her sister's chances at happiness by spouting duty and obligation and all the other things that obviously mattered to him far more than love.

It was just as well the vicar's arrival had put an end to her artistic endeavours, Emma thought moodily. Her creative urges had vanished, leaving her no more able to see the beauty in the lily pond than she could in a warty frog. She was angry and upset, yet she knew that directing her anger at Lord Stewart really made very little sense. Had *she* not questioned the inequity of the match herself? Was *she* not the one who had expressed concern over Linette's ability to take responsibility for her decisions? The one who had told her father that Linette was changeable by nature?

Why, then, was she angry at Lord Stewart for having said *exactly* the same things?

Mr Tufton did not stay long. A quiet gentleman with agreeable manners, he was careful not to wear out his welcome. After enjoying a cup of tea and a slice of seed cake, he spoke to Emma's father and Aunt Dorothy, saying how pleased he was to meet them and how much he looked forward to seeing them on Sunday. Then, after exchanging a few words with Linette and offering congratulations on her betrothal, he left.

Emma was not sorry to see him go. Not because she disliked the man. There really wasn't anything about Mr Tufton one *could* dislike. But the entire time he had been seated in their parlour, Emma had lived in fear of his bringing up Lord Stewart's visit and *that* would have been awkward since she had no intention of telling Linette Lord Stewart had called.

'Had he come to talk about the dinner?' Linette would surely have asked. Or 'Had he come to speak to her father about the upcoming wedding?' And the thought of having to tell her sister the truth made Emma shudder. Such an admission would only have brought on grief and uncertainty, and tears were most effective at destroying harmony in a house.

Then her brother Ridley came home—and that fragile harmony vanished for good.

He arrived at eight o'clock in the evening. Dinner was over and they were all sitting quietly in the drawing room when the door burst open, causing the dogs to start barking as though the four horsemen of the Apocalypse had appeared, and then Ridley blew in like a westerly.

'Well, here I am,' he announced dramatically. 'The prodigal son returned. Have you all missed me dreadfully?'

'We can scarce speak for emotion,' Mr Darling said in a dry voice.

But Aunt Dorothy was already on her feet, anxious to greet her favourite nephew. 'Ridley, dear boy, of course they've missed you. And I haven't seen you in an age,' she said, kissing him soundly on both cheeks. 'But what *have* you done to your hair?'

'It's all the rage in London,' Ridley said, grinning. 'What do you think, Em?'

Emma looked up. 'That you look like Caesar and you know what happened to him.'

'Darling Emma,' Ridley said fondly. 'I can always count on you to say the nicest things. And here is little Linette,' he said, turning to his sister and pulling her to her feet. 'Who I vow is even more beautiful than when I left.'

'Don't be silly, Ridley, you've only been gone a few months,' Linette said, blushing.

'Nevertheless, there does seem to be an additional bloom on the rose and I suspect that has much to do with the fact you are soon to marry the venerable Mr Peter Taylor,' Ridley said. 'Well done, Linny. If all goes well, you might just end up a countess.'

'Highly unlikely,' Emma drawled, 'given that there is an older brother in line for the title.'

'Ah, yes. Alexander the Great.'

Emma blinked. 'I beg your pardon?'

'Alexander Taylor. Lord Stewart,' Ridley explained, flopping down in his favourite chair. 'The lads call him Alexander the Great because he's a cracking good rider and a dashed hand with a whip. I won't mind having him as a brother-in-law, I can tell you.'

'You must be hungry, Ridley,' Aunt Dorothy said. 'Shall I ask Cook to prepare something?'

'You may indeed. I did stop for a bit of overdone beef on the way, but I wouldn't mind a slice of Mrs Dunstan's excellent apple pie if there is any to be had.'

'I'm sure that can be arranged. Ring for Jenks, would you, Emma?'

'So, when are the nuptials to take place?' Ridley enquired, fondling Rory's silky head.

Linette blushed. 'We haven't set a date yet.'

'What? I thought you would have been anxious to reel him in.'

'Really, Ridley!' Aunt Dorothy exclaimed. 'The man is hardly a fish to be landed.'

'Of course not. He's already been hooked and I am very proud of my little sister for having done so. Imagine Linette snapping up the youngest son of an earl. It certainly trumps anything you or I have been able to pull off, Em. Unless there's something you haven't told me?' He grinned. 'Turned any gentleman up sweet yet?'

'If I had, I'd know better than to tell *you*,' Emma said, returning to her chair. 'You would likely tease the poor man to death.'

'Naturally. What are brothers for?'

'To tell you the truth, I haven't quite worked that out.'

'All right, stop bickering, you two,' Mr Darling said. 'Ridley, how are you going on with your studies? Finding the intricacies of the law to your liking?'

For the first time, Ridley looked a little uncomfortable. 'Actually, I've been meaning to write to you about that, Father.'

'Oh?'

'There's something I have to tell you. And I don't want you getting upset because I have given this a great deal of thought.'

Her father's eyes narrowed. 'Given *what* a great deal of thought?'

'My decision to become a solicitor. Or rather, my decision...not to become one.'

His father dropped his book. 'Not become a solicitor. Why the devil not?'

'Because I'm really not cut out for it.'

'Indeed! Then what, pray tell, *are* you cut out for?'

'Painting,' Ridley announced decisively.

Aunt Dorothy frowned. 'Painting?'

'Yes. As in portraits.'

'Of what?' his father demanded.

'Of society's most beautiful and aristocratic families.' Ridley stood up and affected an elegant bow. 'Of grand lords and titled ladies, of cherubic daughters and stalwart sons. And of their noble dogs and horses, of course,' he said, leaning down to scratch Ranger behind the ear.

There was a moment of stunned silence before Linette said, 'Goodness, Ridley, whatever possessed you to do such a thing?'

'Indeed! Giving up law to dabble in paints and brushes?' his father said stiffly. 'I thought you had more sense.'

'Sense I have in limited supply, but talent I possess in abundance,' Ridley quipped. 'I've already completed five commissions and have five more waiting. And they pay me very well.'

'Then he must be good, Percy,' Aunt Dorothy commented. 'The aristocracy are very particular about who they engage to paint their portraits.'

'Exactly!' Ridley agreed. 'They are *very* particular and I *am* very good. More to the point, those for whom I've done work have passed my name along to others and I actually have more work than I can handle.'

'And I suppose you expect me to clap you on the back and say, well done, sir, well done!' his father demanded.

'That would be nice.'

'Well, I shall not! Being a barrister is a respectable occupation. One that would stand you in good stead for the rest of your days. The same cannot be said for artists.'

'Of course not, because we are all licentious reprobates who drink too much and have naked women lying around our studios,' Ridley muttered. 'God knows, I'll probably be dead by the time I'm thirty.'

'Really, Ridley, such language in front of your sisters!' Aunt Dorothy chastised.

'Indeed, *and* in front of your aunt,' his father added. 'I am not pleased, Ridley. Not at all pleased.'

'But why should you be upset? It's not as though I'm drinking myself into oblivion, or trying to cadge money from you. I make a very good living.'

'But it is not the occupation of a gentleman!'

'And I have never aspired to *be* a gentleman,' Ridley said in exasperation. 'I want to paint. I've *always* wanted to paint. It is the only thing I'm good at and likely the only thing I ever will be.'

The conversation was mercifully interrupted by the arrival of Jenks.

'Ah, Jenks,' Emma said quickly. 'Would you be so good as to bring some fresh tea and either a slice of cake or a piece of pie for my brother?'

'Don't bother.' Ridley abruptly got up and headed for the door. 'I've lost my appetite. I'm going up to my room.'

'We'll talk about this in the morning, Ridley,' Mr Darling called after him. 'Don't think we won't!'

Emma exchanged an anxious glance with her sister, then nodded at the servant who was still standing patiently in the doorway. 'Thank you, Jenks, it seems we won't be needing anything after all.'

'Very good, miss.'

After he left, the room settled into an uneasy silence. Linette picked up a book, Emma reached for a magazine and Aunt Dorothy went back to her tambour, muttering something about mismatched threads and too-tight knots.

'Oh well, that's just splendid!' Mr Darling finally burst out. 'My youngest daughter about to marry into an earl's family and my only son announces he's given up law to paint pictures.'

'Portraits, Father,' Emma corrected tactfully. 'And it is not such a disreputable occupation. Mr Gainsborough and Sir Joshua Reynolds were both highly respected for their work.'

'Ridley is *not* Gainsborough,' Mr Darling drawled.

'You don't know that. You haven't seen any samples of his work.'

'And I have no desire to. Knowing Ridley, I can just imagine what kind of pictures—'

The door opened and Ridley walked back in. Ignoring his father, he handed a framed picture to Emma. 'Lord Mortimer paid me six guineas for that and his recommendation brought in two more commissions for which I shall charge double. You may not like what I've turned my hand to, Father, but you cannot deny I'm good at it.'

With that, he left again, this time closing the door firmly behind him.

Emma glanced at the painting and slowly began to smile. The subject was a little girl no more than three years old. She was sitting on a stool with a spaniel at her feet and a small grey kitten clutched in her arms. Her hair was the colour of ripe corn and she was wearing a pale pink dress dotted with silver stars. She was a pretty little girl, to be sure, but it was the wistfulness of her expression and the innocence of her smile that Ridley had captured so perfectly on the canvas.

'It is excellent,' Emma said, handing the painting to Linette.

Linette didn't say a word, but her eyes opened wide and when she looked up, Emma saw the admiration on her face. Clearly, she'd had no idea that Ridley was so talented. None of them had. The portrait was not the work of a rank amateur. It was the work of a man who deserved to be recognised for his skill and ability.

Unfortunately, thinking about paintings took Emma back to that morning and to the unpleasant confrontation she'd had with Lord Stewart. Pity she couldn't so easily relegate *him* to the back of her mind. But, there he was, front and centre once again, and she had a sinking feeling he was going to stay there until she had decided what she was going to do about this situation with Linette and Peter.

Lord Stewart didn't want his brother to marry Linette and Emma didn't want to see Peter and Linette break up. And now Ridley had given up law to become an artist. Was it any wonder she had a feeling it was going to be a long time before harmony found its way back inside the peaceful walls of Dove's Hollow again?

Chapter Four

Alex had been fortunate enough to enjoy a close relationship with his younger brother ever since they were boys. Always a happy-go-lucky lad, Peter was easy to be around and was never moody or quick to anger. Loyal to a fault, he could be counted on to tell the truth, and though that honesty that had cost him the friendship of several boys who tended towards mischief, it had stood him in good stead in all other areas of his life.

His one failing, if it could be called that, was his tendency to fall too easily in love. Peter often mistook friendship for affection and when a young lady smiled at him, he was prone to reading more into it than was intended. Thankfully, since most of the girls they had grown up with had tended to look upon Peter as a brother rather than a potential suitor, his youthful escapades had not landed him in any serious trouble. But Alex feared his brother's engagement to

Linette Darling now *was* trouble. Trouble of the most ominous kind.

'So how did you and Linette meet?' he asked as the two of them stood reviewing renovation plans the following morning.

'We were introduced at the Christmas fête.' Peter picked up the architect's drawing of the new parlour and held it towards the light. 'Linette was looking after the children. The vicar introduced us and we spent a few minutes in conversation. I thought her delightful.'

'So you went to see her after the fête?'

'No.'

Alex frowned. 'No?'

'I didn't think it would be a good idea.'

'I don't follow.'

Peter put down the drawing. 'Father's always had very high expectations of us and while Linette's birth is acceptable, I knew it wouldn't be good enough for him, so I purposely did not seek her out.'

'Then how did you come to be engaged?'

'A week before Christmas, I was invited to a small dinner party. An informal gathering, the hostess said, with three or four other families to whom they were close. Given that I had nothing else to do that evening, I agreed. Linette was there, along with her father and sister.'

'I see. And did she seek you out?'

'No.' Peter drew forwards another sketch, this one of changes to the formal dining room. 'In fact, she went out of her way to avoid me. She admitted afterwards that she had never associated with anyone of high rank before and that she was terrified of embarrassing herself. But she never put a foot wrong. And, as the evening wore on, I found myself making excuses to be near her. I enjoyed talking to her and I loved hearing her laugh.' He stared down at the plans, but Alex knew he was seeing something quite different. 'I believe I fell in love with her that very night.'

'You didn't think it simply a case of infatuation?'

'Briefly, yes,' Peter admitted. 'But as the months passed and I couldn't stop thinking about her, I realised it was more. And the idea she might be seeing someone else nearly drove me insane. So, I started planning ways in which we might meet. Accidentally, of course. I went to a few of the local assemblies. Started accepting invitations to events I knew she would be attending, and, eventually, I got up the courage to call at her house. And the more I saw her, the more I realised how much I loved her. Finally, I had no choice but to speak to Mr Darling. When I had his approval, I asked Linette to marry me.'

Alex stared at the drawings, aware that the answers weren't at all what he had been hoping to hear. He had expected to find fault with his brother's reasoning, sure there would be something upon which he could hang his hopes of breaking them up. But there was nothing. Peter had used logic and family obligation to try to resist the young lady's charms—and had fallen in love regardless. They were not off to a promising start.

'By the way, I talked to Mother last night,' Peter said.

'Oh?'

'I wanted to know how upset Father really was over my engagement.'

'What did she say?'

'That he doesn't approve and that he expects me break it off as soon as possible.'

'Is there any chance you would?'

'No. It would break Linette's heart, not to mention mine.'

So, he would stand by his decision. Alex sighed. Their father would *not* be pleased. 'Did Mother say anything else?'

'No. Why?'

Surprised, Alex turned and walked towards the window. Why hadn't their mother made mention of their father's illness? Surely she felt it important enough. Why else would she have told *him?* 'No reason,' he said, deciding to leave it for the moment. 'Tell me, what does Mother think of Miss Linette Darling now that she's met her?'

'That she is lovely and sweet and seems to come from a nice enough family.'

'But...?'

'But do I really think I am doing the right thing by marrying her.'

Alex hadn't expected his mother to agree with the betrothal, but neither had he expected her to condemn it as harshly as his father had. Her relationship with Peter wouldn't allow it.

'You haven't told me what *you* think about all this yet,' Peter said.

Alex shrugged. 'Does it matter?'

'Of course it matters. You're my brother. I've always looked up to you. I care about what you think.'

'So if I were to tell you that I agree with Father in thinking you should have done better...?'

'I'd say it's not what I wanted to hear, but that I can understand your reasons for saying it.'

'Unfortunately, understanding what I'm saying doesn't solve the problem, Peter,' Alex said. 'If something were to happen to me, you would become the next earl. Do you really think Linette Darling is suitable to being the next Countess of Widdicombe?'

Peter smiled unhappily."I'm sorry, Alex. But in my eyes, she already is.'

Ridley's startling admission that he had given up law to paint portraits for a living was an endless source of fascination to Emma. It seemed a thoroughly illogical, but totally understandable, thing for her brother to do; curious to find out more about that part of his life, she waited until their father had gone for his daily walk and then went to seek him out.

She found him, not unexpectedly, in the stables, devoid of jacket and with his shirt sleeves rolled up to his elbows. He had a soft brush in his hand and was running it over the sides and back of his chestnut, both he and the horse seeming to enjoy the peaceful occupation. Ridley was different from most gentlemen in that regard. He liked looking after his horses almost as much as he enjoyed riding them.

'Hello, Emma,' he said as she appeared at the stall door. 'What brings you down here?'

'I wanted to talk to you about your painting. Away from the house.'

'Away from Father, you mean.' Ridley resumed brushing. 'At least I know you don't think I'm dicked in the nob for going ahead with it.'

'Not at all. I admire you for having had the courage to follow your heart. But weren't you nervous, giving up your legal studies for something as unpredictable as art?'

'In truth, I was terrified,' Ridley admitted with a smile. 'But only for a day or two. In my heart, I *knew* I was doing the right thing. I wasn't cut out for the law, Em. All those boring precedents and tedious pleadings. I never would have been any good at it. But painting is like breathing to me. It's natural. It's what I need to do to be happy.'

Emma understood that. Though her own enjoyment of painting wasn't the passion it so clearly was for Ridley, she knew the joy of sitting down in front of an easel and getting ready to create, the freedom of allowing her imagination to soar. 'But you said you had commissions. With so many successful portraitists in London, how did you get anyone to hire you?'

'I was lucky enough to be friends with Lord Bickerson's son at Oxford,' Ridley said, moving the brush over the chestnut's hindquarters. 'Tom knew of my interest because I had shown him a few of my sketches. So when he came in one evening and told me his father was looking for someone to do a family portrait, I jokingly suggested that he put my name forward. He told me he already had and that I was to meet with his father the next day to go over the details.'

'How wonderful!' Emma said.

'Yes, it was, rather. So I met Lord Bickerson and told him I'd do the painting, and that if he didn't like it he didn't have to pay me.'

'Very noble of you.'

'Not really. Bickerson knew I'd never done a commission before. He had already engaged an estab-

lished artist before Tom even mentioned my name.
So giving me a chance wasn't much of a risk on his
part. It was something he did as a favour to his son.
And if it turned out I wasn't any good, he'd still have
a painting from someone else and all I would have
been out was the cost of a canvas and some paints.
But, as luck had it, he was delighted with the painting and paid me what I considered to be a very fair
sum. More importantly, he recommended me to Lord
Huston—'

'*Viscount* Huston?' Emma asked on a gasp of surprise.

'That's right. And when Huston saw what I'd done
for Lord Bickerson, he hired me to paint a portrait of
his wife and another one of his two young sons. After
that, I received a commission from a titled gentleman,
followed by one from a lady who wished me to paint
her portrait as a gift for someone.'

Emma smiled. How wonderful to hear that Ridley
was enjoying success in his new career. Why, then,
the faint echo of regret in his voice? 'So you are now
an established artist with enviable credentials and a
growing list of clients,' she said.

'Indeed. But Linette tells me *you* have improved
immeasurably since I left,' he said in an overly hearty
voice. 'When are you going to show me some of your
work?'

'Are you mad? After showing me that delightful

painting of the little girl with the kitten in her arms? Not a chance. I paint for my own pleasure. Not for your eyes or anyone else's!'

But someone else *had* seen her work. Lord Stewart, the morning he had come upon her painting down by the pond. He had complimented on her ability and told her that her work was *impressive.* High praise indeed from a man like that.

Good thing she'd known better than to believe him.

On Wednesday morning, Emma donned a plum-coloured riding habit with a matching bonnet and had Jenks saddle her mare. It was a glorious morning for a ride. The sky was a bright sapphire-blue with a few white clouds drifting by like tufts of cotton. Dark-green hedges criss-crossed lighter green fields dotted here and there with clumps of golden butter-cups and white-and-yellow daisies. A painter's palette of colours! Unfortunately, caught up as she was in her study of the world around her, Emma failed to notice the approaching rider until he was close enough to speak. 'I suspect your artistic eye is seeing all this in a vastly different light than those of us who cannot tell blue from turquoise.'

The voice was teasing, lighter in tone than it had been the last time they'd spoken. Nevertheless, Emma couldn't suppress a *frisson* of awareness at hearing it. 'You surprise me, Lord Stewart. The fact you know there is a difference leads me to believe you already know more about colour than you are willing to let on.'

His smile widened. 'I always try to exceed a lady's expectations.'

'But since I have none, there is nothing to exceed.'

'Come now, Miss Darling, surely you have *some* expectations of the man who will soon be your brother-in-law.'

'Really? I thought you were doing everything you could to prevent that from happening.'

He shrugged. 'If neither party is willing to cry off…'

'Then you have not succeeded in changing your brother's mind?'

'No more than I suspect you have succeeded in changing your sister's.'

'Ah, but I have not tried,' Emma informed him. 'There have been so many other things to occupy my time. Fittings for new gowns. Paying calls on all the people who are desperate to hear details of my sister's upcoming nuptials. Meetings with Mr Tufton to talk about the ceremony.'

'Ah, yes, the dedicated vicar.' Lord Stewart did not smile. 'I wonder if he is taking as much of an interest in *all* of his parishioners as he seems to be taking in you and your family.'

Emma cursed the warmth that flooded her cheeks.

She did not blush prettily. Patches of red stood out on her cheeks like droplets of blood on snow, resulting in her chin and forehead appearing all the more pale. 'It is part of his job to get to know the people of this parish, my lord. And since Linette is to be married in his church, he is spending time with her to familiarise her with the ceremony. As well, he and my father discuss matters of philosophy and religion. The time he spends with Ridley and myself is minimal.'

'If you say so.' He didn't meet her eyes, but Emma could sense his annoyance and for the life of her she couldn't imagine why.

'You haven't answered my question as to what you expect of me as your brother-in-law,' he said, reverting to their earlier topic of discussion.

Wondering why it mattered, Emma lifted her shoulders in a shrug. 'Only that you are good to my sister and mindful of your obligations to her. Although,' she said, hoping to lighten the mood, 'I suppose if you were to occasionally take your mother and two sisters-in-law to lunch at some hideously expensive but exceptionally good restaurant in London, it would not go amiss.'

'Hideously expensive but exceptionally good,' he mused. 'That would have to be the Clarendon. A pricey ticket, but worth it under the circumstances. Have you ever eaten there?'

'No, though Ridley may have. He has a taste for the finer things. What would you suggest?'

'Many believe their Coquilles St Jacques to be without equal and their crêpes Suzette better than those served at the Hôtel Le Meurice in Paris. Personally, I prefer the *langoustine d'anglais,* followed by a tender fillet of beef, and to finish, either a chocolate soufflé or *crème brûlée,*' Lord Stewart said. 'And I would start with a chilled bottle of champagne. I find it stimulates the appetite and lends a rosy glow to the surroundings.'

'Not to mention the diners,' Emma said.

He actually smiled. 'Only if one imbibes too freely. Then a piquant white for the fish course and a robust Burgundy for the beef.'

'Goodness, after all that, I shouldn't think you would be able to taste the food!'

'Ah, but a good wine enhances the flavours,' he informed her. 'As well as lending a certain *joie de vivre* to the proceedings.'

'Yes, I've heard my brother talk about *joie de vivre,*' Emma said drily. 'As I recall, they had to carry him to his room afterwards.'

'That is the result of *too* much *joie de vivre.* A man must know where to draw the line.'

'And I suspect you always know when and where to do that.'

He shot her a sardonic gaze. 'I would have thought

the ability to avoid falling into a drunken stupor something to recommend a man. You make it sound like a failing.'

'Did I? It wasn't my intention,' Emma said with a smile. 'I can think of nothing more demeaning than to see a man tumble into his host's rhododendrons.'

His mouth lifted in a smile. 'So, apart from entertaining you with good food and wine and not falling headlong into the bushes, what other expectations have you of me?'

'None I can think of at the moment. As long as you and Linette contrive to be happy in one another's company, I shall be content.'

'I wonder if the rest of your family's expectations will be as straightforward.'

'Well, my brother expects nothing of himself and even less of others, and my father will only be concerned with Linette's happiness.'

'Then it would seem I have only your opinion to worry about.' Lord Stewart narrowed his eyes against the brilliance of the morning sun. 'Is that your brother I see coming over the brow of the next hill?'

Emma turned to follow his gaze. 'Yes. Ridley arrived the night before last and will be staying for the duration of the spectacle.'

He shot her an amused glance. 'Did I detect a note of sarcasm in your voice?'

'Unintentional, but yes. I find all the pomp and ceremony excessive.'

'Your sister is marrying the son of an earl,' Lord Stewart pointed out. 'Some would say that worthy of ceremony.'

'I suppose, though I would enjoy it far more if it were all a little less grand.' Emma risked a quick glance in his direction. 'Do you like weddings, Lord Stewart?'

'I'm not sure one can like or dislike them. They are a necessity of life. But I enjoy seeing a well-matched pair come together.'

Emma laughed. Had he any idea, she wondered, how much like an old pair of boots he made the bride and groom sound? 'I take it by that you mean a lady and a gentleman of similar circumstances.'

'Of course.'

'Unlike my sister and your brother.'

He shot her a penetrating glance. 'We've already had this discussion, Miss Darling. Why bring it up again now?'

'Forgive me. Perhaps I should look to *your* marriage as the model for all others.'

'Now you are being cruel.'

'Not at all. I am quite sure your upcoming engagement to Lady Glynnis will be, in the eyes of the *ton,* an ideal match. She has all that you require in a wife, and you, all a woman could ask for in a husband. Why would you say I am being cruel?'

'Because on the basis of our brief association, *you* know that I have chosen to put practicality first and *I* know you decry the idea of marrying for anything *but* love.'

Emma tilted her head to one side. 'I said I would rather marry for love, my lord. I did not say it was the only reason for marrying.'

'Yet you mock me for saying that Lady Glynnis and I are well suited, rather than being madly in love.'

'If I mock anything, it is the way in which you say it. And, in truth, I should not mock you at all—while I do not like to think of two people marrying without love, it is, perhaps, the more intelligent reason for them to do so.'

'Have you ever been in love, Miss Darling?' he asked. 'Or know how it feels to have your heart broken?'

'Oh, I have most definitely had my heart broken. When I was seven years old, Johnny Beaton stole my beloved stuffed elephant and threw him into the pond,' Emma said. 'I could not speak of it for days. And I did not speak to Johnny Beaton for several months.'

The smile transformed him, lighting up his face and making him look years younger and far more approachable. 'Now you are teasing me and for that I demand a forfeit.'

Emma snorted, even though her stomach did the silliest flip flop. 'Don't be ridiculous, my lord. Teasing does not warrant a forfeit. I am constantly being teased by my brother and as you are soon to be my brother-in-law, that falls under the heading of family privileges.'

'Nevertheless, until I *am* related by marriage, you owe me for being impolite.'

'I was not impolite!'

'Sarcasm is a gentleman's prerogative. It is not a quality to be admired in a lady.'

'Oh, very well. What is my penalty to be?'

He turned his eyes to the rolling countryside around them. 'A painting. The subject of which will be of my own choosing.'

Emma stared at him. 'Are you mad? I'm not talented enough to do the kind of work someone like you would wish to hang on his wall.'

'On the contrary, what you are *not* is a good judge of your own talent. I like what I've seen of your work and, since I am the one naming the forfeit, I shall be the one who says what it is to be. And if I say I want a painting, you have no choice but to agree.'

'And what would you have me paint, my lord?' Emma asked mockingly. 'A tranquil landscape? A bowl of fruit? A picture of your horse?'

His gaze moved over her face in a way that caused her breath to catch. 'I shall tell you at the ball what I wish the subject to be. But do not think I will forget. I've a far better memory than that. Good day, Miss Darling.' He touched the brim of his hat and turned the bay around, galloping back in the direction of Ellingsworth Hall.

Emma watched him go, trying to make sense of what had just happened. He wanted her to do a painting for him? Ridiculous! A man like that could afford to buy the works of the finest artists in the world. Why on earth would he ask for a painting from an amateur like herself?

Given that Aunt Dorothy and Linette could talk about nothing but the upcoming ball, Emma decided it was a good time to run a few errands. She needed to replenish some of her painting supplies and Mrs Wilbers, who ran the village shop, made a point of keeping most of what Emma required in stock. As well, Aunt Dorothy had asked her to pick up two lengths of lace and the latest fashion magazines from London. Her aunt might not be living in London, but her heart never left the bustling metropolis for any length of time.

Emma enjoyed her trips into the quaint little village. Thatched roofed cottages lined the main street, each with gardens bright with colourful flowers. And while there were only a few shops, they seemed to provide all the residents required. There was a bakery and a linen draper, a bookstore and a greengrocer, and whatever those establishments weren't able to provide, visitors to London could often be called upon to bring back. Consequently, two hours later, with all of her errands done, Emma returned to the trap, her arms piled high with purchases.

'Miss Darling, how nice to see you again. Here, let me help you with your purchases.'

Turning, Emma was surprised to see Mr Tufton walking towards her. 'Thank you, Mr Tufton, but it really isn't necessary—'

'Nonsense, I wouldn't be able to sleep knowing I had allowed a lady to struggle unaided beneath the weight of her purchases.' He relieved her of several of the boxes and placed them carefully in the trap. 'I suspect a good deal of this has to do with Miss Linette's wedding.'

'Some of it,' Emma agreed, 'though just as much is for me. Painting supplies and the like.'

'Ah, yes, your sister told me you were a talented artist. It must run in your family.'

Emma smiled, assuming from his comment that word of Ridley's new profession had also made the rounds.

'Still, there must be a great deal of excitement in

your house,' Mr Tufton went on, 'with your sister about to be married to the Earl of Widdicombe's son.'

A little too much, Emma was tempted to say, but feeling it might sound disloyal, said, 'There is indeed. And with Ridley home, we are quite a houseful.'

'I'm sure you are an admirable hostess and well able to keep everyone under control,' the vicar complimented her. 'You strike me as being a supremely organised young woman, entirely capable of managing a household.'

Emma inclined her head, wondering if he thought 'organised' the type of compliment a woman liked to hear. 'How are you getting on with your visits to parishioners?'

'Very well indeed. I have eaten more cake and drunk more tea in the last two weeks than in the previous six months,' he said with a rueful smile. 'But I have been made to feel welcome and for that I am exceedingly grateful. It is not easy to fill the shoes of a man like Mr Humbolt. He was a gifted orator, loved by one and all.'

Emma was touched by the note of humility in his voice. 'He was vicar here for a long time, Mr Tufton. It is only to be expected that he would garner a loyal following. You will too, given time.'

'You are kind to say so, but there are those who think I am too young to do the Lord's work.'

And likely too handsome. Emma already knew

of several young ladies who had taken to attending Sunday service with a great deal more enthusiasm than they had in the past. 'Never mind, they'll come round. Country folk do not like change and resist it for as long as they can. But you have a very pleasant manner and I feel sure you will be as well loved as Mr Humbolt in no time at all.'

'Thank you, Miss Darling. Your support and your friendship mean a great deal to me. I hope you know that.'

He smiled down at her and Emma saw a glimmer of earnest affection in his eyes.

'Well, I had best be getting home,' she said quickly. 'Thank you for your help, Mr Tufton. It was most appreciated.'

'My pleasure. I look forward to seeing you again in the near future.'

Emma felt her cheeks grow warm as she climbed into the seat. Was it possible Mr Tufton was interested in her? She didn't have a great deal of experience in that area, but it was hard to ignore the warmth in his voice when he spoke to her. The last time they had met, she had assumed his attentions were merely those of a man of the cloth towards one of his flock, but after today's encounter, she wasn't so sure.

Emma flicked the reins and set the mare to a brisk walk. How did she feel about the idea of Mr Tufton courting her? On a practical level, she knew she could do worse. He held a position of respect within the community, had a nice home and garden, and if he was at all ambitious, his chances for advancement were as good was any man's and better than most. And he was certainly handsome enough.

Not, perhaps, as handsome as Lord Stewart, but then she had met very few men who were. But his manner was pleasing and she did not feel as unsettled with him as she did with Lord Stewart. Nor did she feel the need to be on guard with everything she said.

No, Mr Tufton's was definitely the more tranquil presence. Lord Stewart was about as tranquil as a tiger. She couldn't believe she was even *thinking* about the two men in the same light. Lord Stewart was heir to the Earl of Widdicombe, practically engaged to Lady Glynnis Pettle. He clearly had no interest in her, and she certainly had no interest in—

Craacccckkk!

It happened without warning. The trap suddenly lurched to the left. As the mare whinnied, Emma toppled backwards off the seat, the reins wrenched from her hands as she landed on her back, her head hitting the floor of the trap hard.

For a few minutes, she just lay there, staring up at the sky. Though she'd heard that people often saw stars when they hit their heads, she had never experienced that particular sensation until now. And it was not in the least pleasant. Nor was the rest of her predicament. She was lying on an angle, with her feet higher than her head and her dress up around her knees. She was also over a mile from Dove's Hollow. How on earth was she going to get everything home?

She tried to sit up, only to sink back with a moan. Never mind getting home, how was she to sit up when every time she tried, the world started to spin madly around her?

'Miss Darling. Are you injured?'

Oh, wonderful! And now Lord Stewart had happened upon her. Of all the people who *could* have ridden by, why did it have to be him? 'I'm fine, though I'm not so sure about the trap,' she said in a depressingly weakened voice. 'Is Bess all right?'

'If you're referring to the mare, she's fine.' She heard him dismount and, seconds later, saw his face looming over hers. 'The trap's thrown a wheel. Are you sure *you*'re all right?'

Strangely enough, she was—now that he was here. But when she went to sit up, not only did her head swim, but the angle of the trap made it virtually impossible.

'Here, let me help you,' he offered.

'That won't be necessary—'

He brushed her objections aside. Leaning down, he slid his left arm behind her shoulders, and his right arm under her knees. Thank goodness she had pulled her dress down, but the cool air on her ankles told her it wasn't far enough. 'Lord Stewart, I hardly think this is necessary—'

'Put your arms around my neck,' he ordered.

Her cheeks flamed. 'That wouldn't be proper!'

'It might not be proper, but it will make getting you out of the trap a good deal easier.'

'But—'

'Miss Darling. Either do as I ask or I shall leave you here until dark. Which would you prefer?'

Too weak to argue, Emma put both of her arms around his neck and, seconds later, felt herself lifted out of the trap as though she weighed nothing at all. She had never been carried by a man before and she found the sensation startlingly intimate. The scent of fine linen and starch clung to his clothes, the scent of bay rum and lemon to his skin. Unfortunately, when her head suddenly came up higher than her legs, the world began to spin in a most alarming fashion. Perspiration dotted her forehead and stars danced in front of her eyes again. The sound of him calling her name was the last thing she heard before the white light exploded and silence blanketed her world.

Chapter Five

Emma came to slowly, rising from the depths of sleep to an awareness of soft grass beneath her back and a canopy of green leaves over her head. She blinked a few times, waiting for memory to return. When it did, she groaned and went to sit up, only to feel a hand at her shoulder gently pressing her back down.

'You might like to think twice before doing that,' Lord Stewart advised. 'Judging by the size of the lump on the back of your head, you would only pass out again.'

Emma reluctantly subsided, aware that he was probably right. Obviously she'd hit her head harder than she'd thought. She closed her eyes and drew a long deep breath. When she opened them again, it was to see him sitting beside her. 'Lord Stewart, where is your jacket?'

'Folded up beneath your head. I thought the lump needed cushioning.'

That explained the fragrance of lemon. 'It will not be fit to wear.'

'A small price to pay for your comfort. How do you feel?'

'I don't know,' she admitted. 'I should probably try sitting up.'

'Only if you go slowly.'

When she nodded, he slipped his arm beneath her shoulders and carefully brought her to an upright position. Emma kept her eyes closed and took a few deep breaths, trying to ignore the pleasurable feeling of his arm behind her back. Oh, yes, her head was definitely spinning, though whether that was from bumping her head or being in such close proximity to him, she really couldn't say.

'You might like to apply some cold cloths to that lump when you get home,' he advised. 'It will help bring down the swelling.'

'Thank you, I will.' She finally opened her eyes—and found herself staring into his: two clear blue mirrors that reflected her own face back at her. And try as she might, she couldn't look away.

'I've…taken the liberty of disengaging the mare from her harness,' he said abruptly. 'The trap is of no use now. I'll put you up on Thunder and walk alongside with the mare. We can take a few of the packages you'd rather not leave behind, but I'm afraid the rest will have to stay. I'll send someone back for them later.'

Emma nodded. He was being very sensible. Very gallant. Both of which were making her feel very guilty. 'I don't want to be a bother, Lord—'

'Alex.'

She glanced at him. 'Lord Alex?'

'Just Alex. I think we can drop the formality given what's happened. Besides, if I'm to be your brother-in-law, it is perfectly acceptable for you to call me Alex and for me to call you Emma.'

It did make sense. Unfortunately, it also made things a great deal more intimate, at least as far as she was concerned. 'I'm sure it would raise eyebrows if we were to be heard addressing one another in such a manner.'

'You worry too much. I already call your sister Linette. Why should I not call you Emma?'

Because it is my sister who is marrying into your family, Emma wanted to tell him, but she doubted he would understand. She wasn't sure she understood herself.

'I think I am well enough to stand. I need to get home. They will be wondering where I am.'

'Very well. But I shall get up first and help you to your feet.'

Emma nodded her agreement. It would be too embarrassing to try to regain her feet, only to collapse in a heap at his feet. She watched him rise, admiring his ease of motion. For such a tall man, he moved with surprising grace. Once standing, he bent down and placed his hands under her arms, then slowly raised her up.

It seemed right that she should put her hands on his forearms as he drew her to her feet. Even right to leave them there as they straightened together. But it was not right to think about letting them slip around his waist as she leaned into his strength…or to close her eyes and press her face against the warmth of his chest…

Unfortunately, that was exactly what happened. The moment she tried to stand on her own, Emma's knees buckled and the world began to waver… 'Oh!'

His arms went around her in an instant. 'You're not strong enough to ride alone,' he murmured against her hair. 'I'll ride with you.' Changing his position so that his arm encircled her waist, he led her back towards his horse. 'Lean against him while I fetch the mare,' Alex advised. 'And don't worry. He won't move and he doesn't bite.'

Emma did as she was told, thankful the big bay stood as motionless as he did. Alex walked across to where Bess stood flicking her ears back and forth and picked up the reins. He led her back across the grass, then swung up into his own saddle and looped the mare's reins through the leather strap of his saddle bag. 'All right, Emma, up you come.'

He lifted her with no more effort than had she been a child, gently placing her on the saddle in front of him and settling her so that her left side was resting against his chest, his arms on either side of her, holding her steady. Emma couldn't believe she was so weak. Just the act of being lifted on to Thunder's back had made her head spin. 'I'm sorry to be so silly,' she muttered. 'This has never happened to me before.'

'No need to apologise.' Alex pressed his heels gently into the bay's sides. 'It's not always easy to predict the effect a head injury will have.'

In spite of herself, Emma snorted. 'I don't have a head injury. I merely bumped my head. There is a difference.'

'Only if one has an effect and the other does not,' Alex said. 'In this case, you're dizzy and disoriented. Those are signs of a head injury as far as I'm concerned.'

Fearing that arguing might only make her feel worse, Emma subsided into silence. There was nothing she could do. The big horse's gait was surprisingly smooth; as she nestled against Alex's chest, it was all she could do to stay awake. Every time she closed her eyes, her head lolled back against his shoulder.

'Stop fighting, Emma,' he whispered. 'If you want to close your eyes, do so. I won't let you fall. You have my word as a gentleman.'

She didn't doubt him. Not for a moment. She would never fall as long as she was in his arms—but it was just unconscionable that she should enjoy it so much.

Finally, however, she did stop fighting. She lay back against him, aware of the rhythmic beating of his heart; with his arms enclosing her and the mare trotting peacefully behind them, they made their way home.

Alex knew the moment Emma settled into sleep. He felt her body go limp and heard her breathing settle into a deep, even pattern. How small she seemed in his arms. The first time they'd met, he'd thought her more substantial, but today, the top of her head barely reached his chin.

Strange the protective instincts she aroused within him. Alex thought he had experienced the full range of emotions when it came to women—fascination, admiration, lust—but he had never experienced this overwhelming need to protect. Perhaps because he had never been called upon to do so. The women with whom he associated were either the society ladies he flirted with or the demi-reps he bedded. And, given that the latter had no interest in holding anything back, Alex had never felt anything but the need to indulge himself.

Why, then, was this feeling for Emma Darling so different?

Whatever it was, he'd have to get it in hand. His unwelcome awareness of Emma Darling as a woman was something he hadn't anticipated and it definitely wasn't part of his plans. His plans were to propose to Glynnis after the house party and get on with his life. That was what everyone expected.

Certainly it was what Glynnis expected. They had been friends for a long time. When she had first made her debut in society, it was Alex to whom she had turned for guidance and Alex with whom she had danced her first dance. And when, over the course of those first few weeks, she had spent time in the company of other men, she had never taken any of them seriously. She was typically cool and reserved, almost analytical in her assessment of them, and she had always come back to Alex.

Perhaps that's why their relationship had become the eminently suitable partnership it was. Neither of them was ruled by passion. They liked each other and made decisions calmly and intelligently, the way decisions were supposed to be made. Matters were always far less complicated when emotions weren't involved.

Why, then, was he having so much troubling separating the two when it came to Emma?

She awoke within sight of Dove's Hollow. Alex felt her stir, heard the softness of an unguarded sigh, then felt her body stiffen as she realised where she was.

'Relax, Emma, we're almost home,' he murmured against her hair. 'You have nothing to worry about.'

'I'm not worried,' she said huskily. 'But my family will be if they see me slumped against you like this.'

He smiled, aware they would worry far more about the fact the two of them were riding the same horse than they would about how erect her posture was. Nevertheless, he was sorry to see their enforced closeness come to an end. He had enjoyed, more than he cared to admit, the softness of Emma's body against his. Perhaps because it had been such a long time since he'd held a woman in his arms. Once he had made up his mind to marry Glynnis, he had parted company with his mistress, feeling it was unfair to his future wife to carry on with the affair. And naturally, there hadn't been anything of a physical nature between himself and Glynnis. Their time together was usually spent in conversation or in the company of others. They had held hands on more than one occasion, and twice they had kissed, but at Glynnis's request they had gone no further than that.

There would be plenty of time for passion after they were married, Alex assured himself.

Still, holding Emma Darling now was a pleasurable experience beyond any he had ever known. Her hair felt like strands of silk against his chin and he was aware of the most delightful fragrance emanating from her. Something sweet, yet sensual. And not for the first time that day, he was grateful for whatever whim of fate had sent him down that particular path, resulting in his finding a wrecked trap in the road and its winsome owner in desperate need of his help.

As expected, their arrival at Dove's Hollow created quite a stir. Linette ran out first, followed closely by her aunt and then by her father, his face lined with concern as he ran up to greet them. 'Lord Stewart, what's happened?'

'Your daughter is fine, Mr Darling,' Alex was quick to reassure them. 'The trap broke a wheel and Miss Darling hit her head when she fell backwards into the cart.'

'Gracious, it was very good of you to stop and help,' Mrs Grand said.

'Indeed it was.' Mr Darling reached up his arms and, carefully, Emma slid down into them. 'Emma, my dear, are you all right?'

'I'm fine, Papa,' Emma said, even though Alex

suspected the motion set her head to pounding again. 'It's really not at all serious.'

'We'll let the doctor be the judge of that. Linette, send Jenks for the doctor. Ask him to come as quickly as he can.'

'Yes, Papa,' the girl said and promptly disappeared.

'Lord Stewart, we are indebted to you,' Mr Darling said. 'Will you stay and take some refreshment with us?'

'Another time.' Alex had dismounted and was already unfastening the mare's reins. 'I think Miss Darling needs to rest.' He glanced at Emma's white face and knew she didn't need a stranger around right now, especially one of whom she had no reason to be overly fond. 'But I would ask that you send me word of her condition so that I may be assured no complications have set in.'

'We will certainly keep you apprised,' Mr Darling said. 'And again, we are in your debt for having brought her safely home.'

Alex inclined his head as the three of them walked back into the house. He watched until the door closed behind them, but as he swung up into the saddle, he refused to ask himself why it mattered that Emma had not turned to look back at him.

He waited impatiently for word of her condition. He assured himself there was nothing to worry about.

That it had been only a light bump to the back of her head. If it had been more, he would have seen signs of it straight away. Nevertheless, Alex was relieved when he finally received Mr Darling's letter, saying that the doctor had called and that the bump Emma had sustained was not serious. The application of cold cloths had brought the swelling down and she had managed to sleep for most of the afternoon.

He refolded the letter, pleased by the news that Emma was all right, but alarmed at how much better he felt upon receiving it. He had been on tenterhooks all afternoon. A natural reaction, he tried to tell himself, for the young lady whose sister would soon be his brother's wife.

'Ah, there you are, Alex,' Peter said, walking into the billiards room. 'I thought you'd gone up. Is that a letter from Lady Glynnis?'

Alex glanced at the parchment in his hand. It seemed a waste of time to tell Peter about the events of the afternoon now that everything had been satisfactorily resolved. 'No.' He folded it up and slipped it into his jacket. 'Care for a game?'

'Yes, though you'll probably just beat me again.'

'Only if you don't concentrate.' Alex racked the balls as Peter took down his cue. 'You may break.'

Peter did, then stood back to survey the table. 'So, Mother tells me you're planning to ask Glynnis to marry you in the very near future. That must have made Father happy.'

'It did.' Alex also surveyed the table. Bending down, he sighted his cue, then smoothly drew it back. 'He's always thought highly of Glyn.'

'The two of you have been friends for a long time. I remember the day you told Father you were thinking about her as a wife. He didn't stop smiling for a week.'

'I know. He used to tease Glyn unmercifully,' Alex said, watching the ball drop into the pocket. 'Said she was too tall and skinny and that she squeaked when she got excited. But she was never afraid of him. Not like the other girls. ' He bent down to take another shot. 'Glyn always gave as good as she got. That's why he liked her so much. And why I did.'

'No doubt,' Peter said, leaning against the edge of the table. 'So, when were you going to tell me about Father's being ill?'

Alex glanced up. 'If you recall, I mentioned it while we were at dinner with the Darlings.'

'Telling our guests that Father had to stay in London because he wasn't feeling well isn't quite the same as telling me he collapsed as the result of a bad heart. How serious is it?'

'I honestly don't know.' Alex took his shot and then watched the ball roll the length of the table, stopping just short of the pocket. 'Serious enough that Mother had to call in Harrow.'

'Good Lord.'

'I know. Came as a shock to me as well.'

'Do you think it's his heart?'

'That's what Harrow said.'

'But he can't know for sure?'

'Your guess is as good as mine. All I know is that Harrow said Father has to start taking better care of himself.'

'And to avoid stressful situations,' Peter murmured drily. 'God knows I'm not helping in that regard, am I?'

'Well, I'd be lying if I said the circumstances of your engagement haven't caused him some additional aggravation,' Alex said, straightening. 'But I doubt you're the only source of frustration in his life.'

'So what am I supposed to do?' Peter asked, his forehead furrowing. 'End my engagement to Linette just to make Father happy?'

'Is that so unreasonable?'

'It is to me.'

'Maybe you should look at your reasons for wishing to marry her,' Alex said. 'Analyse what you stand to gain from the alliance.'

'My reasons for marrying her are simple,' Peter said. 'I love her. And what I expect to gain from the marriage is the opportunity to spend the rest of my life with the woman I want to be with more than any other. What more *could* a man ask?'

'The respect of his friends and society,' Alex said quietly. 'The knowledge that he has lived up to his obligations with regards to his family and his name. There are those who share Father's concern about the wisdom of this marriage, Peter. People who expected you to do better.'

'I couldn't have done any better. Linette makes me happy.'

'But a man cannot always concern himself solely with his own happiness. Marriages are made for the good of both parties and for the benefit of the family.'

'Your marriage, Alex, not mine,' Peter said quietly. 'I don't need to worry about producing an heir.'

'That's a rather narrow point of view.'

'Is it? I prefer to think of it as being realistic, the same as my acceptance of your superiority at billiards. See? You've won again.'

Alex didn't give a damn about the billiards game. He cared about his brother. And the more time he spent in conversation with him, the more he feared he wasn't going to be able to change Peter's mind about Linette Darling.

'Alex, would you be willing to do something for me?' Peter said, putting his cue back on the rack.

'If I can.'

'Come out with us this week. Spend some time

with Linette and see what kind of woman she is. I guarantee you won't be disappointed. And if you speak up on her behalf, I know Father will feel better about the marriage. He won't listen to me, but he respects your opinion. He always has.'

It was a lot to ask. Alex knew it wasn't so much Linette Darling his father resented, but what she represented. The earl expected both of his sons to marry well-born ladies. Linette didn't fit into that mould. She had been raised and educated in the country. She was not well read, had very little fashion sense and likely hadn't been taught any but the most rudimentary of country dances. She was not a lady born to the role.

And no matter how lovely or pleasant she was, nothing was ever going to change that.

Emma was in the garden sketching when Alex arrived to pay a visit the next morning. Given that her neck and shoulders were still tender as a result of her tumble into the trap, she had decided not to venture out as far out as the pond, but to sit in the shade of the towering oak tree, beneath which stood an old stone angel.

The angel had long been a source of artistic frustration to Emma. Not only was the colour of the stone difficult to replicate, but the details of the angel's features had all but worn away. Only her wings seem to have maintained any semblance of their original texture and Emma was fully engaged in trying to replicate their feathery look when she heard the crunch of gravel and turned to see the gentleman walking towards her.

The quiver of anticipation was automatic—and instantly quelled. She had no right to feel anything beyond the mildest friendship for Alex, but facts were facts and she knew there was no use in pretending otherwise. She liked Alexander Taylor. Worse, she was attracted to him. Not only because he was a remarkably handsome man, but because he was turning out to be a surprisingly compassionate one. She had been startled by the degree of concern he had shown towards her yesterday, and though it was pointless to complain about the way he had brought her home, she certainly couldn't pretend she hadn't enjoyed being held in his arms. He was a man who commanded respect and affection simply as a result of who he was.

And with every day that passed, Emma grew more and more aware of how deeply she was coming to like and admire him.

'Good morning, Emma,' he greeted her. 'I hope I'm not disturbing your concentration.'

'I was already disturbed by my inability to capture the wispy quality of the angel's wings.' Emma kept her sketch pad poised, glad to have something other than him upon which to focus. 'As you can see, it is an ongoing battle.'

He stopped and glanced over her shoulder at the sketchpad. 'But you have captured it.' He leaned forwards to indicate a line. 'See here, how you've made this piece look so wispy and this one so bold. It is exactly how the statue looks.'

Emma tried to ignore the warmth of his arm as it pressed against her shoulder. 'Thank you, my lord, but if you look more closely, you will see that the edge of this wing is too heavy, and up here, there isn't enough shading where the top of the wing curves over. And I've done a terrible job of capturing her expression.'

'On the contrary, it is the angel's expression that is lacking,' Alex said, straightening. 'You have given her a very nice smile. The statue's is somewhat… evil.'

Emma chuckled. 'Only because a piece of her mouth was knocked off during a windstorm. Poor thing. She originally had a very pretty mouth.'

'Not unlike the lady attempting to sketch her.'

Emma's head snapped up. He was smiling at her—and, stupidly, it went straight to her heart. How in the world was she to keep him at a distance if he continued to be charming like this?

She set the sketchbook aside and slowly stood up. 'Thank you for collecting the rest of my packages and having them sent home, Alex. *And* for having the trap fixed. It was very good of you to go to all that trouble. You really shouldn't have bothered.'

'It was no bother. You couldn't have driven the trap the way it was and I didn't like the idea of your packages sitting at the side of the road where anyone could have taken them.'

'I doubt a thief would have been interested in painting supplies,' Emma said drily. 'But I was glad to have them returned. If you have a moment, Papa would like to thank you as well. He was most grateful for everything you did.'

'Never mind that, how are you feeling?'

'Did you not receive Papa's note?'

'Yes, but I wished to know for myself that you are feeling better. You took a nasty spill.'

His concern was flattering, but Emma knew better than to let herself read too much into it. 'I am much better, thank you. Even the swelling has gone down.'

To her dismay, he brought his hand to the back of her head and gently felt for the lump. 'So it has. There is only a slight swelling there now.'

Emma took a short, hard breath. His hand was warm, his fingers gentle against her scalp. The urge to close her eyes and lean into his hand was overwhelming—and indefensible. 'The result of… frequent applications of cold clothes,' she said in a halting voice. She took a step back and watched his hand fall away. 'Shall we return to the house?'

Not surprisingly, it took only a few minutes to gather everyone in the drawing room. Aunt Dorothy and Linette were already there, the latter refurbishing a bonnet, the former embroidering handkerchiefs. Her father arrived shortly thereafter, and upon seeing Alex, stretched out his hand in welcome. 'Lord Stewart, how very good of you to call.'

'I thought to enquire after Miss Darling's health, but she has informed me she is fully recovered.'

'Mercifully, she is, but it is extraordinarily kind of you to be so concerned. And I must ask you to let me know the cost of repairing the trap. I was grateful you repaired one wheel. There was certainly no need to replace all four.'

'We will not talk about cost where the safety of your family is at issue,' Alex said. 'I was told it was only a matter of time before the other wheels went the way of the first and I would not have been able to live with myself had an accident occurred that I had had the knowledge to prevent.'

'Nevertheless, it was an exceedingly generous thing to do,' Aunt Dorothy said. 'Without the trap, we are quite housebound. And though there is little enough to be had in the village, it is nice to be able to get there when one is in need.'

There was a clatter of boots in the hall, followed by the appearance of Ridley at the door. 'Have I missed all the excitement?'

'Not a bit. Your timing is, as always, excellent,' Mr Darling drawled. 'Lord Stewart, my son, Ridley.'

Alex bowed. 'Your servant, sir.'

'Lord Stewart,' Ridley said. 'A pleasure.'

Emma glanced at her brother in surprise. Was it her imagination or did he actually sound a little in awe?

'Lord Stewart stopped by to see how Emma was feeling,' Linette explained.

'Really? Ah, well, you've no worries there,' Ridley said. 'Emma's head is as hard as mine. Takes more than a little bump to keep either of us down. Isn't that right, Em?'

Emma could have cheerfully murdered him. 'I dare say it does.'

Alex just smiled. 'I understand you're an artist, Mr Darling.'

'I am. Gave up chasing the bar to paint portraits of aristocratic gentlemen like yourself,' Ridley quipped. 'I find it far more entertaining.'

'But not nearly as respectable,' his father muttered.

'Now, Percy, let's not start in on that again,' Aunt Dorothy said. 'Ridley has assured us that he is making a good living, and as long as he is in demand, he will no doubt continue to do so.'

'Speaking of which, I've decided what I am going to give you as a wedding present, Linny,' Ridley said. 'How would you like a formal portrait of you and your fiancé in a setting of your choice?'

'Oh, Ridley, that would be wonderful!' Linette said, clapping her hands together. Then, with an anxious glance at her father, added, 'It would be all right, wouldn't it, Papa?'

'I don't see why not,' Ridley said before his father had a chance to object. 'The aristocracy all have portraits painted of themselves and as you are going to be the daughter-in-law of a peer, why shouldn't you have one done too?'

'I think it is a very generous offer,' Aunt Dorothy said. 'And we all know Ridley will do an excellent job.'

'Although you may wish to wait until they *are* actually married before starting on the work,' Alex said.

Emma sent a suspicious glance in his direction. 'Why would you say that?'

'Because it takes a good deal of time to paint a portrait and getting two people together at a time convenient to both during the preparations for a wedding can be challenging. However, once they are married and living in the same house, it will be much easier to arrange sittings.'

'Very sensible, Lord Stewart,' Aunt Dorothy commented. 'And I think a portrait of the newly married couple will make a fine wedding gift. Who knows, Ridley, perhaps Lord Stewart will commission you to do one of himself and his lady once they are married.'

'I should be delighted.' Ridley glanced at the other man with interest. 'But forgive me, my lord, I was not aware you were to be married.'

'My mother was a bit hasty in announcing the engagement,' Alex acknowledged. 'I have not yet actually asked the lady for her hand.'

'But what woman in her right mind would turn down the opportunity to become a countess?'

'I doubt that is of concern to Lady Glynnis,' Linette said. 'She is already the daughter of an earl and has no need to marry in order to acquire a title or status.'

'Lady Glynnis?' There was a brief pause before Ridley said, 'Lady Glynnis Pettle?'

'Yes, that's right.'

'Do you know her, Ridley?' Linette asked, blue eyes bright with excitement. 'I thought you might given that you are moving in such high society now.'

'I do not move in high society, Imp,' Ridley replied. 'I merely bump into them every now and then. But I have heard the lady's name mentioned in conversation. I believe it came up in regard to a charity auction she and Lady Trilby's daughter were arranging.'

'Oh.' Linette's disappointment was plain. 'Then you are not acquainted with her.'

'I am not.' Ridley put his hands on his knees and got to his feet. 'Well, if you will all excuse me—'

'Where are you off to now?' his father asked. 'You've been out more than you've been in since you arrived home.'

'Oh, leave the boy be, Percy,' Aunt Dorothy said. 'You can't expect him to keep you apprised of what he's doing every minute of the day. Think how you would have felt had your father treated you that way when you were Ridley's age.'

'My father *did* treat me that way and it certainly didn't do me any harm,' Mr Darling said. 'You've seen what happens when young men are left to their own devices. Ridley gave up a perfectly respectable occupation to become a painter.'

'I did not *give up* an occupation,' Ridley said in frustration. 'I simply decided not to become something I didn't want to be. If you can't understand that, we have nothing more to talk about.'

He left, slamming the door behind him.

'Oh dear,' Aunt Dorothy said. 'I didn't mean to upset him.'

'I shouldn't worry about it, Aunt,' Emma said, aware of Alex standing quietly off to one side. 'I suspect Ridley didn't want to tell us where he was going because he is off to visit a young lady in the village.'

'I beg your pardon? Which young lady?' Mr Darling demanded.

'Miss Harkness, most likely. Or Miss Stone. I know they were both very excited about the prospect of Ridley coming home for Linette's wedding.'

'And why would they not be excited?' Aunt Dorothy said, relief colouring her voice as she picked up her embroidery. 'Ridley is such a handsome lad. Always has been. Reminds me of a young man I knew once. Albert, his name was. Did I ever tell you about him, Linette?'

Linette smiled. 'No, Aunt Dorothy.'

'Almost married the dear boy, I was that smitten with him. And he wasn't near as handsome as your brother. Still, it wasn't meant to be and I suppose it's just as well. Your uncle came along soon after and he was far better off than poor Albert.'

Emma only just managed not to smile. Aunt Dorothy must have been at the sherry again. She tended to reminisce when she'd had a drink or two and she obviously didn't care that Lord Stewart was still in the room.

Still, at least her anecdote had served to take the attention away from Ridley and Emma was definitely grateful for that. Her suggestion that he had gone to see a young lady in the village had been pure fabrication because she was quite sure his reasons for leaving had nothing to do with having to be anywhere. His expression had changed the moment Lady Glynnis Pettle's name had been mentioned. And the tightening of his jaw indicated something far more troubling than a mild case of surprise.

Ridley had been *distressed* by the mention of Lady Glynnis's upcoming marriage to Lord Stewart. And the reasons behind *that* were neither pleasant to contemplate, nor possible to ignore.

Chapter Six

Emma felt nothing but relief when Alex took his leave shortly thereafter. Not because she wished to see him gone, but because the effort of having to pretend that everything was all right was definitely wearing on her nerves. She had no idea if Alex had noticed the change in her brother at the mention of Lady Glynnis's name, but he was not a stupid man and she knew better than to underestimate his powers of observation. Until she knew why Ridley had left so abruptly, she was happier keeping Alex at a distance than she was at having him close.

They walked outside together and found the bay waiting patiently, his reins having been tied to the hitching post. 'Strange,' Alex said. 'I don't recall leaving him tethered.'

'That's likely Jenks's doing,' Emma said with a smile. 'He isn't used to horses being left to their own devices. Certainly none of our horses are so well behaved.'

'Thunder is unusual in that regard, but it does come in handy when one takes a spill in the hunting field,' Alex said, patting the big bay's neck. 'Nothing worse than having to trek miles back to the house on foot, especially in the rain.'

'That cannot be good for one's boots.'

'Most definitely not.' Alex untied the horse's reins. 'Emma, my brother tells me there is to be an assembly held tomorrow evening at a house on the outskirts of the village.'

'Yes, at Mr and Mrs Jacobs's. Linette mentioned it to me the other day.'

'Were you planning to attend?'

'I thought I might. The Jacobs are good friends,' Emma said. 'They have a large house and they enjoy holding dances in it. We always have a good time.'

'Then perhaps I shall see you there.'

Emma gasped. 'You're *going?*'

'Yes. Do you find that strange?'

'Well, yes, I suppose I do,' Emma said, at a loss for a tactful reply. 'It will surely pale in comparison to the elegance of the soirées you normally attend in London.'

'Perhaps, but I thought it might make for an interesting diversion. There is not a great deal to do here in Little Moreton.'

Emma sighed. No, there really wasn't, especially for a man like Alex. To him, Little Moreton must seem almost paralytically boring because it wasn't his world. *His* world was in London, with the beautiful Lady Glynnis Pettle at his side. An assembly at the Jacobs's would be, at best, a pale imitation of what he was used to. 'Well, I dare say you'll find something with which to amuse yourself,' Emma said. 'There will be cards for those who don't like to dance.'

'But I do like to dance,' he told her. 'In fact, I hope you will reserve a dance for me. A waltz, if I may be so bold.'

Stupidly, her pulse quickened. He wanted to dance with her…and not just any dance: a waltz, that most intimate of ballroom dances. He would be required to take her in his arms and to twirl her around the room, with one hand at her waist and the other holding her hand. And throughout it all, she would be expected to remain calmly indifferent and commendably aloof.

She *had* to remain that way. There would be far too many eyes watching them to permit any other kind of expression.

'I shall make a note of it on my card,' Emma said lightly. 'Until tomorrow, Lord Stewart.'

He stared at her for a long time. Then, with a brief but unusually genuine smile, he swung up into the saddle and touched the brim of his hat. 'Until tomorrow, Miss Darling.'

* * *

No sooner had Alex disappeared than Emma went in search of her brother. It was better she face *him* down than let her thoughts dwell on Alex. In that direction dwelt heartache and disappointment. The less time she spent longing for the unattainable, the better.

Ridley was another matter entirely. Emma was convinced there was more going on between her brother and Lady Glynnis than he was letting on, and for everyone's sake, she had to find out what it was, though Lord knew if he'd tell her. Her brother could clam up tighter than an oyster when it suited him.

She found him in the conservatory, sitting on a stone wall, his sketchpad open in his hands. 'Ridley?'

He flushed and quickly turned the page over. 'What do you want?'

'Only to talk. I was concerned when you left the drawing room so abruptly.' She sat down on the wall beside him. 'I wondered if someone had said something to offend you.'

'You mean other than Father *demanding* to know where I was going?'

Emma laughed. 'He did not demand that you tell him.'

'He would have,' Ridley muttered, 'had Aunt Dorothy not stepped in to intervene. Thank God she'd been at the sherry again. I doubt she would have said anything if she'd been sober.'

'Probably not. But you and Papa have never seen eye to eye about the proffering of information.'

'And I doubt we ever will. He doesn't seem to understand that I'm not a child any more,' Ridley grumbled. 'I'm old enough to do as I please and I don't appreciate having to account for my whereabouts every time I set foot outside the door.'

'But you didn't have anywhere to go, did you, Ridley? You just wanted to leave the room. Why?'

'No particular reason.'

Emma shrugged. 'As you wish.' She glanced at the sketchpad. 'What are you drawing?'

'Nothing. As you can see, the page is blank.'

'I mean on the one you just flipped over.'

'Oh, that. A poor rendition of a folly I came across on Lord Garrickson's estate,' he said in an offhand manner.

'Lord Garrickson,' Emma repeated, impressed. 'You *are* moving in illustrious circles these days, Ridley. Hobnobbing with Lord Bickerson. Accepting commissions from Viscount Huston. And now whiling away the hours on Lord Garrickson's estate. No wonder you're acquainted with people like Lady Glynnis Pettle.'

Nothing altered in Ridley's face. Not so much as an eyebrow flickered. But Emma saw his fingers

tighten on the piece of charcoal. 'I have no idea what
you're talking about. I've already said I don't know
the lady.'

'But I believe you *do* and better than you would
have any of us believe,' Emma said softly. 'And not
just as a result of hearing her name mentioned in
conversation.'

'It would be impossible for me to give you an accounting of *all* of the people I hear spoken of in a
day, Emma.' Ridley began to sketch the wicker chair
opposite, making quick, bold strikes with the piece
of charcoal. 'We would be here until doomsday.'

'But we weren't talking about a lot of people. We
were talking about Lady Glynnis Pettle. Now stop
prevaricating and tell me the truth, Ridley. Have you
met the lady or not?'

He hesitated briefly. 'What if I have?'

'Why didn't you want to admit it in front of Lord
Stewart?'

'Because it's none of his business.'

'None of his business? Ridley, Lady Glynnis is
going to *marry* Lord Stewart. I would say that *makes*
it his business, wouldn't you? And since there is no
getting around the fact that you and the lady are
going to *be* in the same house together, I suggest
you stop playing games. Now, what's the real reason
you didn't want Lord Stewart to know that you were
acquainted with Lady Glynnis?'

Ridley sighed in exasperation. 'Damn it, Emma, you are no less a badger at four-and-twenty than you were at six. Even then you refused to let anything go.'

'Then you should know better than to try to keep things from me now.'

'I wasn't trying to keep anything from you. I simply didn't want to tell Lord Stewart that I knew Lady Glynnis, because…I didn't want him to know that I had painted her.'

Emma blinked her surprise. 'She *sat* for you?'

'Remember I told you a lady had hired me to paint a portrait of her as a gift for someone else? Well, that was Lady Glynnis.'

Emma stared at her brother in bewilderment. He had run out of the room as though the hounds of hell were after him…because the woman Alex was going to marry had hired him to paint her portrait? 'You're not making any sense, Ridley. You are an artist and Lady Glynnis wanted her portrait painted. Where is the harm in admitting that *you* were the one she hired to do it?'

'Because I was afraid such an admission would have spoiled the surprise.'

'What surprise?'

'Did I not just tell you the portrait was to be a gift?'

'Yes.'

'Did it not occur to you that the person Lady

Glynnis had in mind for the gift might just be Lord Stewart?'

'Oh!'

'Exactly.' Ridley resumed his sketching. 'It wouldn't have been very sporting of me to spoil her surprise. Now, may we please move on to another topic?'

'What did the two of you talk about?'

'Emma!'

'I'm just curious to know more about her. After all, she is going to be related to us through Linette's marriage to Peter.'

Ridley's face darkened. 'Then you'll have to ask her yourself. I don't remember what we talked about.'

'Did she mention Lord Stewart at all?' Emma persisted.

'No.'

'Strange. You'd think she would have if the painting was to be a gift for him.'

'Sometimes there's just no accounting for the ways of the aristocracy.'

'Was she pleased with her portrait?'

'I believe so.' He glanced from the wicker chair to his sketchpad, his hands constantly moving. 'I painted her in the rose garden at Devonwood. She said she preferred that to a more traditional setting.'

'How long did it take?'

'A few weeks.' Ridley deftly drew a few more lines

so that, as Emma watched, not only the chair but the entire corner began to take shape. 'She asked me to come at different times of the day so it was difficult to finish the painting without having to keep retouching the background. Mid-morning light is entirely different from afternoon light. It took me several days to get the warmth of her complexion and the variations of her hair colour just right.'

'Yes, I'm sure it was,' Emma murmured, watching his face. 'You know she's going to be at the ball.'

'I suspected as much.'

'Will you be all right with that?'

'Of course. The lady engaged me to paint her portrait. I did. Nothing more to it.'

'So when you see her again, there won't be any feelings of awkwardness between you?'

'Why should there be? I completed the commission and we parted. Most likely, she won't even remember my name.' Ridley closed the sketchpad and stood up. 'People like that never do.'

He walked away, hands in his pockets, the sketchpad tucked under his arm, as though he hadn't a care in the world—but Emma didn't believe it for a moment. Ridley had always been good at making others believe what he wanted them to, but she had always been able to see through him because she knew where to look. The truth was there in his eyes.

They were open and honest—sometimes in direct contrast to what came out of his mouth.

And the truth had been there just now, when he had talked about his feelings for Lady Glynnis. His mouth had said one thing, but his eyes had said something entirely different.

For once, Emma desperately wished that she could have believed the former.

The next afternoon, Emma sat with paintbrush in hand, staring at her own blank canvas. She wanted to believe that her inability to paint was the result of a lack of creative thought, but that was like trying to convince herself that the sky was purple and the clouds red.

How *could* she paint with everything that was going on around her? Her sister was about to enter into a marriage the groom's parents didn't approve of. She was unable to shake the feeling that Ridley hadn't been honest with her about his previous encounters with Lady Glynnis Pettle. And, worst of all, *she* had to deal with the inappropriateness of her feelings for Alex.

If all that wasn't enough to stifle creativity, she didn't know what was!

Still, while there was nothing she could do about Linette's or Ridley's situations, there was definitely something she could do about hers—and that was to stop thinking about Alex. The man was all but engaged to another woman. A woman his family approved of and who was eminently more suited to being his wife than she ever would be.

She didn't even know why she *couldn't* stop thinking about him. It wasn't as though she was lonely, or in need of male companionship. Emma was proud of her ability to find contentment without the presence of a man. Why, then, was *his* face the first thing she saw upon waking and the last thing she thought of at night?

It made absolutely no sense. Apart from that one afternoon when he had come to her rescue, Alex's treatment of her had been utterly cordial and predictably correct. He had given her no encouragement, nor had she looked for any. And yet, the thought of seeing him at the Jacobs's assembly tonight, and the knowledge that they would be dancing together, made her pulse race in a most alarming fashion. How silly that the thought of being held in his arms, that the anticipation of his hand closing around hers, should make it so difficult to breathe. Unfortunately as the carriage drew to a halt in front of the Jacobs's sprawling house later that evening, Emma realised it was all she was able to think about.

'Oh, look, Emma,' Linette whispered as they made their way into the ballroom after greeting their host and hostess. 'There's Mr Taylor. And Lord Stewart is with him.'

As her sister raised her hand to wave at her fiancé, Emma smiled and glanced in the other direction. Linette could wear her heart on her sleeve if she wished, but she didn't have that luxury when it came to Alex. She had to clamp down on these ridiculous urges and get them under control. She couldn't risk making a fool of herself in front of everyone she knew.

Worse, she couldn't make a fool of herself in front of him.

For that reason, she was exceedingly grateful when relief presented itself in the form of Mr John Tufton.

'Good evening, Miss Darling,' he said, coming up to them. 'Miss Linette. How lovely you both look this evening.'

'Thank you, Mr Tufton,' Emma said. 'I didn't expect to see you here.'

'I enjoy gatherings of this sort,' the vicar said. 'And though I don't usually dance, it is very pleasant to watch others do so.'

'Mr Tufton,' Linette said, 'I hope you won't think me rude, but I would like to go and speak to Mr Taylor.' She glanced at her sister. 'Emma, do you mind?'

'Of course not. I shall catch up with you later.'

Linette smiled and left them, all but skipping across the room in her eagerness to join her fiancé.

'Your sister seems very happy,' Mr Tufton remarked.

'I have never seen her happier,' Emma said softly. 'I suppose that is a true indication of love.' She watched them and was suddenly reminded of what Linette had said about the way people in love act. She saw Peter smile down at her, saw them briefly lean towards one another and touch hands, and then both blush and pull away again. Oh, yes, there was a very strong connection there. And to think Alex had asked her to try to break them up—

'…excited about the wedding.'

Emma turned her head, aware that Mr Tufton must think her abominably rude. 'I'm so sorry, Mr Tufton. What were you saying about the wedding?'

'Only that your sister must be very excited about it.'

'You would think so, but in fact, she is dreading it.'

The vicar looked shocked. 'She is?'

'The ceremony,' Emma said quickly. 'Linette wants nothing more than to be Mr Taylor's wife, but she is terribly shy and would much rather it be done without a great deal of fuss. However, she is marrying into the Earl of Widdicombe's family and that calls for a certain amount of formality.'

'Yes, I see what you mean,' Mr Tufton said. 'I should think it would be daunting for anyone, let alone someone as shy as Linette, to face the challenges that lie ahead. Especially given the dissension that I hear exists within the family over the marriage.'

Emma turned to look at him. 'Dissension?'

'There are those who say the earl is not pleased with his son's choice of bride and that he is not going to attend the wedding. There has even been speculation that he isn't here because of his refusal to meet her.'

'The reason my father is not here,' said a cold voice behind them, 'is as a result of his ill health. It has *nothing* to do with his reluctance to see my brother and Miss Linette celebrate their engagement.'

Emma blushed hotly. It was impossible to miss the note of irritation in Alex's voice and Mr Tufton clearly had not. 'Forgive me for speaking out of turn, Lord Stewart,' he said quickly. 'I was only repeating what I had heard.'

'Then I suggest you verify your facts before passing along gossip. It does no one any good for lies to be taken as fact, Mr Tufton. You of all people should know that.'

Chastised, the vicar inclined his head. 'Indeed I do, my lord. And I shall be more mindful of what I say in the future.' With that, he bowed and walked away.

Emma, feeling decidedly sorry for the man, said, 'You could have been more tactful.'

'And he could have been more circumspect,' Alex snapped. 'I don't care for a clergyman who gossips. Why my father isn't here is no one's business but his own.'

'On the contrary, your brother is about to marry a woman your father hasn't even met and on the two occasions where he might have done so, he was noticeably absent,' Emma said boldly. 'Questions are bound to be raised in other people's minds.'

'I repeat, my father is not well.'

'But he has not even sent her a letter saying how sorry he is that he has had to miss both occasions. So naturally, Linette is imagining all manner of reasons as to why he hasn't come. She believes he has taken her in dislike.'

'Does that surprise you?' Alex replied. 'Have I not already told you that neither he nor my mother are happy about the marriage?'

'But if your mother can set aside her feelings, why can your father not do the same? You said yourself the marriage *is* going to take place.'

'Only because Peter will consider nothing else.'

'Then does it not behove *both* of your parents to come to terms with the arrangement as quickly as possible? For the benefit of all concerned?'

Emma hated arguing with him, but she simply

could not let his father's continued absence at these gatherings go unchallenged. Surely he could see that other people must find it questionable in the extreme.

'Good Lord, Emma, what are you and my future brother-in-law talking about?' Ridley said, suddenly appearing on the scene. 'If looks could kill, I swear you'd both be lying dead on the floor.'

Emma felt her cheeks burn, but Alex rose to the occasion masterfully. 'It is nothing to be concerned about, Mr Darling. Your sister and I were simply discussing the painting she has agreed to do for me.'

Emma glanced at Alex in horror, but Ridley was even more shocked. 'Emma is doing a *painting* for you? Good Lord, and here I thought I was the only artist in the family.'

'You *are* the only artist!' Emma said, blushing furiously. 'Lord Stewart happened upon me one day as I was painting a dragonfly and said he wanted one of my paintings—'

'Of a dragonfly?'

'No, silly! Of something of his own choosing.'

'And you *agreed?*'

'Not exactly.'

'But he just said you were discussing the painting you agreed to do for him. How is it you were going to sell him a painting when you're not even willing to *show* me anything you've done?'

'Lord Stewart isn't buying the painting, Ridley!'

Emma said, cursing Alex for having brought it up. 'He mistakenly believed I insulted him and that I owe him a painting as a forfeit.'

Ridley's surprise quickly turned to incredulity. 'You insulted our future brother-in-law?'

'Of course not! I said he *thought* I'd insulted him, when in fact I did nothing of the kind—'

'I think,' Alex cut in smoothly, 'it would be best if we were to continue this discussion at a later date, Miss Darling. I do believe this is our waltz.'

Sure enough, the orchestra had begun to play and the opening strains of the waltz could be heard drifting throughout the room. With Ridley looking on, Alex extended his hand.

Emma stared at it, furious at having been backed into a corner. She hated having to explain herself and she didn't like having to defend her actions to Ridley. He was already watching them with far more interest than was called for and the last thing she needed was to give him more ammunition with which to tease her. But neither could she refuse to dance with Alex. She had given him her promise and if she reneged on that now, he would likely only end up demanding another forfeit. And God only knew what *that* might be!

And so, keeping her smile firmly in place—while wishing them both a long and lingering malady—she placed her hand in his, raised her chin and in chilly silence let him lead her on to the floor.

Alex did not regret his decision to attend the Jacobs's assembly. While lacking in the number of titled guests, it could not be said to be lacking in any other way. The refreshments were far superior to those served in many of the best London houses and the warmth of his host and hostess was undeniable. Now he was on the dance floor with Emma Darling, a woman who aroused more conflicting emotions in him than any woman he'd ever met. She was a baffling mixture of innocence and independence—a woman who could freeze with a glance or charm with a word. He couldn't remember the last time he had been so fascinated by a woman. Or so aware of one. 'You dance very well, Emma,' he said, hoping to break the tense silence between them. Since they had stepped on to the floor, she had scarcely spoken a word.

'Did you think I would not know how?' she shot back.

For some reason, her anger amused him. 'Not at all. I had no reason to believe you would not be as accomplished in feminine undertakings as any other lady of my acquaintance. But while the waltz is accepted in London, I thought it might not have received widespread approval in places like Little

Moreton. A fact borne out by the expression on *that* lady's face.'

Emma turned her head to glance at the woman in question, and struggled not to smile. 'Mrs Proctor is not as forward thinking as some, my lord. She doesn't approve of single ladies and gentlemen…touching.'

'Then I dare say she would be shocked by some of the dances I saw during my travels in Spain.'

'Why? How do they dance in Spain?' Emma asked.

'Provocatively,' he whispered against her ear. 'They dance as though they were lovers.'

He wasn't surprised when she gasped, but when she tried to pull away he merely tightened his grip. 'You asked me a question, I answered it.'

'But surely there was no need to be so descriptive,' she threw back at him.

He laughed, a fact which only angered Emma more. 'Stop it, Alex! Mrs Proctor is staring at us.'

'Let her stare. I don't care about Mrs Proctor, Emma,' he murmured. 'We're not doing anything wrong. Our bodies aren't touching, only our hands.' But as if to make matters worse, he curled his fingers around hers, pressing his thumb into the centre of her palm, gently caressing the creamy-smooth skin. And when he saw her swallow, he knew she wasn't immune to his touch.

'Did you…dance any of those dances?' she asked. 'The ones you saw in Spain.'

'No, but I enjoyed watching them. The Spanish are a passionate people. They are not afraid to demonstrate that passion when they dance.' He glanced at the stiffly erect bodies moving around them. 'We English have a long way to go.'

Emma said nothing more for the rest of the dance, but Alex knew she was aware of him, and in a way she hadn't been before. Her breath was coming faster, her colour was high, and when they were bumped by an overly-enthusiastic pair, he heard her gasp as she was pushed up against him, the softness of her breasts crushing into his chest. It made him think of those sultry nights in Spain and the whispers in the darkness of the night.

It would have been worth it, he thought, to take her there. If for no other reason than to watch the expression on her face when the Spaniards danced.

At the conclusion of the waltz he escorted her back to the sidelines, aware that a number of people were still watching them. Emma must have noticed it too. 'Thank you, Lord Stewart.'

'My pleasure, Miss Darling. I can't tell you how much I enjoyed it.' He would have said more had the vicar not suddenly appeared and extended his hand to Emma.

'I believe this is our dance, Miss Darling.'

Uncharacteristically annoyed, Alex said, 'I thought clergymen didn't dance.'

Mr Tufton's handsome face creased in a smile. 'I don't as a rule, but Mrs Jacobs has been most persistent, given the number of single ladies in attendance. I thought it would not hurt to make an exception this one time.'

Alex watched the blush rise in Emma's cheeks and silently cursed the vicar's charming manners. He watched them take their positions on the floor and while he knew he should have asked one of the other single ladies to dance, he suddenly wasn't feeling that charitable. Instead, he signalled the waiter for a drink and then stormed out into the garden.

His brother found him there some time later. 'Ah, so this is where you ran off to,' Peter said. 'Are you not having a good time?'

Alex took a mouthful of wine. 'No. Are you?'

'I am enjoying myself immensely.'

Of course he was, Alex thought darkly. His brother had danced as many dances as was polite with Linette, and had then turned his attention to the other ladies. He had even danced with Emma, allowing Alex the opportunity of observing her as she moved gracefully through the steps, her beautiful smile frequently appearing, without the restrictions she so often placed on those she offered him.

'Emma seems to be having a good time,' Peter said innocently. 'I saw her dancing with Mr Tufton.'

'Yes. The vicar is a man who enjoys getting to know his parishioners. Especially the pretty ones.'

'What's this?' Peter said in amusement. 'Is that jealousy I hear in my brother's voice?'

'Don't be ridiculous,' Alex snapped. 'She can dance with whomever she likes.'

'Yes, she can. And Tufton's a good man. She could do worse than to marry him.'

'Marry a village clergyman?' Alex said derisively. 'Surely she could set her sights a bit higher than that? Her sister set her cap at an earl's son and got him.'

Peter laughed. 'Linette did not set her cap at an earl's son. The earl's son fell in love with *her.*'

'Foolish young man,' Alex murmured. 'You know there will be those in attendance next weekend who will take you to task over it.'

'Yes, I know.' Peter sighed, his easy smile fading. 'And Father's not coming, is he? Even if he's well enough.'

It wasn't really a question and they both knew it. 'I think it would be best if you didn't get your hopes up,' Alex agreed.

'It isn't fair,' Peter said quietly. 'His absence will send a message.'

Yes, it would. Soon, everyone in London would know that the Earl of Widdicombe did not approve of his son's marriage to Linette Darling and, sadly, she would be treated accordingly. Not by the people of Little Moreton with whom she had grown up, but by those in society who knew of the earl's antipathy towards her and who would naturally take his side. They would eat shy little Linette for breakfast and spit out her bones.

'Peter, have you given any thought to what it's going to be like for Linette if you do get married without Father's approval?' Alex asked, feeling sorry for the girl in spite of himself. 'If he doesn't acknowledge her, society never will, and doors that have always been open to you will suddenly be closed in your face. Linette will not be welcomed by those it is necessary she be welcomed by and you will be forced to live on the fringes of society.'

'I don't care. I'll never set foot in London again if that's the way we're treated. We can live here, where Linette is loved and admired for the woman she is. I don't need society's approval.'

'And what of your children? Would you have them shunned because of their mother?'

Peter blanched. 'That's not fair.'

'Life isn't fair, but we have to deal with it on its own terms,' Alex said. 'I'm not saying Father will do any of this, but the possibility exists. Think carefully about this, Peter. Because it's not only *your* life that is going to be affected by your decision.'

* * *

Emma did not dance with Alex again, though she was painfully aware of his presence in the room. She felt his eyes on her several times throughout the evening, watching with whom she danced and with whom she spoke. Once or twice, she even looked up in time to catch his thoughtful gaze resting upon her, but he was always the first to turn away and eventually she stopped looking. But her nerves were on edge regardless.

There was also no question that Alex's presence at the assembly was a tremendous coup for the host and hostess. Mrs Jacobs had been delighted at the prospect of having the youngest son of the Earl of Widdicombe in attendance, but to also have the eldest son there was an unexpected boon. The fact he was charming and handsome and single only added to his cachet.

The young ladies, of course, flocked to him like bees to honey. Since no one knew of his plans with regard to Lady Glynnis Pettle, he was seen as an eligible bachelor and both the young ladies and their mothers were anxious that good impressions be made. After all, Mrs Jacobs whispered to Emma later that night, if dear Linette could capture the heart of one of the earl's sons, why should Mrs White's daughter or Mrs Feeny's niece not secure the other?

* * *

By midnight, Emma was more than ready to leave. Her head was pounding and there was a queer, unsettled feeling in the pit of her stomach. Needing a moment's quiet, she slipped out on to the terrace, welcoming the freshness of the cool evening air against her cheeks. Perhaps she shouldn't have eaten the lobster...

'Emma, are you all right?'

She turned, and her heart plummeted. *Dash it all!* Why did the man have to keep on finding her? 'I'm all right.'

'Are you sure?' Alex said. 'You're as white as a sheet.'

'Perhaps I'm just a little tired.' Despite her best intentions, his concern touched her and she mustered a shaky smile. 'I must be out of practice. I haven't danced this much in years.'

'Yes, I noticed the vicar claimed two dances,' Alex muttered.

'Then you probably noticed he also claimed two dances with all of the other ladies present,' Emma told him. 'And his attentions were very well received. I thought Miss Brown seemed particularly taken with him.'

'And here I thought clergymen didn't dance,' Alex mumbled.

Emma laughed and leaned in closer. 'It would appear this one does.'

It was a mistake. When Alex abruptly turned, Emma found herself only inches away from his face. And when he glanced down at her lips, her heart gave a most unsettling lurch. 'Oh!'

'You're not well.' He grasped her arm, his long fingers curving gently around her elbow. 'Let me get you a chair.'

'No, I'm all right. Really,' she assured him, aware that her skin was burning where he touched her. 'I just need to go home.'

'Are you sure?'

She closed her eyes, nodding. 'My head is hurting. Perhaps a leftover from the bump I received.'

His eyes darkened with concern. 'Is the rest of your family ready to leave?'

'I don't think so. Papa and Aunt Dorothy are playing cards and I hate to take Linette away when she is having such a good time.'

'Then I shall send you home in my own carriage.'

'Oh, no, I couldn't—'

'Yes, you could. I shall go and let your father know you are leaving.'

Wearily, she nodded. 'Thank you.'

A few minutes later, Emma found herself standing outside the Jacobs's front door. She could see the line of carriages winding out into the driveway, but even at this distance, Alex's was easy to pick out. Not only because it was the only one drawn by four perfectly matched blacks, but because it was the only one bearing a coat of arms. A coat of arms that signified how truly different they were—and how ridiculous were the direction of Emma's daydreams.

'Thank you, Hobbs,' Alex said when the coachman finally brought the elegant equipage to the door. He carefully helped Emma inside, then surprised her by climbing in after her.

'My lord, this really isn't necessary—'

'I wish you wouldn't call me that when we're alone,' he said. 'And you can let me be the judge of what is and isn't necessary.' He settled the fur rug over her lap. 'I'm sorry the bricks aren't warm. Your feet must be cold, standing on the front step all that time.'

And before Emma could object, Alex had slipped off her left slipper and was cradling her foot in his hands.

Shock waves ran up her leg. Dear Lord, was the man part-god of fire? His hands were blissfully warm, his touch unbelievably gentle. She could feel the cold recede as welcome heat seeped back into her skin. He massaged her toes through her stockings, the gentle caress bringing them slowly back to life.

'Does that feel better?' he enquired.

Emma gazed at the dark head bent over her foot, about to tell him she had never felt anything better in her entire life when he suddenly reached for her other foot and slipped that shoe off as well. Oh, no, this was definitely *not* a good idea. While rubbing someone's foot wasn't exactly a prelude to making love, Emma was finding it incredibly intimate and it was made even more so by the privacy of the carriage.

She bit her lip as she listened to the sound of his breathing, aware that she was alone in the carriage, that both of her feet were bare, and that Alex was caressing them in a way that was making her head spin. If someone were to see them now...

'Alex, I really think you should...stop,' she whispered.

'Yes, I know.'

But he didn't stop. He went on touching her, his long fingers curving around the base of her ankles, caressing the sensitive spot just beneath the bone before running his thumbs along her insteps and then back.

Emma closed her eyes, lulled by the sensual massage. She heard the tempo of his breathing quicken as his fingers climbed higher, gently kneading the flesh of her calves. She wanted to groan out loud at how blissful it felt, but she knew such a sound would send the wrong message entirely. Thank goodness the carriage was dark. His touch was making her warm all over, her body strangely heavy and lethargic. But she had neither the will nor the desire to stop him.

She gazed down at his head, fighting the urge to put her hands in his hair, to run her fingers through the ebony strands. She wanted to touch him. To hold him. To—

No, no, *no!* She was mad even to think it. He wasn't hers. He *never* would be hers. And every step she took down that treacherous path only made the return journey that much more painful. 'Stop it, Alex,' she whispered harshly. 'For pity's sake, *stop.*'

It was the anguish in her voice that finally stilled his hands. She held her breath as he looked up, the space between them crackling with tension. She was sure he must be able to hear her heart. It was pounding so hard it deafened her to everything else.

Slowly, he drew back his hand and even more slowly he sat back, and slowly he backed out of the carriage. But he did not stop looking at her. Not as he folded in the stairs. Not as he closed the carriage door. Not as he stood and gazed in at her through the window. Only when he stepped away and the carriage moved off did she finally lose sight of his face, and only then did Emma close her eyes and lay her head back against the cushions.

In the space of five minutes, her entire life had changed. From this moment, there was no going back. But sadly, there was no going forwards either.

Chapter Seven

Emma heard the carriage with the rest of her family arrive home later that night, though she couldn't have said at what time it did. She heard, shortly thereafter, a light knock at her door, followed by the flickering brightness of a candle as someone pushed the door open a crack. But she kept her eyes closed and said nothing, too afraid of the words that might have tumbled out had someone given her the chance.

She was falling in love with Alexander Taylor. Of all the idiotic, imbecilic things to do, that had to be at the top of the list. All of her life, Emma had prided herself on being the sensible sister. The one who scoffed at the idea of love at first sight and who said passion was the purview of poets and dreamers. Then Alex had come along and she'd discovered that she was no more impervious to Cupid's arrows than anyone else.

But she had to be! She had to be strong for everyone else's sake. Linette was marrying a man whose family didn't want her. Ridley had feelings for a woman who could never be his. And somewhere along the way, *she* had been stupid enough to fall in love with a man who was promised to another. Surely one of them had to save themselves from the arrows of that scheming little monster!

Morning came, and with it the memory of everything that had happened the night before. Emma gazed at her reflection in the glass and saw all too clearly the ravages of a sleepless night. Faint purple shadows lingered in the hollows beneath her eyes and there was a noticeable pallor to her complexion.

She prayed her family would be too caught up in their discussions of the dance to notice that her appearance was considerably less than vibrant.

'Ah, there you are, Emma,' her father said as she walked into the breakfast parlour. 'Feeling better this morning?'

'Yes, thank you.' She managed a faint smile and quickly went to the sideboard where breakfast had been laid out.

'Dashed good of Lord Stewart to send you home in his carriage,' Ridley said between mouthfuls of ham.

'Yes, it was,' Emma said, keeping her answers as non-committal as possible.

'Well, I think he's quite the gentleman,' Aunt Dorothy observed. 'Welcoming Linette into the family the way he did. Taking care of Emma not once, but twice now. I can tell you he made a very big impression on everyone who was there last night. Mrs Jacobs was positively over the moon at having *both* the Earl of Widdicombe's sons at her assembly. Definitely a feather in her cap!'

'Poor Lord Stewart,' Linette said. 'He was positively besieged by the ladies. Mrs Connelly cornered him every time he was alone and Mrs Hewitt followed him around the entire night, trying to introduce him to any one of her three daughters.'

'As if he'd be interested in any of them,' Ridley said with a snort. 'Not a pretty face amongst them.'

'Now, Ridley,' Aunt Dorothy chided. 'A pretty face isn't always a guarantee of a sweet disposition.'

'Perhaps, but if she hasn't a pretty face, why bother to look? I know I wouldn't.'

'No, because *you* put entirely *too* much stock in a lady's appearance,' Mr Darling criticised. 'And given your chosen field, you'll be lucky to have *any* woman look at you, let alone one worthy of attracting.' He went back to his paper. 'You should have stuck to the law.'

'Jupiter, Father, are you never going to let that go?' Ridley asked. 'At least I can paint pictures of my future wife. What can a barrister do but bore her to death with legal pleadings?'

Emma was thankful the conversation did not require her to take part. She sat down at the table next to her sister and applied herself to her eggs.

'Did you have a good time before you went home?' Linette leaned over to whisper.

'Yes, of course,' Emma said. 'But you were the belle of the ball!'

Her sister blushed. 'I wasn't that at all. Cynthia Brown was. Everyone was talking about how lovely her gown was and how very pretty she looked. Even Mr Tufton seemed to notice. But I did have a nice time and I'm so sorry you weren't feeling well. Was it the bump on your head?'

That, and Alex tenderly massaging her feet in the darkness. Oh Lord, there went her stomach again. 'I think it must have been.'

'Lord Stewart seemed very concerned about you,' Linette said, reaching for the salt cellar. 'He said you were in a bad way and that sending you home was the kindest thing he could have done.'

Emma tried very hard not to remember the other kindness he had shown her. Some things just didn't bear thinking about. 'It *was* good of him and I was very grateful for his assistance, but I'm all right now and I think we need say no more about it.'

'He really is a very nice man though, Emma. He spoke to me last night, you know.'

'He did?'

'Yes. After you left and when Peter was dancing with Loretta Jacobs. He came over to me and asked me about myself and what it was like living at Dove's Hollow. I told him I couldn't have imagined a nicer place to grow up and when he asked me about London, I said I really had no desire to go there at all. He said he could understand that, and then I told him about Ridley, and we actually laughed about it together. He didn't seem in the least intimidating. In fact—'

'Linette, please!' Emma said in desperation. 'I really have heard quite enough about Lord Stewart for one day, thank you.'

Unfortunately, her comment fell into a lull in the conversation.

'What's this?' her father asked as all eyes turned in her direction. 'Have you taken Lord Stewart in dislike, Emma?'

'That doesn't seem very charitable after he was good enough to send you home in his carriage,' Aunt Dorothy added.

'I have not taken Lord Stewart in dislike!'

'Then why don't you want to talk about him any more?'

'Very well. Talk about him all you like. I really don't care.'

A strained silence followed her words. Her father looked at Aunt Dorothy, Ridley and Linette exchanged a glance, and then everyone returned their attention to their plates.

Not surprisingly, Emma felt the onset of another headache.

The eleven o'clock service on Sunday morning was very well attended. Not only because it was a lovely morning or because Mr Tufton was presiding, but because it was a wonderful opportunity for people to gather and discuss what had taken place at Mrs Jacobs's assembly.

It was generally agreed that the assembly had been one of the most successful ever held, mainly because no one could remember an event where not one, but two members of a peer's family had been present. It was also agreed that Lord Stewart's presence at the event made it that much more memorable, especially to the young ladies who'd had the good fortune to speak with him, or to those who had been even more fortunate in being asked to dance with him. And though it did not go without notice that Lord Stewart had waltzed with Miss Emma Darling, or that he had demonstrated a marked partiality for her company, it was also agreed that because the gentleman's brother was engaged to Emma's sister, the family connection warranted a closer association than might otherwise have been allowed.

Emma, who refused to offer any comment with

regard to the gentleman's attentions towards her, her sentiments about him, or what he was like to waltz with, sat quietly in the pew, leafing through the pages of her hymn book as she waited for the service to begin. A few minutes before it did, however, the church doors opened and Lady Widdicombe, Lord Stewart and Mr Taylor walked in.

Emma heard the muffled gasps, predominantly female, and saw heads turn to watch the late arrivals make their way up the aisle. The front pew was always reserved for the aristocracy and as the three settled into their places, she heard the whispers begin. Mr Tufton merely smiled down at them from his pulpit. 'Good morning. I am delighted to see all of you here on this fine day. And I bid special welcome to those visiting us for the first time.' He nodded at Lady Widdicombe and her sons. 'Please open your hymn books and let us begin with "Hail the day that sees Him rise."'

It was a moving service about sin and forgiveness and Mr Tufton spoke passionately about man's need to forgive his fellow man for wrongs committed. Several young ladies surreptitiously wiped tears from their eyes, but Emma simply allowed the comforting words to wash over her, enjoying the sense of peace she so often found in the old stone church.

John Tufton was an eloquent speaker. He did not drone on about God's unending mercy, or speak in that boring monotone that threatened to put people to sleep. His voice was musical, almost lilting, as it touched on man's vices and virtues. Sometimes, he drew on humour to illustrate his point; other times he called on pathos to drive his message home. But no one fell asleep during his sermon and, at the conclusion, Emma stepped out into the sunshine feeling much better than she had going in, because listening to Mr Tufton's words had allowed her to examine her feelings for Lord Stewart and to put them in perspective.

She wasn't in love with Alexander Taylor. She admired and respected him, yes, but she certainly wasn't in love with him. True love took months to develop, sometimes even years. She had known Alex less than two weeks! Obviously, she had been caught up in a girlish infatuation and swept away by his dashing good looks. She wasn't proud of that, but at least she could explain it. And she could forgive herself for it, as Mr Tufton advised.

'Excellent sermon, Mr Tufton,' Mr Darling said as he greeted the vicar on the steps of the church. 'Always a thought-provoking topic, forgiveness.'

Mr Tufton smiled, his eyes sparkling with amusement. 'Thank you, Mr Darling. I have always thought so.' He turned to Emma and smiled. 'I hope you enjoyed the sermon, Miss Darling?'

'I did, Mr Tufton, very much. It came at a most appropriate time.'

She gave him a warmer smile than she had in the past and was surprised to see his cheeks redden. 'Yes, well, I like to think my words help many people through difficult or challenging times,' he said. 'Ah, good morning, Lady Widdicombe. Lord Stewart. Mr Taylor.'

'Good morning, Vicar,' Lady Widdicombe said. 'Excellent sermon.'

'Thank you, your ladyship.'

'Mr Darling,' the countess said, turning to regard Emma's father. 'I am pleased to see that you and your family honour the Sabbath.'

'We always have, Lady Widdicombe,' Mr Darling replied. 'Sunday is a day for quiet reflection and contemplation. To thank the Lord for all He has given us. Speaking of which, how does the earl go on?'

'I believe he is feeling better,' Lady Widdicombe said. 'I had a letter from his physician yesterday and he seems quite pleased with my husband's progress.'

'Then it is possible he may be here for the ball?' Linette asked impulsively.

Emma spared a glance for her sister's hopeful face, before looking at Alex. She was surprised to see compassion rather than annoyance reflected there. 'I'm sure if he is feeling well enough to attend, he will be here, Miss Linette.'

'Of course he will,' Peter said, reaching for her hand. 'Nothing would please him more. Mr Darling, may I have the pleasure of walking your daughter home?'

'I have no objection if Linette does not,' Mr Darling said.

Linette beamed. 'I would like it very much. Good day, Lady Widdicombe, Lord Stewart.'

On the heels of their departure, Lady Widdicombe set off in the carriage and Mr Darling resumed his conversation with Mr Tufton, Aunt Dorothy went to speak to Mrs Brown and her daughter, Cynthia, and Emma found herself alone with Alex.

'Are you feeling better, Miss Darling?' he asked in a casual tone.

'Much better, thank you.' Buoyed by the strength of Mr Tufton's words and by her new awareness of how silly her brief infatuation was, Emma offered him a genuinely warm and engaging smile. 'I am most grateful for your kindness last night, Lord Stewart. I hope it did not delay your departure from the assembly for too long.'

He looked down at her and shook his head. 'The moment I returned I was set upon by Mrs Jacobs and Mrs Connelly, both enquiring after your health. Word of your accident seems to have spread throughout the village, and when they noticed you looking so pale, they were concerned that you might have suffered a relapse. I was called upon to give my medical assessment of the situation.'

Emma frowned. 'But you're not a doctor.'

'As you and I know, however, they questioned me as though I was and I assured them that you had revived somewhat upon venturing into the cooler night air and that I was sure you would be feeling much better by the morning. So, as you can see, my time was fully occupied until my carriage returned.'

Emma smiled. 'I heard you were also kept very busy on the dance floor. The residents of Little Moreton cannot stop talking about the assembly. Indeed, I suspect it will be the topic of conversation for months to come.'

His mouth lifted at one side, making him look somewhat rakish. 'I'm sure it will grow tedious long before then. But I shall remember the evening too, Emma...' he looked at her and his smile changed '...though I venture to say for reasons far different than anyone else's.'

And just like that, Emma's newfound conviction vanished. He couldn't have been more clear had he said the words aloud, and her heart ached within her breast. 'Well, I had best be returning home. Good day, Lord Stewart.'

'Emma.' He put his hand out, stopping her. 'There's no one around. No one to overhear us.'

'I know.' Emma knew exactly what he was referring to. She glanced in the direction of her father and the vicar, relieved to see that they were still enjoying their conversation. 'But I think it better that we maintain a more formal distance between us.'

'Better for whom?'

'For everyone.' She gently disengaged her arm. 'Life is complicated enough, my lord. It will not benefit either of us to complicate it any further.'

She didn't wait for his answer, but turned and started in the direction of Dove's Hollow. It was over a mile and her father would no doubt question her decision to walk home, but at the moment, she needed to be alone. She needed time to sort through her feelings.

In a little less than a week, she would be seeing Alex again, but this time, it would be in the company of Lady Glynnis Pettle. The woman he was going to marry. If she did not ready herself for that, if she was not mentally prepared for the sight of Alex with another woman, she didn't know how she would be able to bear it. She was already so confused, so out of her depth.

'…I shall remember the evening too, Emma, though…for reasons far different than anyone else's…'

What was he saying? That he, too, had enjoyed the time they had spent alone in the carriage? That he remembered with fondness the intimacy of caressing her feet and calves? Surely that was wrong. Surely a man in his position knew what he invited by dwelling on such memories. He certainly knew better than anyone the impossibility of their relationship. Was he not the one who had counselled her to have Linette end her engagement to his brother on the grounds of her unsuitability? And Peter wasn't even the heir. The future of the line didn't depend on him. It depended on Alex. What possible chance could there ever be of the two of them having a life together?

More to the point, why was she suddenly beginning to think that she was not the only one asking that question?

After a bruising ride across the hills, Alex returned to the stables at Ellingsworth no happier than when he'd left. He had striven to banish all thought from his mind by flinging himself and his mount at hedges and turnstiles with a careless abandon not at all in keeping with his usual sense of responsibility. But even then he'd found no peace. He didn't even know why his mood was so foul. Only that it was and that it hadn't been improved by the sight of Emma smile so engagingly at Mr Tufton this morning. Surely it was not her intention to encourage the man. Surely she knew she could do a thousand times better than a simple country parson.

And yet, why the hell should he care? If she wanted

to marry the local butcher, that was entirely up to her. He hadn't any more say in who she married than did a fly. Because *his* future was settled...or would be as soon as he asked Glynnis to marry him.

'Give him a good rub down,' he said to the stable lad who came running out. 'And an extra ration of oats. He deserves it.'

The young lad tugged the edge of his cap, then turned to lead the steaming bay into the stable. Alex headed in the direction of the house, his thoughts on Glynnis as an image of her face appeared in his mind. He'd always thought her beautiful, with those aristocratic features, lithe, slender body, and bright, golden hair. It was longer than Emma's and fell in a shimmering ribbon almost to her waist.

By contrast, Emma's hair was shorter and far less disciplined. Wispy tendrils all too often escaped to dance around her face, blowing across her eyes and cheeks so that she constantly had to push them back. The colour was darker, too. Richer.

He tried to remember the colour of Glynnis's eyes, but all he kept seeing were Emma's: that soft, melting brown, reminiscent of molten chocolate. And when she smiled, dimples popped out in both cheeks. He didn't think Glynnis had dimples, though he couldn't be sure.

He couldn't be sure of anything any more...

'Alex, dear, did you have a good ride?'

Alex turned to see his mother approaching and quickly marshalled his thoughts. 'I did, thank you. I'd forgotten how beautiful the countryside around here is.'

'I've always thought it the most picturesque in England,' Lady Widdicombe said. 'But then I grew up not far from here so my roots are in Hampshire.' She tilted her head to one side and looked at him. 'What's wrong? You seem unsettled.'

'Do I?' He gave her a rueful smile. 'Maybe it's just everything that's going on between Peter and Father. I don't like to think of them at odds with one another.'

'I know. It makes me unhappy too.' His mother sighed. 'As a child, Peter adored your father. And Richard couldn't spend enough time with him. He loved carrying Peter on his shoulders. You never liked being carried. You preferred to walk beside him.'

'I did?'

'Mmm. Said you were too big to be carried. That you might hurt him.'

Alex tried to remember those days, but they were lost in the annals of time. 'Is it truly such a bad thing, Peter marrying Linette Darling?' Alex asked. 'She is a lovely girl and the family seems respectable enough.'

His mother sighed. 'I know. I've tried to find something to object to in Linette's conduct, but I really cannot. The older girl is a touch bold and a little odd, but Linette is quite sweet and I've come to like her very much. And when I see her and Peter together...' The countess pressed her lips together, tears forming in her eyes. 'I love him so much, Alex,' she whispered. 'I just want him to be happy. That's all I've ever wanted. Especially after...what happened.'

Alex nodded and drew his mother into his arms. Few people knew the story of Peter's childhood accident. It was one the family had taken pains to conceal, but it burned in his mother's heart like acid. Because on the one day she had left Peter alone in the nursery, the unthinkable had happened. She had only been gone a moment, but it was long enough for the little boy to have climbed out of his crib and fallen down.

He hadn't cried. He had knocked himself unconscious. And when his mother had come back in and seen him lying motionless on the stone floor, she had believed him dead and started screaming.

Naturally, the servants had come running. They had stood in the doorway, horrified by the sight of the countess clutching her youngest son in her arms, his body limp, his eyes closed, blood pouring from a gash on his face.

Thankfully, the diagnosis had been good. Peter had suffered a mild concussion, but he had regained consciousness soon after and had gone on to lead a normal healthy life. But the memory of that scare and the knowledge that, because of her inattention, her youngest son could have died stayed with Lady Widdicombe all through the years. It was the reason she could deny him nothing. Whatever Peter needed to make him happy, she was more than willing to give.

'This can't be helping matters between you and Father,' Alex said, knowing it wasn't the first time his parents had experienced differing opinions when it came to Peter.

'It isn't, but we are dealing with it as best we can.' She straightened, and pulled away. 'Your father doesn't understand why I cannot see his side in this. Why I won't stand with him in refusing to allow Peter to marry Linette. But I cannot.' She turned bright eyes towards Alex. 'I simply cannot.'

'I understand. But if Father chooses to make matters difficult for them, there won't be much any of us can do. He could revoke Peter's allowance and leave him without anything upon which to live. And given that Peter hasn't shown any inclination towards the law or the church, he will have no occupation.'

'I know,' his mother whispered. 'I would give him some of my own money, but your father would be furious and that would only make matters worse.' She hung her head. 'I really don't know what the answer is, Alex. I don't know what to do.'

'Well, why don't we see how matters go over the weekend?' Alex suggested. 'Everyone is coming to celebrate the engagement so the mood should be festive. Besides, Glynnis will be here; if she speaks favourably about Linette to Father, perhaps it will be enough to change his mind.'

'That would be a blessing,' his mother agreed. 'Your father has always been so fond of Lady Glynnis. She's like a daughter to him.' She shook her head. 'If only Peter had been able to find someone like that, everything would have been so much easier.' She laughed softly. 'I've often thought it a pity Glynnis didn't have a sister.'

'Yes, I suppose it is,' Alex murmured. 'Though there's no saying she would have turned out as well as Glynnis.'

'No, that's true. And there is no point wishing for the impossible,' the countess said. 'At least we know you are going to make a marriage of which your father approves. He keeps asking if I know when you plan to propose. Naturally I've said that's up to you. But I know he's looking forward to it.'

Alex nodded, trying not to allow an image of Emma's face to intrude. As his mother said, there was nothing to be gained by wishing for the impossible. 'I thought to ask her after the house party,' he said. 'Perhaps when we all return to London.'

'That would be wonderful, darling. I know it will

make your father so happy. Both of us, really. I've always liked Glynnis. Such a sensible, down-to-earth girl. Well, I suppose I'd best get back to work. There are still many things to do before the weekend. Thank you, Alex,' she said, kissing him on the cheek. 'I don't know what I would do without you. You've always been so strong. You stand firm while the rest of us crumble. No wonder your father's so proud of you.' She raised her hand and brushed it across his cheek. 'And in case I haven't said it lately, so am I.'

All too soon, the weekend arrived and with it the ball to celebrate Peter and Linette's betrothal. Guests began arriving early on the Friday afternoon, or so Emma was informed by Mrs Connelly when she went into the village to purchase a length of lace. Of course, Mrs Connelly was in the perfect position to see the carriages as they rumbled through town, given that her shop fronted on to the main street. Some had borne elaborate coats of arms, while others were just very stylish as they clipped along behind teams of matched black, grey, or brown horses.

And of course, the occupants had been very fashionably turned out, Mrs Connelly had assured Emma. She had caught glimpses of stylish bonnets and elegant travelling gowns in many of the carriages, and such handsome gentlemen riding such very fine horses! It was clearly going to be a very exciting weekend. And to think it was all in honour of little Linette and that Emma's entire family were going to be there. Wasn't she just beside herself with excitement?

Emma had smiled, agreed that she could scarcely think straight and had then taken her leave. Mrs Connelly would have given her right arm to be a guest at the betrothal ball, but that honour had been reserved for invited guests only. While a general invitation had gone out to the residents of Little Moreton to attend the outdoor festivities planned for tomorrow, only family and friends would be in attendance at the grand ball tonight.

Mrs Connelly would have to be satisfied with that.

As expected, by the time Emma got home, Linette was in a rare state of nerves. Several times throughout the afternoon, Emma had to repeat herself as a result of her sister staring off into space, oblivious to what was going on around her. She was terrified of the evening ahead and there seemed to be nothing Emma or Aunt Dorothy could say that could change how she felt.

Emma had to admit she wasn't looking forward to the evening either. Thanks to the summer she had spent in London, she was more at ease with strangers than her sister, but she knew that many of the guests would be titled and that all of them would be well to do. At such a gathering, her family would naturally be out of their league. If they managed to acquit themselves with only a few *faux pas,* Emma would think them lucky.

As a result, she took more care with her appearance than usual and at the last minute had decided not to wear her favourite gown of white India muslin, but to bring out a new dress she hadn't worn before. The gown of pale ivory shot through with gold thread had been a present from Aunt Dorothy, brought with her from London for Emma to wear during her stay in Bath. But because it was far more daring than the gowns Emma usually wore, she hadn't taken it with her.

Now she put it on and gasped at the amount of smooth white skin visible above the neckline. It was bordered in two inches of the finest lace but it was also far more revealing than anything she'd ever worn before and the sight of her breasts all but popping out over the top took some getting used to.

'Oh, Miss Emma, what a beautiful gown!' her maid said. 'You'll surely be turning heads, looking like that.'

Emma glanced at the girl, wishing she felt a little more confident and a little less exposed. 'Are you sure, Jane? It does seem a trifle…immodest.'

'Of course it does, miss, but that's what all the fine ladies are wearing in London.'

Yes, judging by the latest magazines Aunt Dorothy had been reading, it was—which meant it was also what most of the ladies at Ellingsworth would be wearing tonight.

With that in mind, Emma decided to grin and bear it—literally. She even allowed Jane to arrange her hair in a more elaborate style than usual. Fortunately, the girl was as much an artist with a brush and comb as Ridley was with his paints, and the upswept hair-style, fastened with a pearl-studded comb that had belonged to Emma's great-grandmother, could not have been more flattering. With excitement lending a natural blush to her cheeks, Emma knew she looked her best. But would it be enough for the discerning eyes of Lord and Lady Widdicombe and their guests? For Alex?

Ridley was already in the drawing room when Emma went down. He was standing by the window gazing out and, even to her eyes, he looked remarkably handsome. Somewhere along the way, the boy had disappeared and the man had taken his place. His body had filled out and his clothes looked to have been cut by one of London's better tailors.

It seemed they had all grown up, almost overnight.

Ridley turned as she walked into the room, a thoughtful frown quickly replaced by a smile of approval. 'I say, Emma, you're looking quite the thing. You might just outshine our little sister.'

Emma's mouth twisted. 'Thank you, Ridley, but we both know there's as much chance of that as there was of you being named first in your class.'

'You wound me,' he said, pretending to be hurt. 'I never thought you could be so cruel.'

'Do you disagree with what I said?'

'Not a bit, but that doesn't make it sting any the less.'

Moments later, the door opened and Linette and Aunt Dorothy walked in. 'Oh good, you're both here,' Aunt Dorothy said, looking rather more flushed than usual. 'Jenks is bringing the carriage around. Pour me a sherry, there's a good boy. I take it we do have time for a drink?'

'Not really, but if you're quite quick…' Ridley walked over to the decanter and poured his aunt the requested glass.

'Thank you, Ridley. Never hurts to have a little liquid courage, I always say.'

As long as it was only a little, Emma thought. Aunt Dorothy enjoyed a drop of sherry. More than a drop, though no one in the family had been tactless enough to mention it. But tonight was an occasion—something out of the ordinary. It definitely wasn't the time for Aunt Dorothy to end up lying face down in the trifle.

'Good Lord, Linny, are you going out like that?' Ridley asked.

Linette gasped, her lovely face turning white. 'Like what?'

'What *are* you talking about, Ridley,' Aunt Dorothy asked. 'Linette looks beautiful.'

'I didn't say otherwise.'

'But you said—'

'I simply asked her if she was going out like that,' Ridley said, his mischievous grin flashing. 'I didn't say she wasn't beautiful.'

'That's horrid, Ridley!' Linette complained, suddenly looking close to tears. 'I thought you were criticising me.'

'Then take that as a lesson, my dear,' he said. 'Never jump to conclusions until you've heard everything a gentleman has to say and don't try to read something into his meaning that isn't there.'

'Most important of all,' Emma said drily, 'never try to read *anything* of intelligence into anything Ridley says. That would most definitely be a mistake.'

The good-natured bickering carried on until Mr Darling appeared, but for once Emma was glad of it. They were all a little on edge, and why would they not be? It wasn't every day one's sister was guest of honour at a ball hosted by an earl and a countess. A ball where lords and ladies would be in attendance and where all eyes would be focused on her from the moment she stepped into the room.

How would Linette handle such intense scrutiny? Her exposure to the upper crust had been virtually non-existent and Emma knew how deeply a careless word or a thoughtless gesture could wound. Would there be awkward silences as common ground was sought and found lacking, or would the conversations flow easily, as they did at home? More to the point, what would Linette do if she began to suspect she was falling short of everyone's expectations? Or that her future brother-in-law, a man she had come to like and admire, even to trust, might well be leading the pack?

Chapter Eight

Ellingsworth was ablaze with lights when the Darlings' carriage arrived in the courtyard. Liveried servants were on hand to help the ladies and gentlemen alight, to take capes, hats, canes and gloves, and to generally make sure the guests' arrivals went as smoothly as possible.

Having been in the house before, Emma thought she knew what to expect, but even she was unprepared for the splendour that greeted her eyes upon arrival. It was evident the servants had been up since before dawn preparing the house. There were flowers everywhere, their sweet fragrance perfuming the air and serving as a bright dash of colour against the pale walls. Brass-and-silver candleholders glowed warmly in the candlelight, the floors had been polished so that one could see one's reflection in the black-and-white tiles and there wasn't a speck of dust or dirt anywhere.

Peter and his mother were waiting to greet them

in the hall. Lady Widdicombe looked magnificent in a gown of rose-coloured silk, a glittering diamond necklace encircling her throat and long white gloves covering her arms. Peter was equally dashing in formal black and white, his embroidered waistcoat a tribute to the tailor's art. But Lord Widdicombe was still noticeably absent and Emma's heart plummeted when she realised that Alex was missing too.

'Mr Darling, Mrs Grand, how nice to see you again,' Lady Widdicombe said. 'And Miss Linette, you look charming. Miss Darling, you look very well too.'

Emma dipped one knee in a curtsy. 'Thank you, your ladyship.'

Mr Darling stepped forwards. 'Lady Widdicombe, allow me to present my son, Ridley.'

The countess inclined her head. 'Mr Darling. I understand you've come down from Oxford just for the occasion.'

'Yes, your ladyship,' Ridley said. 'To see my little sister marry into such a grand family I would have sailed all the way from America.'

The countess raised an eyebrow, but said nothing as Ridley was likewise introduced to Linette's fiancé. Emma stood back and watched the exchange of greetings with interest, surprised by how easily Ridley seemed to fit in. In fact, with his dashing good looks and elegant clothes, he appeared right at home with the lords and ladies drifting through the beautiful rooms. But then, he moved in this sort of crowd now, Emma reminded herself. His clients were drawn from the ranks of the wealthy and titled and he was used to moving amongst them.

Linette, on the other hand, was like an anxious little bird, constantly looking around for the reassuring presence of her fiancé. Thankfully, he never went far from her side, preferring to stay with her as his mother moved off and the rest of them made their way into the Chinese drawing room. And finally, Emma saw Alex. He was standing alone by the fireplace, with a glass in his hand. He was watching her over the rim and Emma saw his eyes darken as they swept over her gown.

For the space of a heartbeat, she allowed herself the simple pleasure of looking back at him. What would it have been like, she wondered, had *she* been the one anticipating his proposal of marriage? She had been the object of his affections? Would she still feel this breathless every time he came near? Would her heart still hammer in her chest every time he stepped into a room? Or would she look at him the way so many other women regarded their husbands or lovers? Complacently. Smugly. Unemotionally.

The way Lady Glynnis Pettle might one day regard Alex.

Emma didn't want to believe it would be that way.

In fact, it was hard to imagine *any* woman not falling in love with Alex given half the chance. He was
easily the most handsome man in the room and certainly the one with the most presence. But it was also
Alex who had told her there was very little romance
in his relationship with Lady Glynnis. Was she wishing for something that didn't exist? Something he
couldn't give?

Unconsciously, Emma found herself looking
around for Lady Glynnis Pettle. Having no idea of
the lady's appearance, it was impossible to make a
positive identification, but Emma had a feeling she
would know the lady when she saw her.

Her observations came to an abrupt end when Alex
came over to join them.

'Miss Darling, you and your sister would make
lovely subjects for a painting of spring,' he said after
greetings had been exchanged. 'Or perhaps you have
already done such a study.'

'Actually, I seldom paint people,' Emma said. 'I
find facial expressions very difficult to capture.'

'But she is good at birds and insects,' Ridley said
helpfully. 'Be thankful you haven't wings or you
might find yourself sitting for her.'

Alex laughed, but Emma's father was less than
amused. 'I hardly think your sister is about to become
the second artist in the family, Ridley. Not as long as
I have anything to say about it.'

And then, laughter, as melodious as silver bells, rang out, the sound drawing all eyes to the lady who had just entered the room in the company of Lady Widdicombe. She was tall and slender and impossibly beautiful, wearing a stunning gown of shimmering lilac silk. Her golden hair was arranged in an elegant chignon caught up with pearls and roses and she moved with the unconscious grace of a lady born and bred.

This, surely, must be Lady Glynnis Pettle, daughter of the Earl and Countess of Leyland.

'Behold, the lady cometh,' Ridley whispered in Emma's ear.

Emma turned to look at him. His complexion was pale, but otherwise, he seemed composed. 'Are you all right?' she whispered.

'Of course. Why wouldn't I be?'

Emma had a few ideas of her own on that score, but knowing this wasn't the time or the place, she turned back to watch Alex's future bride approach. Lady Glynnis was clearly very comfortable at Lady Widdicombe's side, and judging by the expression on the countess's face, the feelings were mutual. But then, Lady Glynnis had grown up with these people. She was the daughter of an earl. Just as Alex was the son of one.

'Ah, there you are, Alex,' his mother said, catching

sight of him. 'I was just telling Lady Glynnis about our evening at the Parkinsons'.'

'I am so sorry to have missed your performance, my lord,' Lady Glynnis said with a beautiful smile.

Alex sighed. 'I should have known you would be in a hurry to volunteer that information, Mother.'

'Now, you mustn't blame your mother,' Lady Glynnis said. 'I did hear rumours to the effect that you had reluctantly agreed to play and that you gave an outstanding performance. But since I could not find anyone to confirm which *étude* you played, I was forced to ask your mother.'

Emma just stared at him. Alex played the piano? He had never made any mention of that to her. But then, why would he?

'Lady Glynnis,' he was saying now, 'may I present Mr Darling and his sister, Mrs Grand, as well as Mr Ridley Darling, Miss Emma Darling, and of course, my brother's fiancée, Miss Linette Darling.'

'Goodness, so many Darlings,' Lady Glynnis said, her voice sounding just a little breathless. 'I am very pleased to meet all of you. And congratulations, Miss Linette. I hope you and Mr Taylor will be very happy.'

Linette blushed, but Emma could see that she was pleased, and why would she not be? Lady Glynnis was beautiful, and charming and kind, with just a hint of the reserve that would be expected from the daughter of an earl. She smiled at each of them in turn, though when she came to Ridley, Emma noticed she didn't meet his eyes. Instead, she turned her head to ask a question of Emma. 'Lord Stewart tells me you are an accomplished artist, Miss Darling. Is that true?'

'Not at all, Lady Glynnis. I merely dabble with colour and brush and my efforts are those of an amateur. My brother is the true artist in the family—'

Too late Emma realised the inappropriateness of the remark. A scarlet bloom appeared on Lady Glynnis's cheeks, but it was Lady Widdicombe who stared at Emma in surprise. 'Your brother is an artist?'

'Yes, your ladyship.'

'Mr Darling, I thought you told me your son was studying law.'

'He was, Lady Widdicombe,' Mr Darling acknowledged reluctantly. 'But upon arriving home, he informed us that he had given up his studies to become…a portraitist.'

'Really? That is not the usual occupation for a gentleman's son.'

'No, my lady,' Mr Darling agreed with a decided lack of enthusiasm. 'It is not.'

'But he *is* very good at it,' Aunt Dorothy piped up, clearly not wanting anyone to think less of her nephew's abilities. 'He has already received a number of commissions from members of society and apparently he has several more lined up. And he would not be so gainfully employed if he was not—good heavens, what is all that noise?'

The commotion was coming from the direction of the hall. Emma turned, as everyone else did, to see what the cause might be.

'Oh, dear Lord!' Lady Widdicombe whispered. 'He's *here?*' She glanced at Alex with something akin to panic in her eyes. 'I had no idea he was coming.'

'Perhaps he thought you would try to discourage him,' Alex said softly. 'I wonder if the doctor knows.'

'Chances are good he does not. Pray excuse me,' Lady Widdicombe said with an apologetic glance at her guests before heading quickly towards the door.

Alex glanced at his brother. 'I think we had best go too.'

'Peter, what's wrong?' Linette asked quickly.

'Nothing.' Peter raised her hands to his lips and fervently kissed them. 'I shall return as quickly as I can.' Then, he turned and followed his mother and brother out of the room.

'How strange,' Aunt Dorothy said. 'I wonder what that was all about?'

Lady Glynnis was still gazing in the direction of the door; it looked to Emma as though she was trying not to smile. 'I cannot be sure, but judging from the look of surprise on Lady Widdicombe's face, I would say that the unexpected has happened

and that, contrary to opinion, the Earl of Widdicombe has most definitely arrived.'

Alex was two steps behind his mother as they
walked quickly into the hall. Just in time to see his
brother's butler and valet helping his father get up
off the floor.

'Richard!' his wife cried. 'Is it your heart?'

'Don't be silly, woman, it's these damned slippery
floors,' the earl grumbled. 'I simply lost my footing
and fell.'

'Perhaps you should lie down for a moment, Father,'
Alex suggested.

'I didn't come here to lie down.' The earl rose to his
full height, shaking off the butler and valet. 'I came
to see what kind of a mess my son is making of his
life!'

Alex felt Peter stiffen at his side. 'Then I'm afraid
you've wasted your time, sir. I am very happy with
my life. In fact, I am having a grand ball tonight to
celebrate it.'

Aware that his mother was about to say something,
Alex said, 'Why don't we retire to the drawing room?
I don't think our guests need witness any of this.'

Recognizing the wisdom in the suggestion, the four
of them repaired to the nearest saloon. Alex shut
the door and then turned to face his parents, aware
that his father had already poured himself a glass of

whisky and that his mother was looking none too pleased about it.

'Is that a good idea, Richard?' she said.

'Harrow wouldn't think so, but since he's not here I don't give a damn.' The earl raised the glass and tipped back the contents. 'Damn fine whisky, that.' When he'd emptied the glass, he smacked his lips in satisfaction. 'Damn fine. Now, about this engagement—'

'I won't hear anything said against Linette,' Peter said, quietly defiant. 'I love her. And I am going to marry her!'

'Not without my permission.'

'I don't need your permission. I am old enough to make my own decisions.'

'So you would defy me in this!'

'If you pushed me to it, yes,' Peter said. 'It is not what I would like to do, Father, but I will if you force my hand.'

'Force your hand? Of all the—!'

'Father, if I may,' Alex interrupted. 'I understand your taking exception to Linette Darling based on what little you know of her, but she is here tonight and anxious to meet you. Why not spend some time with her? I venture to say you will be surprised.'

His father's eyes narrowed. 'What's this? Has the chit charmed you as well?'

'I like her, yes,' Alex said simply. 'But, more importantly, Peter has already said he intends to marry her with or without your permission, and if the latter happens, the rift between you will never be healed. All I'm saying is that surely it is worth a few minutes of your time to speak to Linette and find out what kind of person she is.'

'And if I spend a few minutes with her and don't like what I see, what then?' The earl turned his gaze on his youngest son. 'Would you respect my wishes and walk away?'

Peter swallowed hard. 'No, sir, I would not. I have given my promise to Linette. I will not go back on my word. Not even for you.'

Alex felt the atmosphere in the room grow explosive. He watched his father's mouth begin to work and saw him stiffen as he turned away. 'Then it would seem we have nothing more to say to one another.'

'But you will meet her?' Peter said.

'No, sir, I will not. Nor will I acknowledge her family.'

'Richard!'

'Don't bother, my dear.' The earl's voice was coldly pre-emptive. 'I am still the head of this family and I say how matters are to go on. For your sake, I will not malign her, but neither will I speak of her in the terms you might wish me to.'

'You can't do that, Father,' Alex said quietly.

'Can't I? I'm not the one who's chosen to turn

his back on the morals by which we live,' the earl snapped. 'The morals that have guided this family for generations. Your brother knows what kind of woman I expected him to marry. The kind of life I expected him to lead.'

'There's nothing to say he can't still lead that life,' Alex said, catching a glimpse of the despair on his brother's face. 'Miss Linette Darling is a lovely young woman. The least you can do is take a moment to meet her.'

'Why? Your brother's already told me he doesn't give a damn about my feelings.'

'That's not what I said!' Peter was stung into replying.

'Wasn't it? Did you not say you would marry her regardless of my opinion? That you would pay no mind to my concerns about her lack of position or breeding?'

'She may not have a title, Richard, but that doesn't mean she has no social graces,' Lady Widdicombe objected. 'Her appearance and manners are most pleasing and she plays the pianoforte very well.'

'That's right,' Peter spoke up. 'Because Linette is the daughter of a gentleman.'

'She is the daughter of a former tutor who lives in a house obtained as a result of gambling,' the earl threw back. 'That does not make her a suitable bride for any son of mine.'

Lady Widdicombe gasped. 'Gambling?'

'Yes. Apparently, Mr Darling's older brother was something of a Captain Sharp. He won the house and everything in it at the faro table. When he died in a drunken brawl, it passed to his only brother, along with a tidy sum of cash that enabled him to give up teaching and settle down to the life of a gentleman. Not the most honourable way for a man to acquire the roof over his head.'

'You can hardly condemn the daughter for something the uncle did,' Peter said.

'Ah, but there's more. Mr Darling has two sisters, a younger sister living in Bath and an older one who lives in London. Both have a known propensity for drink, especially the widowed sister in London, while the husband of the sister in Bath is reputedly engaged in a scandalous affair with the woman next door.'

'Never!' Lady Widdicombe said. 'How do you know all this?'

The earl flushed. 'Never mind how I know. It is enough that I do. I should also tell you that the son, Mr Ridley Darling, has given up his studies of law to take up painting and that he has set himself up in a studio in London. And you know what they say about the morals of an artist.'

'In this instance, I can guarantee that whatever you've heard are exaggerations,' Alex felt disposed to say. 'I have made the acquaintance of Ridley Darling and he is good mannered and extremely affable.'

'I'm sure he is. No doubt he uses that affability to persuade impressionable young women to come and sit for him in his private studio.'

'Richard, really!'

'All I'm saying, my dear, is that the Darlings are not the genteel family they would try to make you believe they are. And if you'll take my advice, you will stay well away from them. All of them!' He glanced at his younger son, adding, 'And you, sir, would do well to take a page out of your brother's book. *He* is marrying a lady worthy of him. A woman who can hold her own with dukes and duchesses. Can your little country chit do that?'

Peter raised his chin. 'I would present her at Court if I could and be proud to do so.'

'Then you would embarrass yourself and the rest of your family by your efforts,' the earl said in disgust. 'Alex, for God's sake, try to talk some sense into him. Obviously nothing I say is having the slightest effect.'

'Only because you are being narrow minded and cruel,' Peter said.

'You would call me cruel, sir!'

'I would, because Linette has done nothing to deserve your condemnation!' Peter flung at him. 'You'd know that if you took even a moment to speak with her.'

'Enough,' Alex said sharply. 'This evening is not about debating the wisdom of the relationship. It is about celebrating Peter and Linette's betrothal. And since people know you are here, Father, you have no choice but to make an appearance and to put a good face on it. Unless you wish to bring down upon all our heads the type of embarrassment you fear Peter's association with Miss Darling will.'

'Alex is right, Richard,' Lady Widdicombe said. 'Whatever your feelings, you must put them aside for this evening. To cut the Darlings in your own son's home would be the height of ill manners and it would not be forgotten by those who are here to witness it.'

The earl muttered something about that not being his fault, but finally seeing the wisdom in Alex's words, reluctantly agreed to meet the family and to try to be civil whilst doing so. Alex could see that his mother, while relieved, was also anxious as to exactly how civil her husband was likely to be. He had got it into his head that Linette Darling was unsuitable and Alex knew he wouldn't give that up easily.

He was quite sure he wasn't the only one holding his breath as the four of them headed back to the ballroom.

Emma was also doing battle with family issues. Shortly after Alex and the rest of the family had left the ballroom, Ridley had excused himself on the pretext of securing refreshments for her and Lady Glynnis. An excuse that would have been believable had he actually returned with any.

'I cannot think what has happened to my brother,' Emma said some ten minutes later. 'He is usually most attentive.'

'Perhaps he stopped to speak to someone,' Lady Glynnis said, avoiding Emma's eyes. 'It really doesn't matter.'

Emma couldn't help thinking that the lady seemed relieved by his absence and she wasn't at all surprised when the earl's daughter bid her a clipped good evening immediately after.

As soon as she did, Linette appeared. 'Emma, do you mind if I slip upstairs for a moment? I've a mind to press a cool cloth to my face.'

'Are you all right, dearest?' Emma asked in concern.

'I'm not sure.' Linette bit her lip, looking far from happy. 'I don't know whether to be relieved or alarmed that Lord Widdicombe is here. Peter didn't look at all pleased upon hearing of his arrival.'

'Now don't start creating problems where none exists,' Emma cautioned. 'By all means, go upstairs and do whatever you need to settle your nerves. A cooling cloth will help. Your colour is a touch high. I shall find Ridley and, together, we will deal with whatever happens.'

* * *

She found her brother in one of the smaller saloons a short while later. He was standing by the window, staring out into the night. 'Ridley? What are you doing in here? You were supposed to be bringing back refreshments for Lady Glynnis and myself.'

'Yes, I know.'

'Then why didn't you?'

'Because I thought it would be better if I did not.' He pulled his gaze from the night and turned, his brow furrowed. 'Easier.'

'Easier for whom?'

'For me.' He sighed, and raised his head. 'And for her.'

Emma's heart did a flip. 'Lady Glynnis?'

She watched him nod, the candlelight accentuating the blue-black highlights in his hair. 'I haven't been entirely honest with you about my dealings with her, Emma. I led you to believe our relationship was strictly a business arrangement. That I didn't have any…personal feelings for her.'

Emma felt her breath freeze in her throat. 'So what are you telling me now? That you do have feelings for her?'

He glanced at her, then away. 'I'm afraid so.'

'Oh, Ridley. How could you? If you knew she was promised to someone else—'

'I didn't. Not in the beginning,' he said quickly.

'When she first came to sit for me, that's all she was. A client who wished me to do a painting of her. We didn't even talk about anything of a personal nature for the first few days. But as the hours passed and we came to know each another better, I found myself growing more and more fond of her.'

'Did you ever tell her how you felt?'

'Of course not! She is the Earl of Leyland's daughter. Who am I? A man who'd dropped out of Oxford to paint society portraits. Not exactly an equitable match.'

'So how did you part when the painting was done?'

Again, Ridley shook his head. 'I wish I could say we parted as friends, but the truth is, the last time I saw her, she was furious with me.'

Emma felt herself go pale. 'Why? What did you do?'

Ridley breathed a deep sigh. 'I let someone else see the finished portrait.'

'Someone else?'

'A friend. He often comes by the studio to see what I'm working on. Then we usually go out for a bite of supper and on to his club.'

'And he saw the painting when he came to collect you.'

'Yes. It wasn't even that I made a point of showing it to him.' Ridley's eyes were dark with misery. 'It was simply still on the easel when he walked in. I wanted to make sure it was completely dry before I framed it.'

'What did he say?'

'That it was stunning. The best piece of portraiture I'd ever done. Frankly, I didn't think anything of it. Tom's seen most of my work; as he was personally acquainted with Lady Glynnis's family, I didn't think it would be an issue. But when I delivered the painting to her two days later and happened to mention that a mutual friend had seen it, she tore a strip off me,' Ridley said unhappily. 'Told me I'd had no right to show it to anyone and that I had completely betrayed her trust.'

Something was missing, Emma thought. It made no sense that the lady would be so angry just because Ridley had allowed someone to see what was obviously a very beautiful portrait of her. 'You said this fellow was a mutual friend?'

'Yes. Lady Glynnis knows his sister quite well. That was another reason it never occurred to me that it would be a problem.'

'Ridley,' she said slowly. 'You didn't harm Lady Glynnis's reputation in any way by showing this fellow her portrait, did you?'

'Of course not. She was fully clothed and seated on a garden bench. It couldn't have been more proper.'

'Then why did she object so strenuously to his seeing it? Surely it would be no different than someone coming to her house and seeing it hanging on a wall. Portraits *are* for public viewing.'

Ridley sighed and turned back towards the window. 'That's what I tried to tell her, but it didn't make any difference. She took the painting, told me my professional ethics were lacking and made it clear she never wanted to see me again. That's why I thought it would be easier if I didn't linger in her company tonight. She was polite in her greeting of me, but it can't have been easy. I know it wasn't for me.'

'Unfortunately, you *will* have to see her again, dearest,' Emma said softly. 'Even if you manage to avoid her for the rest of this weekend, there's still Linette's wedding to get through, and any future family events and engagements we may be called upon to attend.'

Including Lady Glynnis's marriage to Alex, Emma thought sadly. An occasion that was going to be exceedingly difficult for both her and Ridley.

'Do you think I haven't thought of that?' Ridley ground out. 'I didn't want this to happen. In fact, it's the last thing I'd wish on anybody. It's just that… sometimes you meet someone at the wrong time in your life. And when you suddenly find yourself developing feelings for them, you can't just turn them off.'

A chill rippled through her body. 'Ridley. You're not…in love with Lady Glynnis, are you?'

He laughed, a harsh sound that was an unconvincing as the words that followed. 'Of course not. And it wouldn't matter if I was. She's going to marry Alexander the Great. And I am going home.'

'Home!'

'Yes. I have no intention of staying here and ruining Linette's special evening.'

'Now you listen to me, Ridley Octavius Darling,' Emma said firmly. 'I don't care what's happened between you and Lady Glynnis, you are *not* going home. Linette needs you right now. She needs all of us.'

Ridley frowned. 'Why?'

'Because Lord Widdicombe has just arrived and Linette is absolutely beside herself with worry. She's upstairs trying to calm herself down, which means you and I have to go back out there and lend her whatever moral support we can.'

'Shouldn't Mr Taylor be doing that?'

'Probably,' Emma admitted with a sigh. 'But to be honest, right now, I think supporting Linette is more than even he is capable of doing.'

Thankfully, Linette had not returned to the ballroom by the time Emma and Ridley arrived back, but a quick sweep of the room showed her that Alex and Peter had. The former was speaking quietly to Lady Glynnis, their heads close together. The latter hurried across the room to join them. 'Where's Linette?' Peter asked straight off.

'Upstairs,' Emma told him. 'She should be down soon.'

'Is she all right?'

'Nervous, but fine other than that.'

'I'm not surprised.' Peter looked decidedly unhappy. 'My father wishes to meet her. All of you. In the Chinese Salon.'

Oh, wonderful, Emma thought with a sense of fatalism. A meeting in a room filled with fire-breathing dragons and those sword-wielding warriors. She couldn't help wondering if the earl had chosen it for that very reason. 'Very well. As soon as Linette returns, we will make our way there.'

Peter smiled at her and Emma saw the look of gratitude in his eyes. He knew what this was costing Linette—probably what it was costing all of them— but there was nothing he could do. His father was the head of the family. All he could do was stick it out and hope that everything turned out for the best. He bowed and withdrew, likely to make his way to the Chinese Salon.

No sooner had he done so than Alex approached with Lady Glynnis.

'Oh, hell!' Ridley whispered.

'Courage, dearest. Remember, you're not the only one suffering over this,' Emma said, knowing her brother would think she was referring to Lady Glynnis—but she wasn't. She was talking about herself—about having to face the painful truth that the beautiful woman on Alex's arm would soon be his wife. A realisation that was causing Emma more pain than she would ever have believed possible. Her feelings for Alex were such that she could not bear thinking about him being with any one else. The thought of the tender moments they would share and the loving words they would exchange was tearing her apart because, in her heart, *she* wanted to be the one Alex turned to for intimacy and warmth. The one he turned to for love.

But that wasn't going to happen. She'd had the misfortune to fall in love with the wrong man at the wrong time. And sadly, there was never going to be a right time for her.

'Mr Ridley, Miss Darling,' Alex said now. 'My father has arrived and wishes to meet you and the rest of your family in the Chinese Salon.'

'Yes, so your brother just informed us. Ridley,' Emma said, 'why don't you go and find Papa and Aunt Dorothy and tell them what is happening?'

Clearly relieved to have a reason for making himself scarce, Ridley nodded. 'Yes, of course.'

After he left, Lady Glynnis said, 'Where is your sister, Miss Darling? She should be here, mingling with her guests.'

'I know, but she is not used to being the centre of attention.'

'If she is to marry into this family, she will have to get used to it,' Lady Glynnis said, though not harshly. 'She will be expected to take her place in society.'

Emma looked up and saw the expression of sympathy on Alex's face. Did he know how she was feeling? She had to believe that Lady Glynnis knew of his opinion with regard to the relationship between Peter and Linette, indeed how the entire family did. So was her question now an indication that she agreed with his assessment of the situation, even to wondering why the engagement was proceeding?

Emma managed a smile. 'I'm sure she will be fine once she gets used to it. This is all so new to her.'

'Emma?'

And then, thankfully, Linette was there. Her cheeks were still pale, but she held her head high and wore a valiant smile. No one looking at her would ever guess that her knees were knocking beneath her gown. 'We are to meet Lord Widdicombe,' Emma said. 'In the Chinese Salon.'

Linette's eyes went wide. 'All of us?'

'Yes. Ridley has gone to find Papa and Aunt Dorothy.'

'We may as well head that way now,' Alex said.

With an encouraging smile at Linette, Lady Glynnis put her hand on Alex's arm and the two of them turned to lead the way. Stifling the pain the sight of the proprietary gesture caused, Emma linked arms with her sister. 'Are you ready, Linny?'

'I don't have a choice,' Linette whispered. 'This is the meeting I've both longed for and dreaded. What will I do if he doesn't like me?'

'Of course he's going to like you. And Peter will be there to support you and you know he loves you madly. And really, in the end, that's all that matters.'

'I know it's all that *should* matter,' Linette said, her face softening. 'But will it be enough?'

Lord and Lady Widdicombe were standing by the taller of the two lacquered cabinets when Emma and her sister walked into the salon. Alex and Lady Glynnis had entered ahead of them and, glancing to the left, Emma saw that Ridley, her father and Aunt Dorothy had also arrived and were standing by one of the ornate Chinese pagodas.

Peter, who had been standing beside his mother, came towards them as soon as they entered. Lady Widdicombe touched her husband's shoulder and, slowly, the earl turned to face the assembled group.

The Earl of Widdicombe was an impressive-looking man. Tall and somewhat gaunt as a result of his illness, he was still a commanding and authoritative figure. He was faultlessly dressed, a tribute to the finest tailors in London, and his colouring was as dark as Alex's. Emma saw his gaze touch briefly on his eldest son before moving over to her, and then finally to Linette. Peter took Linette's hand in his and gave her a reassuring smile.

But it was not Linette or any other member of the Darling family to whom Lord Widdicombe spoke first. It was the lady at Alex's side.

'Lady Glynnis,' the earl said warmly. 'I am very pleased to see you again.'

'Lord Widdicombe.' Lady Glynnis executed a perfect curtsy. 'I'm glad you were feeling well enough to join us.'

'Thank you. Are your parents here?'

'They are, but I don't believe they have come down yet.'

'I look forward to seeing them again,' the earl said. 'It has been far too long since Leyland and I enjoyed some shooting together. We will have them out to Widdicombe Hill once the Season is over.'

'I know my father would enjoy that,' Lady Glynnis said with the ease of one talking to a long-established friend. 'Mama has always said Widdicombe is one of the last truly gracious country houses in Kent.'

'Father?' Peter said during a lull in the conversation. 'Pray allow me to introduce our guests. This is Mr Darling and his sister, Mrs Grand.'

Emma watched her father and aunt step up to make their greetings. Aunt Dorothy was visibly shaking, but Emma was pleased to see that her father acquitted himself well. The earl nodded, but the smile that had warmed his face during his conversation with Lady Glynnis was noticeably absent. 'Mr Darling,' he said. 'Mrs Grand.'

'And this is Mr Ridley Darling and his sister, Miss Emma Darling,' Peter continued.

'Ah, yes, the artist,' Lord Widdicombe said, his eyes narrowing.

Emma felt Ridley stiffen at her side and prayed he wouldn't do anything stupid. But obviously aware of the repercussions such a response would generate, he let the remark pass. The earl's glance rested briefly on her, but his interest was already on Linette.

'And this,' Peter said, drawing her forwards, 'is my fiancée, Miss Linette Darling.'

Emma hadn't realised she was holding her breath until Ridley nudged her gently in the ribs, forcing her to let it go. Linette walked the few steps towards Lord and Lady Widdicombe, and then, smiling up at the earl, made an elegant curtsy. 'Good evening, Lord Widdicombe.'

Her lovely face was so innocent, so devoid of artifice, that Emma wondered how anyone could ever believe ill of her. And the intense rush of fierce, protective love she felt in that moment was so strong that she knew if the earl made one single derogatory remark, she would confront him immediately.

'So, you're the one,' Lord Widdicombe said, raking Linette with his gaze. 'Very pretty, as expected. Well, what have you to say for yourself?'

'That I am very pleased to meet you at last,' Linette said quietly.

'At last? What's that supposed to mean?'

Linette flushed. 'I simply meant that…I had the pleasure of meeting Lady Widdicombe and Lord Stewart at dinner the week before last, but not you. And I was so sorry to hear that it was due to illness. I hope you're feeling better.'

The earl snorted. 'I'm here, aren't I?'

It was a deliberate put-down and Emma felt her blood begin to boil. How *dare* he speak to her like that! Linette was doing everything right and still that wretched man was trying to make things difficult for her. And nobody was saying anything.

And then, to her astonishment, two people did.

'I think you are being overly harsh, Father,' Alex said. 'Linette meant no offence.'

'Indeed,' Lady Glynnis added quickly. 'She was being introduced to her future in-laws for the first time. Naturally, she would regret not meeting you at the same time and be concerned that it was your health that caused you to miss the dinner.'

It was the perfect response, Emma thought dispiritedly, and it couldn't have come from a better person. Lady Glynnis Pettle was clearly adored by both Lord and Lady Widdicombe. Even Alex was gazing at her with approval.

'Think that, do you, missy?' the earl said gruffly.

Lady Glynnis actually smiled at him. 'Yes, I do.'

'Then perhaps I shall give it some consideration. For your sake.' The earl turned to stare at Linette, his expression not quite as intimidating as it had been before. 'It seems you have a champion, young lady. Two, in fact, and a better pair I could not imagine. Perhaps we will speak again, you and I. But not to-night.' He glanced at his wife before briefly closing his eyes. 'I think I would like to retire. The journey must have been...more tiring than I thought.'

Lady Widdicombe immediately stepped forwards to take his arm. 'I shall accompany you upstairs and then Murdoch can look after you. Peter, you have a houseful of guests. Please extend our apologies. If anyone asks, tell them your father is not fully recovered from his illness.'

'Of course.'

The earl did not look at Linette again, but somehow Emma knew the worst was over and that the atmosphere had lightened. As soon as the earl and countess left, she gave her sister a fierce hug. 'Linette, dearest, you were wonderful.'

'I was?'

'Yes, and I am so very proud of you.'

'Indeed,' Lady Glynnis said, coming over to join

them. 'I doubt there are many young women who could have withstood the earl's intimidation as well as you did.'

Linette bit her lip. 'But I have *you* to thank for that, Lady Glynnis. You spoke up for me. You and Lord Stewart both,' she added with a grateful glance at Alex. 'I was so nervous when Lord Widdicombe first spoke to me. But I desperately wanted him to like me. For Peter's sake. So I kept on trying. But what you said changed his mind. I know it did.'

'Lord Widdicombe can be as prickly as a hedgehog at times,' Lady Glynnis said with a fond glance at Alex. 'But I've always believed his bark to be worse than his bite. Wouldn't you agree, my lord?'

'Yes, though I'm not sure a bark like that can't do as much harm as a bite. What say you, Mr Darling?' Alex asked Ridley as the door opened and a butler walked in with a tray of drinks. 'I thought for a moment he was going to start in on you.'

'I would have preferred that to watching him take a bite out of my sister,' Ridley murmured, reaching for two glasses of champagne and handing one to his aunt. 'We appreciate you stepping in. For a moment I wasn't sure who was going to go for him first, Emma or myself.'

'Ridley, really!' Aunt Dorothy said. 'I'm quite sure neither of you would have done anything so outlandish.'

Ridley laughed. 'Then you don't know either of us very well, Aunt.' His gaze rested briefly on Lady Glynnis's averted face. 'We are none of us exactly what we seem.'

For a split second, Lady Glynnis turned to look at him—and Emma sucked in her breath.

Dear Lord, had anyone else in the room been witness to that naked gaze? Was she the only one to have seen the expression of anguish in the young woman's face? The desperate longing in her eyes?

Apparently so. Mr Darling was already talking to Aunt Dorothy, who was happily tipping back her glass of champagne. Alex and Peter were speaking quietly between themselves and Linette was gazing in Peter's direction. She was the only one to have witnessed it and she could only thank her lucky stars that such had been the case. Whereas before she had only suspected this might be a weekend fraught with difficulties, now she knew it was going to be.

Her brother was in love with the woman Lord Stewart was planning to marry. And if Emma didn't miss her guess, Lady Glynnis was not entirely without feelings of her own!

Chapter Nine

Word of Lord Widdicombe's illness was accepted without question by the guests gathered for Linette and Peter's engagement ball, and when at midnight, the toast was offered by Alex rather than his father, not a single well-groomed eyebrow was raised. Most of the guests knew the earl had not been well, so it came as no shock that the rigours of the journey had forced him back to bed. They simply expressed their concern at hearing of his discomfort and sent wishes for his speedy recovery.

As for Linette, her future father-in-law's absence provided some much-needed breathing space; contrary to what Alex had feared, she was not shunned by the guests who were introduced to her, but was now welcomed by them, most probably because no outright rift between her and the earl had been declared. Everyone seemed to know that a meeting had taken place between the two families earlier in the evening, but, given that no obvious signs of condemnation had followed, the guests accepted as fact the earl's approval of the match.

And in light of that acceptance, Linette blossomed. The pride on her face at being introduced as Peter's fiancée lent her a new and even more beautiful glow. Emma could hardly believe that the confident young lady moving around the room was the same nervous girl who had quaked at the thought of being the centre of attention only a few hours ago.

An opinion shared by more than one person in the room.

'Your sister is utterly charming,' Alex said quietly at Emma's side later in the evening. 'I am beginning to understand why my brother has fallen so deeply in love with her.'

They were the words Emma had been longing to hear—the words she had never expected to hear. But hearing them from Alex now made her pleasure in the evening complete. 'I admit, she has exceeded even my expectations,' Emma said. 'Linette has always been so quiet and unassuming. Completely unpretentious. She wears her heart on her sleeve; while she can fly as high as a kite, she can also be cut down by an unkind word. But I have never seen her rise to an occasion the way she did tonight, or shine the way she is shining now.'

'Obviously, love *does* work miracles for some people,' Alex commented drily.

Emma sent him a curious look. 'You sound as though you still doubt the power it wields.'

'Oh, I know full well its power. Wars have been waged over it. Kingdoms lost and reputations forfeited because of it. All as a result of man being a constant victim to his stronger desires.'

'But why do you see only the harm that it does?' Emma asked, turning to face him. 'Men have done miraculous things in the name of love. They have created masterpieces of art and music. Built magnificent castles and crossed vast expanses of land and ocean, all because they were inspired by something bigger than themselves.'

His gaze softened as he looked at her. 'You truly are a romantic, aren't you, Emma?'

'No!' His caustic tone made her flush. 'But neither am I deaf or blind to what has been accomplished in the name of love.'

She watched the play of emotions across his face. 'I wonder,' he said softly.

'What?'

'I wonder what you could achieve if you were ever to fall as deeply in love with a man as your sister has. I'd like to be there to see that.'

Her heart thudded once, painfully, the echo of it reverberating throughout her entire body. *I'd like to be there to see that.* It hurt, more than she could ever have expected, the knowledge that he didn't see himself as that man. And while she dearly wished she could have responded to his statement in as casual a manner as he'd made it, even that simple act was beyond her.

'I like to think I would be able to accomplish such things with or without the presence of a man in my life.' Emma gazed up into his face, saw everything she had come to love and admire about him, and said, 'We are all capable of great achievement, my lord, limited only by our own imaginations and by the resources we have at our disposal.'

'But you do not believe that love is necessary for the achievement of all things.'

'Not all things, no. But consider what a mother will do for her child,' Emma said. 'Most would move mountains if they thought it would make the lives of their children easier.'

'You speak of selfless love,' Alex said.

'But is not all true love selfless? Do you not think that what Linette and Peter feel for one another is selfless? Your brother has gone against your father's wishes in order to be with the woman he loves, and such rebellion does not come without cost. But he has chosen his path and will not be diverted from it.'

'He says he can do nothing else,' Alex said.

'Exactly. That is what true love does. It inspires one to be better.'

His smile was infinitely gentle. 'Then I do not think

I could bear to see you when you do find that man, Emma. Because try as I might, I cannot imagine you being any better than you already are.'

After another sleepless night due in large part to Alex's enigmatic remark, Emma arrived in the breakfast parlour the next morning to find her father, brother and aunt happily discussing the events of the previous evening.

'I always thought Linette had more spunk than we gave her credit for,' Aunt Dorothy said, spreading a liberal helping of lemon curd on her toast. 'She's just never had an opportunity to shine. But last night, she was given that opportunity and I think I can safely say that she made all of us proud. Wouldn't you agree, Percy?'

'She did indeed,' Mr Darling said, turning the page of his newspaper. 'She is much like her mother in that regard.'

'And I thought Lady Glynnis Pettle was very impressive too,' Aunt Dorothy went on. 'I know old Widdicombe's fond of her and that she is going to be Lord Stewart's wife, but it takes courage to stand up to a man like that. I vow he had me trembling in my boots when we first walked into that room.' She looked up and frowned. 'You're very quiet this morning, Ridley. Feeling a bit poorly after all the excitement last night?'

Emma glanced up from her toast, not particularly surprised when her brother didn't answer. Aunt Dorothy just frowned. 'Ridley?'

He finally looked up, his expression blank. 'Pardon?'

'Dear me, and here I thought only old ladies and lovelorn young women were prone to wool gathering. I asked you if you were feeling poorly.'

'No. I feel all right,' he said, glancing around the table. 'I was merely thinking about a new painting I've been engaged to do.'

'Oh, yes, I'm sure that takes a great deal of thought,' Mr Darling muttered into his paper.

'As a matter of fact, it does,' Ridley said stiffly. 'I have a family grouping to do and they have asked me to come up with a list of possible settings or locations other than those usually employed for such portraits.'

'You could put them in a boat,' Aunt Dorothy suggested. 'Floating on a tranquil pond.'

'And I would stand where?' Ridley asked. 'On the gunnels? Tricky keeping the easel upright.'

'What about a folly?' Emma asked. 'You could use your sketch of the one on Lord Garrickson's estate.'

He stared at her without comprehension. 'A folly?'

'Yes, the one in your sketchbook. The one—'

Emma stopped. Ridley was looking at her as though she was spouting Greek—and suddenly, she knew the reason why. Her brother didn't *have* a sketch of Lord

Garrickson's folly in his sketchbook. He had a sketch of something he hadn't wanted her to see.

Unfortunately, given what Emma had seen of his behaviour with Lady Glynnis Pettle last night, it wasn't all that difficult to puzzle out what—or who—that might to be.

A wide range of outdoor events had been planned for the entertainment of the guests at Ellingsworth on Saturday, and by the time Emma and her family arrived around one o'clock, many of them were already underway. Emma saw targets for archery contests, buckets of water for apple bobbing, even a jousting course for anyone bold enough to try their hand at the medieval sport. There were also a lot more people milling around the grounds. Peter had kindly extended a general invitation to anyone in the village who wished to participate in the afternoon celebrations, and, always glad for a reason to hobnob with the well to do, many of them had come out.

Standing on the balcony looking out over the proceedings, Emma recognised Mr and Mrs Jacobs, as well as many of the guests who had been at their last assembly, strolling about the manicured lawns. Mrs Connolly was good-naturedly taking part in a three-legged race with Aunt Dorothy, while Mr Darling and Mr Connolly laughed and looked on.

Ridley had chosen to stay at home, saying he preferred to work on his new commission to running around fields playing silly games. Emma hadn't tried to change his mind. She suspected his reasons for not wanting to come had more to do with avoiding a certain lady than they did with shunning any of the festivities to be found. Ridley was usually a great lover of games.

There were also the well-dressed ladies and gentlemen who had been present at the ball the previous evening and who were staying at Ellingsworth for the weekend. Friends of Peter's and Alex's, all of whom were laughing and having a very good time, aided, no doubt, by the glasses of punch and beer the servants were busy handing around.

Peter played the part of the genial host to perfection, welcoming all of the guests as they arrived. Lord and Lady Widdicombe did not participate in any of the events, but sat comfortably on chairs on a private terrace at the back of the house, talking to Lord and Lady Leyland and the Marquess and Marchioness of Huffton.

Alex moved freely amongst all the guests, often with the beautiful Lady Glynnis at his side. At the moment, she was looking particularly fetching in a dark-green riding habit with a stylish, high-top bonnet that trailed long green ribbons down her back. Clearly she had been riding and hadn't gone up to change. But neither did she need to. She was breath-taking just as she was…

'She *is* lovely, isn't she? And she will make him a beautiful bride,' Linette said at Emma's elbow. 'Pity she doesn't love him.'

Emma's head spun around. 'What on earth are you talking about?'

'I watched them last night,' Linette said. 'They didn't exhibit any of the required signs. Not once did they stare longingly into one another's eyes, or make excuses to stand close to one another. They didn't even hold hands.'

'It *was* a rather harrowing evening,' Emma pointed out. 'As I recall, Lady Glynnis was more interested in defending *you* than she was in clinging to Lord Stewart.'

'I know, but in times of stress, two people in love will always look to one another for support and comfort.'

Linette's unexpected intuition might not have made such an impression had Emma not remembered the conversation she'd had with Alex about his relationship with Lady Glynnis shortly after meeting him. The one in which he had admitted that the basis for their marriage was not love.

'You were meeting Lord Widdicombe for the first time and Lady Glynnis was meeting our family for the first time,' Emma reminded her sister, trying to put the memory of that conversation aside. 'Surely such an evening would tend to make people act differently. I suspect Lady Glynnis was nervous.'

'She wasn't nervous at all,' Linette said. 'Lady Glynnis is the daughter of an earl. She is used to moving in society and to meeting all manner of people. She might have been a little on edge when she first met us, but she certainly wasn't nervous.'

No, she wasn't, Emma acknowledged bleakly. She'd had no reason to be. She was beautiful and well born and she was going to be Alex's wife. Not only that, her future father-in-law adored her. What on earth had a woman like that to be nervous about?

Emma turned to watch Alex approach the archery range. He was dressed for the outdoors and when he turned to smile at something Lady Glynnis said, Emma felt her heart turn over. Had she ever known a more handsome man? Or did he only seem so handsome because she loved him so much?

She glanced at Lady Glynnis's laughing face and decided she must have misread the situation with Ridley last night. Lady Glynnis would have to be mad to think of giving up a life with Alex to be with Ridley. As much as Emma loved her brother, he simply wasn't in the same league.

'Emma, can I ask you a personal question?' Linette said.

'Of course.'

'Do you have feelings for Lord Stewart?'

Emma coloured fiercely. How on earth was she to answer that? If she spoke too quickly, she risked sounding defensive, but if she took her time, Linette might think she was trying to concoct an answer. She decided on a half-truth. 'Of course I have feelings for him, Linette, just as I have feelings for Peter. They are both going to be related to me.'

'That's not what I meant. I meant do you have *feelings* for him. Of a romantic nature.'

Not even a half-truth would suffice here, Emma thought dimly. This called for an out-and-out lie. 'Of course not. Why?'

'Because remember what I said about how you can tell when two people are in love?'

'Yes.'

'Well, that's how you and Lord Stewart were behaving last night.'

Emma felt her face burn. 'We were not!'

'Yes, you were,' Linette said calmly. 'You were standing quite close together, looking as though there was no one else in the room. He spoke to you and you blushed, and when you spoke to him, you leaned in towards him ever so slightly.'

'I did?'

'Yes. Then at the end, *he* leaned in close to you and said something that made you look at him as though—'

'Stop it!' Emma said quickly. 'Immediately. Before you embarrass us both. I do *not* have feelings of a romantic nature for Lord Stewart. I like him as a person, but that's all. He is as good as engaged to Lady Glynnis and I am not so foolish as to risk my heart on someone who is not free to return my affection.'

'But they are not engaged yet,' Linette said softly. 'And if he has feelings for you—'

'He does *not* have feelings for me, Linette. He has feelings for Lady Glynnis. And he is going to marry her as everyone expects he should.'

And *she* would go to the wedding and throw rice at the newlyweds, and act as though she couldn't be happier. And with any luck, the more times she told herself that, the sooner she would come to believe it.

For that reason, Emma contented herself with watching Alex from a distance, admiring the fine figure of a man he presented. It was a lovely afternoon and, like most of the other gentlemen, he had shed his jacket and now stood in shirt sleeves, breeches and boots, aiming a very impressive-looking bow at a straw target set up some fifty feet distant. She saw him take his stance, spreading his legs to balance his weight, then watched him nock the arrow and raise the bow. Slowly he drew it back, his extended hand and his draw hand parallel to the ground. When his lips lightly touched the strings, he released the arrow. Emma watched it fly, straight as a die, landing just above centre in the red-and-white target.

A cheer went up from several of the ladies, including Lady Glynnis, who clapped her hands in approval.

'Well, at least she seems to like and admire him,' Linette observed. 'I suppose that will have to be enough.'

'People do marry for reasons other than love, you know,' Emma murmured, keeping her eyes on the archers.

'Yes, but love is still the only reason that matters.' Linette watched Peter step up to the mark and take up his bow. 'I suppose I'd hoped that given how much love matters to Peter, it might be of importance to his brother as well.'

'Need I remind you that *you* were the one who pointed out how different Lord Stewart and his brother were,' Emma said. 'And time has proven you right.'

'Actually, it hasn't,' Linette said. 'The more I come to know Lord Stewart, the more I think he is like his brother in many ways. He simply doesn't show it. Likely because the role he has always been called upon to play demands that he keeps his deepest feelings hidden. But I believe love matters to him every bit as much as it does to Peter. Oh, well done, Mr

Taylor!' Linette cried, clapping her hands as her fiancé's arrow struck the target about two inches from the centre. 'I had no idea he was so good. I must go down and compliment him.'

Emma and Linette waited until the bows were safely set aside before making their way on to the archery course. Lady Glynnis, Emma noticed, had already turned and started in the direction of the refreshment tent with two other ladies, leaving Alex alone.

'Ah, Miss Darling,' Alex said, slipping his coat back on. 'I thought I saw you watching me from the balcony.'

Flustered that he should have noticed, Emma attempted a quelling smile. 'I was not watching *you*, Lord Stewart. I was observing all of the archers. Including your brother, who I must say shot very well.'

'Peter's a keen sportsman,' Alex said without rancour. 'Where my talents at school ran more to the academic, his always tended towards the physical.'

Strange, Emma thought, given that Alex's build was the more muscular. 'You have nothing to be ashamed of. You acquitted yourself quite well.'

'Quite well.' His smile was slow and deliberate. 'Thank you, Miss Darling. I am at a loss for words in the face of such blatant flattery.'

Emma felt colour scald her cheeks. 'It was not intended as a slight, my lord. I was simply making a comment.'

'Of course you were. Just as if I were to say that you look *quite* charming in that dress, or that I've always thought your hair *quite* a lovely colour, there would be no danger of it going to your head because I would simply have been...making a comment.'

He thought she looked charming? And that her hair was pretty? 'It is not the same at all. I am making a judgement as to your ability. A comment about my dress or my hair addresses something over which I have no control.'

'On the contrary, does a lady not specifically choose clothing to flatter her figure and complexion?' Alex retorted. 'Does she not style her hair in a manner most becoming to her face? Of course she does. Because the whole point of the exercise is to attract the attention of a male.'

Emma frowned. 'You make us sound rather predatory.'

'We *all* are. What do you think the purpose of these gatherings is, Emma, if not to allow us to be seen at our best by members of the opposite sex? The goal of married couples is to provide venues like this so that those of us who *are* single are quickly absorbed into the wedded state. There is nothing a married man likes better than to see a happily single man trapped in the parson's noose.'

'And what about a happily single woman?'

'I doubt such a thing exists.'

'Odious man, of course it does! A woman loses everything when she marries. Her property. Her money. Her identity.'

'Ah, but look at what she gains,' Alex pointed out. 'A man willing to protect her virtue and honour her name. A banker who will pay her debts and keep her in the style she might not otherwise have known. And, if she is lucky, a man who will love her and make her happy in every way a man should.'

She wanted to mock him, but the words died on her lips. He hadn't been smiling when he had spoken those last words. He had been looking right at her. Daring her to disagree. Or waiting for her to tell him he was right...which, of course, he *was.* What did any woman want but a man who truly loved her? A man to whom she meant everything. She might not have believed that a month ago, but she believed it now. Linette had found that connection with Peter Taylor. Emma had not found it with anyone. Nor had Alex, who was marrying Lady Glynnis Pettle because she was suitable. Dear Lord, was there ever a colder, more emotionless reason for doing something so important? So life altering...

'My lord,' Lady Glynnis said, rejoining them, 'what has been keeping you? I was waiting for you at the tent.'

Alex looked round and quickly apologised. 'Forgive me, Glyn, Miss Darling and I were engaged in a verbal battle.'

'Oh?' Beautiful violet eyes turned to gaze at Emma. 'Dare I ask who the winner was?'

'I'm not sure there was one,' Emma said, afraid to look at Alex with Lady Glynnis watching her so closely.

But Alex only laughed. 'I think Miss Darling is right. It was more an exchange of opinions than an argument and it is difficult to establish a winner when there is no point to be won or lost. But now, shall we join the others in the tent for refreshments? This shooting of innocent bales of straw has made me devilishly hungry.'

On the way to the tent, Linette and Peter joined them, and somehow Emma found herself walking with Lady Glynnis behind the other three. She enjoyed watched the antics going on all around her: young men making fools of themselves in three-legged races, young girls skipping rope and tossing bowls, Aunt Dorothy imbibing champagne...

'I am surprised your brother did not come with you this afternoon, Miss Darling,' Lady Glynnis said casually. 'I would have thought this type of gathering the sort of thing he would have enjoyed.'

Surprised to hear her speak of Ridley, Emma said,

'He told me he had to do some preparatory work for a...project he has in London.'

'A new painting, perhaps?'

When Emma turned to look at her, Lady Glynnis smiled. 'It's all right, Miss Darling. You don't have to pretend you don't know. You and your brother are very close. I'm sure he told you he did a portrait of me.'

Glad for the opening, but nevertheless aware of a need for caution, Emma said, 'He did mention it in passing, Lady Glynnis.'

'You must have been shocked to learn he had taken up painting as a living.'

'We all were, given that he started out with the intention of becoming a lawyer.'

'But he is very good. Has he shown you any of his work?'

'He brought home a painting of a little girl with a kitten. I thought it excellent.'

Lady Glynnis smiled. 'Lord Forrester's daughter. He was just finishing that one when I came to talk to him about my portrait.'

They proceeded on in silence for a few minutes. Lady Glynnis walked slowly, as if to let the other three get ahead of them. 'Miss Darling, did your brother tell you anything about the painting he did of me?'

'Only that it took him a long time to get it exactly right.'

'So you don't know anything about the nature of the painting?'

'No.'

'I commissioned it as a gift for Lord Stewart. You must have heard that we are promised to one another.'

Emma swallowed, but kept her eyes straight ahead. 'Yes.'

'The arrangements were made by our parents some time ago, of course, but I had no complaint. I've known Alex for years. Ever since we were children, in fact, and I've always been fond of him. I don't suppose there was ever any question that we would marry other people. And, this last year, we have talked about it several times. That is how I know he will be proposing very soon and why I decided to have a painting done of myself. As a wedding present. And I wanted it to be...beautiful.'

'How could it be anything else?' Emma asked.

To her surprise, the lady blushed. 'You are too kind, Miss Darling. I have never thought of myself as beautiful. My cousin is the acknowledged beauty in the family. But Alex has a keen eye for such things and I wanted him to have a portrait that he would be pleased to look upon. After seeing a sample of your brother's work, I knew he was the one to do it.'

There was a wistfulness to her voice, a sadness,

that prompted Emma to say, 'Ridley told me you were happy with the finished portrait, Lady Glynnis. Is that not the case?'

This time, it was Lady Glynnis who kept her eyes forwards. 'The painting was…exquisite. It captured a side of me I didn't even know existed. Yes, I was pleased with it. And had I taken it with me the day he showed it to me, everything would have been well. But he said he needed a few extra days to frame it and that he would deliver it in person to my home.' Lady Glynnis slowed to a stop, forcing Emma to do the same. 'Unfortunately, before I finally did receive the painting, he did the unforgivable.'

The sadness was back, along with the wistfulness. Emma knew it would be wrong to pretend she didn't know. 'He let someone else see the portrait,' she said quietly. 'That's why you were so angry with him.'

'The painting was to have been a gift for my fiancé, Miss Darling. As such, I felt Alex should be the first man to see it. I thought I could trust your brother in that regard. When he told me he had shown the painting to someone else, I felt betrayed. As though the level of trust I had placed in him had been misplaced.' Lady Glynnis started to walk again. 'I'm sure you can understand that.'

'I can understand your disappointment at your fiancé not being the first to see the painting,' Emma said slowly, 'but not your anger towards my brother for having let someone else see it. Ridley told me the gentleman, who is known to you both, simply dropped by the studio one evening and happened to see it sitting upon the easel where it was waiting to be finished. And I understand that his remarks about the portrait were highly complimentary.'

'All of that is true, Miss Darling. But the painting revealed…a state of mind,' Lady Glynnis said, a delicate rush of pink staining her cheeks. 'A very private state of mind. Had it been just a painting of a woman in a garden, I would not have cared, but your brother's painting gave away more of my feelings than I was comfortable sharing with other people.'

'But surely there is no embarrassment in seeing the face of a woman in love,' Emma said. 'Is that not how you wish Lord Stewart to see you when he looks upon the painting? Or anyone else who sees it.'

When Lady Glynnis made no reply, Emma sighed. She did not understand why the lady was reacting the way she was. All she could be sure of was that whatever she thought she had seen on Lady Glynnis's face in response to Ridley's comment last night must have been a mistake. Clearly, the lady was very much in love with Alex.

'I am sorry, Lady Glynnis,' Emma said finally. 'I know Ridley had no intention of hurting you and that it has upset him greatly to know that he has. He is not a cruel or mean spirited man.'

'I never believed he was,' Lady Glynnis said quietly. 'That's why I was so surprised when I found out he had shown the painting to Mr Towbridge.'

'And I must repeat that it was not intentionally done,' Emma said. 'My brother did not invite Mr...'

'Towbridge.'

'Mr Towbridge to come and see the painting—'

'I understand that, Miss Darling. And I am well aware that Mr Towbridge is a good friend of your brother's and that he was responsible for your brother receiving his first commission. But Alex...Lord Stewart, should have been the first man to see it,' Lady Glynnis repeated. 'The only man.'

Emma sighed. Obviously nothing she said was going to have any effect on the lady's opinion. 'Then I can only say again how sorry I am, Lady Glynnis.'

'I realise this has...nothing to do with you,' Lady Glynnis said as they drew closer to the tent. 'But I wanted you to know so that you would understand the tension between your brother and myself. To understand why it is so...difficult for me to be in the same room with him.'

'I do understand. And I shall not speak of this to anyone else.'

'You're very kind. And despite the difficulties, I do hope your sister and Mr Taylor are able to find happiness together. They are both dear people and I honestly believe they should be allowed to marry.'

'I think what you said last night helped in that regard,' Emma said.

By now they had caught up with the others and were soon absorbed into the crowd of people moving along the tables weighted down with refreshments of all kinds. But Lady Glynnis's words stayed with Emma long after they had parted, as had the tone in which they had been spoken. There had been anger, but there had also been regret, as though the lady was sorry matters had turned out the way they had. But why should she feel that way? Emma kept asking herself. Why would a lady who was as good as engaged to the heir to an earldom feel regret that a relationship between herself and the man hired to paint her portrait had ended so badly?

At the conclusion of the afternoon's festivities, the villagers returned to their homes to talk about all the things they had seen and done, and the invited guests returned to Ellingsworth to prepare for the formal evening events. Alex had seen Emma and her family leave, though he had not gone over to say goodbye. He knew it was best he maintain a distance from her now. She was a lovely young woman and he knew himself well enough to know that he was attracted to her and that the attraction was only going to get stronger. She had such a refreshing and uncomplicated way about her. The afternoon he had arrived at Dove's Hollow to find her painting in the garden, she hadn't made any apologies for her appearance. She had smiled when he had offered the expected compliment, but he had seen in her eyes her awareness of its intention. He knew she hadn't believed him, which was a pity since he really *had* meant it.

He'd found her appearance that day utterly charming. The white painter's smock spattered here and there with splotches of both green and yellow paint had fit loosely, but had done nothing to disguise the sweetness of her figure. The straw bonnet had been casually undone, allowing tendrils of hair to escape, and her lips had been slightly parted as she had gazed intently at the canvas, her arm extended, bent a little at the elbow, as she moved the brush lightly over the canvas.

She'd had absolutely no idea that to him, *she* had been the work of art.

And when he had spoken and she had looked up at him, for an unguarded moment, he had seen surprised pleasure in the depths of those soft brown eyes. It had vanished the moment he had begun to explain his reasons for coming to see her, of course, but just for an instant, it had been there and he wanted very much to see it again. To see her smile at him like that again.

That was the reason he knew he had to back away now. The attraction was there, tangible and strong, but an attraction was all it could ever be. He had a duty to his name and he had made a promise to a lady. A lady who, even now, was waiting for his offer of marriage.

'Thank you, Barker,' Alex said as his valet finished brushing his jacket. He turned to face the glass and saw a composed face staring back at him. No trace of indecision was reflected there. No indication of the age-old battle being waged within. The battle against desire.

The battle to do what was right.

Chapter Ten

Dinner started out as a surprisingly enjoyable affair.
Alex had come to dislike large formal gatherings,
but tonight everyone seemed to be in good spirits.
The guests expressed their pleasure over the events
of the afternoon and many a laugh was shared over
misfortunes encountered and games won or lost.

Seated three chairs down from him and on the
other side of the table, Emma was too far away
to converse, a fact that was both a source of relief
and disappointment to Alex. He had been rendered
almost speechless by the sight of her this evening, her
voluptuous curves magnificently displayed in a gown
that could only have been made by one of London's
most fashionable modistes. Emma could have taken
her place in any of the grandest of London houses,
had such been her wish.

Instead, she was here, looking supremely composed and radiantly beautiful as she conversed with
Lord Mallard on her left and Anthony Slayter on her

right. Mallard was in his late fifties, recently widowed and looking for a wife. Slayter, younger and far more handsome, was looking for a mistress. Alex knew those facts to be well known in society, but he doubted word of them had spread to Little Moreton. A fact that made him less than pleased at seeing both gentlemen paying Emma far more attention that the length of their acquaintance warranted.

'So, what about you, my lord?' Tom Towbridge asked in a genial tone. 'Why aren't we celebrating two engagements this weekend, rather than just one?'

Alex mustered a smile. He liked Tom Towbridge. Though younger than him by a good few years, Tom was a sensible fellow who took his responsibilities seriously. 'Because, Mr Towbridge, this *is* my brother's celebration and the last thing I would wish to do is steal his thunder.'

'But you are still planning to marry Lady Glynnis?' Lady Gregory demanded from across the table.

Alex raised an eyebrow. He might have taken exception to the remark except for the fact that Lady Gregory was a close friend of Glynnis's Aunt Mary and knew how matters stood between the families. But he found he was not as comfortable talking about his marriage now that the direction of his feelings had changed. 'Our arrangement hasn't changed, Lady Gregory. I simply haven't found the right moment to ask her.'

'Good, because everyone knows how anxious your father is to see Lady Glynnis become the next countess.'

'Well, all I can say,' Tom said, 'is that I hope when it comes time for me to choose a wife, I am fortunate enough to find a woman who loves me as deeply as Lady Glynnis loves you.'

Surprised by the remark, Alex said, 'How do you know she does?'

'Good God, man, you only have to look at the painting to know how she feels about you. If that's not a portrait of a woman in love, I don't know what is.'

'The portrait?'

'Yes, the one she had—' Suddenly, Towbridge went white. 'Oh, God. Don't tell me…she hasn't given it to you yet.'

'Given me what?'

'Oh, *hell!*'

'Tom?'

'Forgive me. It was meant to be a surprise. Pretend we never had this conversation,' Towbridge said desperately. 'If anyone asks, say you know nothing about it.'

Alex sat back, frowning. 'That won't be hard since I have absolutely no idea what—'

The whoop of feminine laughter cut across Alex's words and brought the quiet murmur of conversation up and down the table to an abrupt halt. Alex glanced to his left, saw that Emma's face had gone deathly pale, then looked past her to find the source of the laughter.

At the lower end of the table, Mrs Grand was talking with great animation to Sir Stanford Buckle, an affable gentleman and recent widower who was clearly enjoying the lady's attentions. Both were looking a little flushed, and when Mrs Grand picked up her glass and tipped back the contents Alex understood why. It seemed his father had not been mistaken in suggesting that certain members of Emma's family were fond of a tipple.

He glanced quickly at his mother and father sitting at either end of the table, saw the horror-stricken expressions on both their faces, and then, seeing Peter's face, realised he wasn't any happier. Linette's face was crimson, as was her father's, who was seated across the table from his sister.

Thankfully, the last cover had been removed and without waiting for the butler to sweep the table, Lady Widdicombe abruptly got to her feet. 'Ladies, please join me in the Green Drawing room.' Without another word, she turned and led the way out of the room.

Emma and Linette quickly got to their feet and went immediately to their aunt's side.

'Come along, Aunt Dorothy,' Emma said, helping

the lady to her feet. 'It is time for us to leave the gentlemen to their after-dinner pleasures.'

'Really? What a pity.' She giggled. 'Sir Stanford and I were having a most interesting conversation about—'

'Aunt, *please,* we really must go,' Linette whispered in mortification.

It was only then, as Mrs Grand looked around the table and saw how many of the guests were staring at her with disapproval, that her laughter abruptly died. She glanced at her nieces, the expressions on their faces giving her an awareness of what she had done, and her joy evaporated. 'Oh, yes. Yes, of course.'

Alex watched the girls help their aunt to her feet, noticed her teeter a little as she backed away from the table, then saw them quickly escort her from the room. The moment the door closed behind them, the buzz of conversation resumed. Alex watched his father get up from the table and abruptly draw Lord Leyland aside. Several other gentlemen also stood up to stretch their legs, but Mr Darling stayed where he was, his body rigid, his eyes downcast.

Alex went over and sat down next to him. 'Mr Darling, would you care to join me for a—?'

'I am so sorry, Lord Stewart,' Mr Darling said in a choked voice, his eyes never leaving the table. 'I cannot imagine what came over her.'

'A little too much champagne, I expect,' Alex said,

trying to downplay the seriousness of the event. 'It happens to the best of us.'

'But not to a lady. *Never* to a lady. And certainly not at such an important occasion as this.' Mr Darling's face was a study in regret. 'One meant to celebrate her niece's engagement to the son of a peer.'

'Perhaps it was the nature of the event that compelled her to imbibe a little more freely than she normally would,' Alex said. 'Drink does tend to help settle one's nerves.'

'Yes, but all too often it also results in the loss of one's inhibitions and this is the *last* place such a thing should have happened.' The older man sighed deeply. 'Do you know what the sad part of this is, my lord? My sister has been more concerned with making a good impression on your family and friends than any of us. She knows how important this is to Linette and she was most insistent that we present ourselves in the best light possible on each and every occasion our families came together.'

'And you have.'

'Until tonight,' Mr Darling said ruefully. 'Your mother and father were not pleased by Dorothy's conduct and who can blame them? She behaved in a manner totally unbecoming to a lady. I dearly wish Emma and Linette had not been here to witness it.'

'But they are, I think, aware of your sister's tendency to drink,' Alex said as tactfully as he could.

'If it is an ongoing condition, they must have seen evidence of it in the past.'

'Yes. I dearly wish I could say that was not the case, but I would only be lying to both of us.' Mr Darling finally raised his head, but he did not meet Alex's eyes. 'My sister changed after her husband passed away, Lord Stewart. I think it shocked her, his dying so young, and she was totally unprepared for life on her own. She had servants, of course, but she was suddenly the one in charge and I know she missed him dreadfully. So she started taking a glass or two of sherry in the afternoon, just to settle her nerves. I didn't say anything in the beginning. After all, where was the harm? I thought. Why shouldn't she dull her loneliness a little in whatever manner she had at her disposal?'

Alex smiled. 'I suspect we've all done that at one time or another.'

'I know I have,' Mr Darling admitted. 'After the children's mother died, I often found myself heading for my study for a few hours spent in a whisky-induced haze. It was an easy way to escape the less pleasant aspects of one's life. But, eventually, I realised I had a family to look after and that I had to set an example. I saw what happened to my brother when the drink took over and I was damned if I was going to let that happen to me. So I stopped drinking then and there. Unfortunately, Dorothy didn't have anyone to look after, or to turn to for solace.'

'She has no family of her own?'

Mr Darling shook his head. 'She was never blessed with children.'

'But you have, I believe, another sister living in Bath. Could Mrs Grand not have gone and stayed with her?'

'It would never have worked,' Mr Darling said with a sad smile. 'Even as children, they fought. Always jealous of what the other had. Both wanting more than what life had given them. I doubt being together would have helped either of them.'

Alex managed a smile. 'They say misery loves company.'

'And never a truer word spoken,' Mr Darling agreed. 'But sometimes it is wiser to stay clear of someone else's unhappiness when you are so low in spirit yourself. Rather than buoy each other up, I fear they would have dragged the other down.' Then, as if realising who he was talking to and how he had been going on, Mr Darling abruptly stood up. 'Forgive me, my lord. This cannot be of the slightest interest to you and I am the last person in the world who should be monopolising your time.'

'On the contrary, I'm glad you felt you could talk to me about it.' Alex likewise got to his feet. 'I can assure you, I understand completely.'

'Thank you for saying that,' Mr Darling said. 'I only hope Dorothy's behaviour tonight did not reflect too badly on Linette and the rest of our family.'

Alex clapped the man on the shoulder, offered him as reassuring a smile as he could and then walked towards the French doors. The room had grown uncomfortably warm; needing a breath of fresh air, he stepped out in the night, only to overhear another conversation taking place between three gentlemen standing on the balcony.

'…haven't heard a laugh like that since my father took me to the fair and I went to see the Fat Lady,' Anthony Slayter was saying. 'Anyone know who she is?'

'A Mrs Grand, I believe,' said Lord Baird. 'Widowed aunt of young Taylor's fiancée.'

'An aunt? By Jove, they'd best hide the sherry when *she* comes to call lest she drink them out of house and home.'

'Old Buckle seemed quite taken with her,' Lord Whitby said.

'And why wouldn't he?' Slayter said. 'He's well known for bending the elbow himself and he *is* looking for a wife. They'd make a fine pair, as long as Buckle's income don't run out.'

'Speaking of a fine pair,' Baird commented, 'you seemed rather taken with the young lady sitting next to you, Slayter. Isn't she the older sister?'

'She is.'

'Tasty little piece,' Whitby said. 'Got more meat on her bones than most society chits. I wager she'd keep a man warm in his bed.'

Alex had heard more than enough. 'I would advise you to keep a civil tongue in your heads, gentlemen,' he said, stepping out on to the balcony. 'The ladies you refer to will soon be members of my family.'

Lord Baird and Lord Whitby looked decidedly uncomfortable, but Slayter just laughed. 'Oh, come on, Stewart, we were simply having a little fun.'

'At someone else's expense.'

'Of course, we certainly wouldn't want it at our own. But you can't deny that the Darlings are an interesting family. Getting foxed in front of your father wasn't the smartest thing the aunt could have done.'

'I agree it was not the most prudent course of action, but Mrs Grand is not accustomed to moving in society,' Alex said. 'I expect she sought a way to calm her nerves.'

Slayter's smile was more of a sneer. 'She did that very nicely. Unfortunately, just a touch too vocally.'

'So what do you know of the family, Stewart?' Whitby asked. 'I'd never heard of them before receiving the invitation for this weekend.'

'I understand the father used to tutor Lord Gaylord's son,' Baird volunteered. 'But that he gave it up when he acquired a house and moved down here. And his own son recently became an artist. He painted that portrait of Forrester's youngest daughter.'

'*That's* where I heard the name!' Whitby said. 'Has the makings of a damn fine artist from all I hear.'

'And then there's the youngest daughter, presently engaged to your brother,' Slayter said, his smile as cold as his pale blue eyes. 'Tell me, Stewart, are your mother and father pleased about the engagement?'

'They are pleased my brother has found someone about whom he cares deeply, yes.'

'But it's not quite the same thing, is it?' Slayter said. 'I hear the earl has refused to give his permission for them to wed.'

'Then you heard incorrectly. And I suggest you stop listening to gossip and innuendo.' Alex's voice was cold, the warning implicit. 'It is most unbecoming in a gentleman.'

Slayter's expression clouded in anger, but Alex didn't give a damn. The man was an arrogant dandy who cared more about other people's business than he did his own and who was constantly running up gambling losses at the tables and the racecourse that frequently had to be covered by his family. Alex was surprised he had even been invited to the gathering, until he remembered that Sir Roger and Lady Slayter were good friends of his parents.

'Alex,' his father said, coming up behind him now. 'A word, if you don't mind. Excuse us, gentlemen?'

The other three bowed and drifted back into the dining room. Alex ignored the smug look on Slayter's face as he closed the doors and waited for his father to launch into his tirade.

It wasn't long in coming. 'Well? What have you to say about *that?*' the earl demanded.

'I take it you mean Mrs Grand?'

'Of course I mean Mrs Grand! Did you see any other lady at the table drinking and flirting outrageously with one of the guests?'

'I realise it was not becoming behaviour—'

'Not becoming? It was humiliating for everyone who had the misfortune to witness it!' his father snapped. 'And this is the family Peter has chosen to marry into. How do you think that reflects on us?'

Alex sighed. 'I agree it should not have happened, but there is nothing we can do now but try to look at it in the best light possible!'

'There is no light in the *world* that could make this look good!' the earl said. 'Now, I think I have been patient, Alex, but your brother must be made to see that marrying into such a family is simply not acceptable.'

'Peter is marrying Linette Darling, Father. Not her aunt.'

'He is still tying himself to a family of drunkards and gamblers.'

'You exaggerate.'

'Do I? I told you how they came to be in possession of Dove's Hollow, and now you've seen proof that they have no social conscience whatsoever! How much more proof of their unsuitability do you need?'

The French doors opened and Peter appeared. He looked from one to the other and Alex saw the despair in his eyes. 'I think you should come back in. Your absence is being commented upon.'

The earl simply grunted and marched past his younger son without a word.

Alex sighed and glanced at his brother. 'Are you sure you know what you're doing, Peter? There are other young women out there. Women who would be more suitable to being your wife.'

'You mean women who would make Father happier than he is right now.'

'That too.'

Peter shook his head. 'There could never be anyone for me but Linette. I'm more sure of that every day. She is good and kind and she loves me. Not what I own or who my family is. *Me.* And I won't give her up, Alex. Not for Father. Not for you. Not for anyone. The only way I would give her up is if she asked me to.'

'Be sensible, Peter. You know Father's health is failing and this tension between the two of you isn't helping.'

'I know and I'm sorry. But if he cared more about

patching things up between us, he wouldn't have suggested that I set Linette up as my mistress and look
for a more suitable woman to be my wife.'

Alex swore softly. 'He said that?'

'Just now, before he came out to see you. Thank
God I was the only one who heard it, but how do you
think that made me feel, Alex? What does it say when
your father suggests that the woman you've asked to
be your wife is only suitable to being your mistress?'

'It just confirms what he's been saying all along.
That he doesn't believe Linette Darling is good
enough for you,' Alex said. 'That he never *will* believe she's good enough for you. And that if you proceed with this marriage, the two of you will remain
at odds until one or the other of you dies.'

It was a sobering reality, Alex reflected as he
watched his brother walk away. Because it also meant
that Emma Darling would never be good enough for
him. No matter how he'd come to feel about her, any
type of relationship, other than the one his father had
just suggested, was impossible. He was next in line
to the earldom, which meant he had even less leeway
than his brother when it came to giving away his
heart. He owed his family his loyalty; an obligation
that had been instilled in him since he was a boy.
Honour. Duty. Responsibility. The pride one took
in one's name and one's position in society. He was

doing the right thing by marrying Glynnis because it was what everyone expected.

Why, then, did it suddenly feel as though it couldn't have been more wrong?

There was not a great deal of happiness to be found at Dove's Hollow the next morning. Aunt Dorothy, painfully aware of the grievous *faux pas* she had committed the night before, refused to come out of her room. She would not be swayed by her brother's pleas that she come downstairs and talk this out, and, when Emma tried to take her a breakfast tray, she steadfastly refused to open the door.

'Aunt Dorothy, please come downstairs,' Emma said. 'We are not angry with you.'

'You should be!' came the unusually frail voice. 'I am furious with myself.'

'But—'

'Go away, Emma dear. I would rather be alone.'

Emma pressed her ear to the door and heard the sound of muffled crying. 'Very well, but I shall leave the tray.'

'Take it away. I don't want anything.'

'I shall leave it regardless.' And Emma did, hoping her aunt would change her mind. Dorothy had always had a good appetite for food.

'How is she?' Linette asked when Emma arrived back downstairs.

'Not good. I left the tray outside her door, but she wouldn't let me in.'

'Oh, Emma, I feel dreadful about all this,' Linette said. 'I never meant to make everyone so unhappy. I had no idea matters would turn out like this.'

Emma drew her sister into her arms and held her tight. 'You have nothing to apologise for. You have no more control over Aunt Dorothy than I did over Aunt Augusta. They lead their own lives and, if they make mistakes, they have no one to blame but themselves. But you have a man who loves you desperately and who wants to marry you. That is what you have to concentrate on right now.'

'But will the earl still *allow* Peter to marry me?' Linette sadly pulled free of her sister's embrace. 'Lord Widdicombe did not look at me once after the gentlemen rejoined the ladies last night. He made a point of staying as far away from me as possible. And when Peter tried to come over to talk to me, his father called him away on some pretence or other. It couldn't have been more obvious that he did not want us to be together.'

That, unfortunately, was true. Keenly aware of the dynamics in the room, Emma had watched the earl effectively ignore Linette for the rest of the evening. Only when she was leaving had he nodded in her direction, but while it was enough to prevent people from thinking he had cut her entirely, it wasn't much more.

And neither had her own situation improved. She hadn't had a chance to talk to Alex at all. It was as though he had decided to ignore her the same way Lord Widdicombe had chosen to ignore Linette. When he had come back into the drawing room with the rest of the gentlemen, he had gone immediately to Lady Glynnis's side and Emma had watched them laughing and talking as though he had been trying to make her aware of the differences between them.

It had all but torn Emma apart. Even when Alex hadn't been with Lady Glynnis, he had stayed in the company of his other friends, part of the gilded circle in which he moved. If ever the differences between their families had been apparent, it was last night. The elegant society people on one side of the room and her family on the other. The gap could not have been wider.

'Well, as far as I'm concerned, you have absolutely nothing to be ashamed of,' Emma said fiercely. 'You were a perfect lady the entire weekend and everyone who was there saw that. If the earl wishes to wash his hands of us because of something Aunt Dorothy did, there is really nothing we can do. But I will not have you think any the less of yourself because *he* cannot distinguish the goodness in you from the weakness in our aunt.'

Emma had no idea if she managed to convince Linette of anything. She wasn't even sure she had convinced herself. But she refused to believe that the earl would force his son to end the relationship simply as a result of Aunt Dorothy's behaviour. Surely anyone looking at the two of them could see how deeply in love they were.

And what did they see when they looked at you? the nagging little voice asked. *Did they see how desperately you wanted to be with Alex?*

Emma closed her eyes and prayed they did not. It would be too humiliating to be seen as being in love with Alex when he was so clearly dedicated to Lady Glynnis. She could just imagine the whispers. *Who does she think she is? Surely she isn't so naïve as to think Lord Stewart would fancy* her? *It's bad enough his brother is consorting with her sister.*

Oh, yes, she knew what the gossips would say. Her brief exposure to society two years ago had given her a very good insight into the ways of the *ton*. Most of them were shallow and conceited and out for their own gain. She had listened to them gossiping in their elegant salons, heard them whispering in music rooms about this person or that, and had seen them laugh at young unsophisticated girls who came to London with stars in their eyes in the hopes of finding the man of their dreams. A man who was oft-times as shallow and conceited as all the rest.

No, it was imperative that she maintain an emotional distance from Alex. She would not embarrass him by asking for something he could not give. And she would not embarrass herself by being seen to want it.

Aunt Dorothy eventually did come downstairs. It was just past one o'clock and lunch was already over, but it soon became evident that food was the last thing on her mind. She headed straight for the library where she knew her brother would be reading, and informed him—as he informed his children shortly thereafter—that she would be returning to London as soon as it could be arranged. She had disgraced the family beyond all hope of redemption and could not bear to show her face to any of them again. Especially to dear Linette, whose future with Mr Taylor she was quite sure she had put in jeopardy.

Mr Darling, not the most effusive or sympathetic man at the best of times, had asked if there was anything he could do, whereupon Aunt Dorothy had assured him there was not and had then returned to her room to pack. The carriage had called for her an hour later and after bidding them all a teary and embarrassed farewell, she left.

An hour later, Peter arrived.

Emma was not surprised to see him. He must have

known how dreadful Linette would be feeling and he had obviously come to Dove's Hollow in the hopes of consoling her, as any loving and dutiful fiancé would do. Mr Darling received him most civilly and after again apologising for his sister's behaviour, he agreed to Peter's request that he be allowed to take Linette out for a drive.

Naturally, Linette was delighted to see him. She took his appearance to mean that Lord Widdicombe had not ordered him to break off his association with her and that all was forgiven. She hurried upstairs to change into something more appropriate and left Emma and Peter to walk out to his carriage together.

'I would ask you to join us, Miss Darling,' Peter said, 'but I have only the phaeton, as my brother is using the carriage to show Lady Glynnis and her parents the countryside.'

'Pray do not concern yourself, Mr Taylor,' Emma said, far more pained by the knowledge that Alex was occupied with Lady Glynnis than she was at having to miss her sister's outing. 'There are things I must attend to here.'

'Of course.'

Emma smiled and blessed the man for not looking as relieved as he probably felt. She was quite sure the last thing he wanted was an older sister tagging along as he tried to reassure the woman he loved that all would be well. And since the last thing Emma *wanted* was to have to sit there and listen to such reassurances, she was equally relieved not to be included. When Linette came downstairs, looking perfectly charming in a gown of lavender-sprigged muslin, Emma was perfectly content to see Peter help her into the high seat and then climb up after her.

'We shan't be long,' he said.

Emma waved them off, then drew her shawl more closely around her shoulders as she turned to regard the old stone house. How must Dove's Hollow look to someone like Peter Taylor, a man who had been raised in such a grand house and who now lived in one equally fine? Or to Lord Stewart, whose London home was said to be splendid, and who would one day inherit Widdicombe Hill, one of the finest houses in Kent? It must appear quite humble, Emma thought.

But then, their family had never pretended to be anything else. Her father was a good man, but far from sophisticated. He was educated and well read, as any man who tutors others must be, but he liked his home and his books far better than anything London had to offer. Emma's mother was the one who had sampled the delights of town. Growing up as the eldest daughter of a well-to-do merchant, she was the one who had taken in the theatre and the museums and the art galleries. She had met Percy Darling at one such place and had fallen quite madly in love with him.

Still, they had been happy. There had always been food on the table and a roof over their heads. The girls had enjoyed lessons with a governess while Ridley had been sent to a school in the village. It was only after they had moved into Dove's Hollow that their father had given up teaching and settled to the life of a gentleman. And all would have been perfect had it not been for their mother's declining health and subsequent passing.

That had been the hardest thing Emma had ever had to endure. She still missed her mother dreadfully. There were so many things she would have liked to talk to her about. Things only a mother and daughter could share, because a mother had special insights into a daughter's heart. While her father did his best, he was just a man. And dear Aunt Dorothy, well, she'd always had her own best interests at heart. She hadn't adapted well to life on her own and had taken to finding solace in drink.

However, everyone had their problems, Emma reflected, and everyone had their own ways of dealing with them. It was just unfortunate that Dorothy's manner of dealing with *her* problems had unwittingly created a problem for everyone else. But, as her father said, there was nothing any of them could do about it. The damage was done. The fact of Peter's coming here today was surely proof that the wedding was going to proceed. If he had come to break it off,

Emma doubted he would have looked so happy at setting off alone with Linette in the phaeton.

Not ready to head back into the house, Emma ambled towards the stable. She thought Ridley might be back soon, having left just after Aunt Dorothy made her announcement, but Chesapeake's stall was still empty and the stable was quiet, the only sound being the contented sound of Bess munching hay.

Emma went to close the door of Chessy's stall when she noticed, of all things, Ridley's sketchbook lying on one of the bales of hay. Why on earth would he have left it down here?

She had her answer when she glanced at the page lying open. Ridley had started a sketch of the chestnut. Perhaps he thought to use it in his portrait for the family in London. He'd certainly done a masterful job. The musculature of the horse's hindquarters was beautifully depicted, as was the length and shape of its legs. More accustomed to seeing her brother's rendition of the human animal, Emma was astonished at how accurately he had captured the details of the horse's form, even to the coarse texture of the mane and tail.

Curious to see more of his work, Emma sat down and pulled the pad on to her lap. There were a variety of sketches within, some of animals, a few of buildings, but most often of people. There were even casual drawings of the three of them going about their daily routine. She saw one of her father absently rubbing Rory's head as he read the newspaper, and one of her working on her embroidery while Linette played the piano in the background. Ridley had a gift for capturing the tiny details other artists would surely miss. The dusting of freckles across the bridge of Linette's nose. The tranquillity of her father's expression, the smile that always hovered so close to the surface. There was even a second one of her, sitting at her easel with her brush poised against the canvas, her brow furrowed in concentration.

Then she turned the page again—and saw Lady Glynnis staring up at her.

Emma gasped. The portrait was uncannily lifelike. Ridley had captured Lady Glynnis during an unguarded moment, her expression soft, her features relaxed as she smiled back at him. She was wearing a simple round gown and her head was bare, her hair casually arranged in soft waves around her face.

Hardly daring to breathe, Emma turned the page and found another sketch of Lady Glynnis, this time a more formal portrait of the lady seated in a wingback chair, elegantly garbed in a sumptuous silver gown with strands of pearls and flowers woven through her hair.

Then another of her in a riding habit, with a crop in one hand and her other resting on the head of a very large black-and-white dog.

And finally, the last sketch, almost medieval in nature. Lady Glynnis was standing in a doorway looking back at the artist. Her hair hung down her back, her eyes were soft, her lips full and inviting. It was a beautiful portrait. Seductive, without being erotic. But it was the expression on her face that Emma found the most disturbing. Because in every sketch, Lady Glynnis was gazing back at the man who had captured her so deliberately on paper and smiling at him in that special way. The way of a woman in love—

'What the hell do you think you're doing?'

Emma's head shot up. 'Ridley!'

He was standing in the doorway, and he was furious. 'You had no right—!'

'You left the sketchbook open on a bale of hay.' Emma got to her feet. 'Anyone could have found it.'

'But no one would have had the nerve to pick it up and look through it.' Ridley walked in and flipped it closed. 'No one else would have been interested.'

'You don't know that! And if you don't want people looking at your secrets, you shouldn't leave them lying around.'

This time, it was her brother who flushed. 'I have no secrets.'

'Oh, Ridley, do you think I'm blind?' Emma opened the book to the last sketch of Lady Glynnis. 'Do you think I don't recognise that look?'

Her brother's dark brows drew together. 'What look?'

'The look of a woman in love. The same look Linette's worn for the last six months!'

'All right, so it's a picture of Lady Glynnis in love. That's nothing to be remarked upon. She *is* in love—with Lord Stewart.'

'But she's looking at *you*.'

'Of course she is. I'm the artist,' Ridley said. 'But she was thinking of *him*. Now if you don't mind—'

'But Lord Stewart is going to *propose* to Lady Glynnis. But if she's in love with you—'

'She is not in love with me!'

'Look at this drawing, Ridley!' Emma said in exasperation. 'Look at the expression on her face. She isn't looking at Lord Stewart now.'

'Leave it alone, Emma.'

'I can't.' Emma knew she was badgering him, but she had to get at the truth. 'This is too important. Especially if there's a chance she's in love with you!'

'Damn it, Emma, she is *not* in love with me. She made that very clear the day she learned I'd shown the painting to Tom. She said she never wanted to see me again!'

'But *why* do you think she was so upset? Aside from the fact that she wanted Lord Stewart to be the first one to see the portrait.'

'I don't know.'

'You told me she was happy with the portrait?'

'Yes. She asked me to make her look beautiful and I did. But I just painted her as I saw her. I didn't have to *try* to make her look beautiful. She *was* beautiful. And the more I came to care for her, the more of my feelings I poured into the painting. Eventually, it became...a portrait for me.'

'Precisely!' Emma said, quietly triumphant. 'And I think Lady Glynnis was afraid Tom Towbridge saw exactly that. The fact that she was in love...but with you!'

'That's ridiculous!'

'Is it? A guilty conscience is a powerful thing, Ridley,' Emma said softly. 'It makes people go through all kinds of wild imaginings. Make them see shadows where none exist. Lady Glynnis was afraid Tom saw how much she loved you, rather than the man she was having the painting done for!'

Ridley shook his head. 'You're wrong. She was angry because I betrayed her trust. If she loved me, she would have *told* me.'

'Oh, yes, just like you told her!' Emma threw back at him.

'It wasn't my place to tell her! She was promised to another man. It wasn't the honourable thing to do.'

'And letting her marry a man who doesn't love her is?'

'Enough!' he shouted. 'I will not discuss this.

Whatever her reasons for being angry with me don't matter any more. She obviously doesn't have any feelings for me or she would have made some kind of effort to speak to me alone. But she hasn't done that, has she? She's stayed at Ellingsworth even though she knew I was here. If that's how a woman in love behaves, I'm better off without her.'

'Ridley, please think about this—'

'No! I've done all the thinking I'm going to,' Ridley snapped. 'In a few days, I will be returning to London and carrying on with my life. Linette will marry Peter Taylor, Lady Glynnis will marry Lord Stewart and everyone will be happy.'

'Everyone except you,' Emma whispered as her brother marched out of the stall with the sketchbook under his arm.

She didn't have the courage to add, *and everyone except me.*

Chapter Eleven

Alex knew it made no sense to want to see Emma again. He had enjoyed a good deal of time in her company over the last three days, but after spending a few pleasurable hours showing Glynnis and her parents the delights of the countryside, thoughts of another woman should have been the furthest thing from his mind. But they were not. Even as he sat next to Glynnis in the carriage, it was Emma he found himself thinking about, Emma's smiles he pictured and Emma's laughter he heard. And the more he thought about her, the more he realised how desperately he wanted to see her. But what possible excuse did he have for going to Dove's Hollow now?

Unexpectedly, his mother provided him with it. 'Oh, there you are, darling,' she said when he walked into the drawing room. 'I wonder if I could trouble you to pick up a few things from the village. I'd go myself, but I don't want to leave the Leylands alone.'

'I understand,' he said, taking the list she held out to him.

'Oh, and if you wouldn't mind, perhaps you could stop by Dove's Hollow on your way back and give this earring to Miss Darling,' she said, handing him a small package. 'One of the maids found it when they were cleaning.'

'Yes, of course. I'm sure Emma will be pleased to have it returned,' he said without thinking.

'Emma?' His mother glanced at him quizzically. 'I wasn't aware you and Miss Darling had established such a close friendship, Alex. Surely such informality should wait until after the wedding? Besides, the earring belongs to Miss Linette Darling.'

Mentally cursing himself for the slip, Alex inclined his head. 'Of course. I simply had other things on my mind. We are all a little preoccupied these days. Speaking of which, have you decided when you and Father are returning to London?'

'No. I thought it might be a good idea for your father to rest here for a bit. His colour was not good at breakfast and Murdoch said he didn't get much sleep last night.' She sighed. 'I expect I shall have to call for Dr Harrow as soon as we get back.'

'Don't worry. Father's too tough to die.' Alex bent down and kissed his mother on the cheek. 'He'll probably outlast us all!'

* * *

Given that there were a few things his mother needed him to pick up, Alex decided to take the carriage into the village rather than to ride. Upon arriving, he was pleasantly surprised to be greeted by a number of people, some of whom he remembered from the Jacobs's assembly, others who had been at Ellingsworth for the festivities on the Saturday afternoon. But they were all very pleasant and Alex was surprised at how much he enjoyed the feeling of being part of the small community.

He thought back to the assembly and slowly began to smile. Was it only last week he had held Emma in his arms and waltzed her around the room? Only last week that he had felt the softness of her hand in his, and caressed her bare feet in the darkness of a carriage? It seemed like an eternity. He needed to be near her again. To bask in the warmth of her smile and to hear the softness of her voice.

He hurried through his errands in the village and then set out for Dove's Hollow.

She was in the garden when he arrived. Not painting. Just standing still, gazing out over the pond, her arms folded across her chest, her brow furrowed in concentration.

'Emma?'

She turned, and to his surprise he saw not plea-

sure, but pain flash across her face. It was gone in
an instant, but the knowledge that he had put it there
caused him more grief than he cared to acknowledge.
'I've come at a bad time,' he said, ready to leave.

'No, no, you haven't,' she hastened to say. 'I was
just…thinking. Trying to come up with answers.'

'For what?'

She looked up at him and didn't even bother to
hide her unease. 'For a situation over which I have
no control and that is going to cause untold problems
for everyone involved.'

He knew better than to accuse her of exaggerating.
Emma was not given to melodrama. 'Can you tell
me who the people are and what the nature of the
problem is?'

'I wish I could. But it is…a private matter.' She
looked up at him. 'I'm sure you understand.'

He nodded, all too familiar with private matters
of a painful nature. 'Then, perhaps we might take
a stroll together? I often find I do my best thinking
when I am walking. Perhaps the answers will come
to you more readily.'

'Perhaps.' She sighed. 'If nothing else, it will be
good to stretch my legs.' She looked at him with
curiosity. 'Is there a reason you came to see me?'

'Hmm? Oh, yes. Mother asked me to return this,'
Alex said, handing her the package. 'Linette's ear-

ring. One of the servants found it when they were cleaning. Perhaps you could give it to her?'

She stared at the small tissue-wrapped package he held out to her. 'Yes, of course.' When she took it from him, he noticed she was careful not to touch him. 'Linette will be relieved to have it back.'

After slipping the earring into her pocket, they headed out of the garden and along the path towards the gate. Pushing it open, they passed into the next field and started up the hill behind the house. The climb was not steep, but it was steady; at the top, Emma paused to catch her breath. 'Oh, my, I haven't been up here in ages.'

'What a spectacular view,' Alex breathed. 'You can see all the way to Little Moreton.'

'I used to run up here a lot when I was a child,' Emma said. 'I loved watching the clouds flying by overhead. I felt like I was standing on top of the world.'

The image of her as a little girl with her hair streaming out behind her, running up the hill with her arms spread wide, made him chuckle. 'It's hard to picture you as a little girl running up a hill.'

'Papa said I ran everywhere. I've never thought of myself as being impatient, but I must have been when I was younger. Always in a hurry to get wherever I was going,' Emma mused. 'I've slowed down in the intervening years.'

'I'd rather say you've acquired patience,' Alex said. 'I'm sure you still do hurry, if the need is really there.'

She flicked him an amused glance. 'Do you always know exactly the right thing to say, Lord Stewart?'

'Obviously not, because I've become Lord Stewart again.' He had hoped to make her smile. He was dismayed when he saw her frown. 'What's really going on, Emma? What's troubling you?'

'Nothing. And everything,' she whispered. 'After what happened with my aunt—'

'There is no need for us to speak of that again,' Alex began, only to see her shake her head.

'There is every need. I know my father apologised to you and that he spoke to your brother when he came to take Linette driving, but I feel I must also offer my apologies for the way my aunt behaved. It was…unforgivable.'

'It was an error in judgement,' Alex said. 'She didn't do it on purpose.'

'Of course not! But the damage is done and the tragic part is that no one regrets it more than my aunt. She went back to London because she could not bear to stay with us a moment longer. She felt her conduct reflected poorly on the rest of us. Most particularly, on Linette.'

Alex argued with himself as to what he should say, but in the end, he decided on the truth. 'I cannot deny that my mother and father were displeased, Emma, but Peter loves your sister very much and he intends to marry her.' He paused, trying to gauge her mood. 'Is there...anything else that's making you unhappy?'

Her sudden flush gave him his answer, but all she said was, 'No. Why should there be?'

He took a step closer, knowing the moment for honesty was at hand. He couldn't go on pretending that he didn't care. 'Perhaps because you are not the only one forced to keep painful secrets.'

Her eyes widened. 'I don't know what you're talking about.'

'Don't you? You must know I'm drawn to you, Emma. That I think about you...far too much.'

He watched her eyes darken in pain. 'Lord Stewart, this is not a good idea.'

'Perhaps not,' he said quietly. 'My father asked me to counsel my brother as to the unsuitability of his relationship with your sister. I shudder to think what he would say if he knew I was also having to counsel myself against my feelings...for you.'

It had to happen. Perhaps it had been building to this right from the start, but the inevitability of the kiss still left Emma breathless. She watched Alex slowly take a step towards her, felt the warmth of his hands as they closed around her upper arms and watched his head bend towards her with unmistakable intent. But when his mouth finally came down on hers, it was not with trepidation that Emma returned his kiss, but with desire, her heart pounding wildly against his chest, her entire body trembling with need.

He kissed her slowly, languidly, his lips moving over hers without urgency or haste. There was only need and longing. And when at length they drew apart, Emma slowly opened her eyes to find him gazing down at her without regret or recrimination. His hands still held her close, the heat of his body still warming her through the thin fabric of her gown. 'Forgive me,' he whispered.

She shook her head, wishing he had said anything but that. 'I can't. Any more than I can forgive myself for wanting it.'

He gazed down at her, his expression so gentle that Emma feared she would cry. They could not undo what they had done or pretend it hadn't happened, but even before he said the words, Emma knew what they would be. 'I'm sorry, Emma. The expectations of me are such that…I cannot go any further with this.'

'I know. But that doesn't mean the feelings don't exist,' she said. 'Or that the longings are any the less painful to bear.'

He raised his hand, trailed his fingers over her temple and cheek to curl around the point of her chin. 'There are so many things I would say to you,' he said. 'So many things I would have you know. But I can say none of them. It would be unfair to everyone involved, but, most particularly, to you.'

Emma nodded. He was speaking to her, but he was referring to Lady Glynnis. 'I know. This was never meant to happen, but it did. And believe me when I say that *no one* is more surprised than I am.'

'I have been fighting it,' Alex admitted. 'Because I didn't want to hurt you. But the strength of my feelings for you is such that…I had to say something. I wanted you to know how I felt. And I needed to know if you felt the same way about me. Perhaps that was wrong—'

'It was,' Emma said, her voice unexpectedly husky. 'It would have been easier not knowing that you cared for me. Because then I could have pretended it was just me being foolish. That no matter what my feelings for you, you could never have felt the same way. But now I can't hide behind that any more because I know you do care for me. And that just makes it that much harder to bear.'

Alex's hand fell away. He took a reluctant step backwards and glanced at the clouds overhead. 'I've never felt this way about anyone before. You know what my feelings about marriage were. How I thought it should be approached. But with you, everything is so…different.' He finally looked back at her. 'Now I *know* how it is supposed to be between two people.

And how cruel being forced to settle for anything less is going to be.'

Emma squeezed her eyes shut, hardly daring to breathe. How was it possible that the words that should have made her so happy were making her anything but? 'I think it would be best if we did not see each other alone again, Alex. It will be hard enough at the wedding, but other than that...'

He nodded. 'I understand. I have no desire to make this any more difficult for you than it is for me.'

He left her then, and Emma felt a pain so intense it stole the breath from her lungs. It was as though a hand was closing around her heart, tearing it out of her chest. She wanted to cry, but the tears wouldn't come, only this horrible, unending pain. This hollowness, as though someone had cut a hole in her soul.

She was in love with Alexander Taylor. And he was going to marry a woman who didn't love him while she was forced to sit by and watch. It was more than she could bear.

It was more than anyone should have to bear.

The pressure on Alex started early the next morning, over breakfast, when his father informed him that the Leylands would be leaving the following day.

'So if there's anything you want to say to Lady Glynnis, now would be the time,' Lord Widdicombe advised. 'They're all expecting it. And it would be a shining way to end an otherwise dismal affair.'

Alex said nothing. He was well aware that Lord and Lady Leyland were expecting him to propose to Glynnis, but it hadn't occurred to him that it had to be done here before they left. After all, the arrangements over settlements had been made, and he had already talked to Glynnis about where they would live. He owned a town house in London and a hunting box near Melton Mowbray, but until now the latter had been a bachelor's home that was sorely in need of renovation. Alex had shown Glynnis through the house months ago and told her she could do whatever was needed to turn it into a welcoming home. They had even talked about curtains, for heaven's sake. Why wouldn't they be expecting him to propose?

Glynnis must surely have been expecting it. As the days went by, Alex noticed her growing noticeably more quiet and withdrawn. She seemed to laugh less when she was around him and the sparkle he had always associated with her was gone. Was her disappointment in him so great that it was affecting her to this degree?

The question pained him deeply. Glynnis didn't deserve this kind of treatment from him. They had always been good friends and, until now, they had been able to talk about almost anything. But now their association seemed strained, the easy laughter and gentle banter gone. Everything was different... because he knew it was Emma he wished to marry, but that it was Glynnis he *must*.

He brought the subject up when they were out riding together after lunch. 'Glyn, is everything all right?'

They were walking their horses through a shady glen. Glynnis looked at him, and roused herself to smile. 'Yes, of course. Why do you ask?'

'Because you don't seem as happy as you did when you first arrived.'

'It has been...an interesting few days.' She turned her attention to the path ahead. 'A great deal has happened that I did not expect.'

'And perhaps something has *not* happened that you did expect?'

He saw the blush race across her cheeks. 'I'm not sure I know what you mean.'

'Don't you?' Alex reached for her mare's reins and drew both animals to a halt. 'You've never been shy when it came to talking about our marriage before, Glyn.'

Her head slowly came round, but she did not smile. 'To be honest, I wasn't sure if you still wished to marry me.'

The note of anxiety in her voice pierced his heart. 'Why would I not? We have been promised to one another these last two years, and we have been friends a good deal longer. It is what everyone expects.'

'Yes, I know. But things have…happened that I thought might have changed your mind.'

Her face gave nothing away, but her words were a clear indication that something was amiss. Was she talking about his feelings for Emma? Had he somehow given himself away? Alex thought hard about everything that had happened over the last few days, but he couldn't isolate one single incident or conversation that might have exposed him.

'Is there something I should know, Glyn? Something I haven't been told?' When she didn't answer, Alex put his hand on her arm. 'Glyn, please. What's this really all about? I have the feeling there's something you want to tell me.'

He waited, aware that even as she kept silent, hope flared within his heart. Had she met someone else? Was she trying to find a gentle way of breaking it off? At one time such a revelation would have caused him considerable concern, but now he found himself welcoming it.

Still, what good would it do him if she *did* wish to end it? He couldn't go running to Emma. His father would *never* approve of him having a relationship with her and would never forgive Alex for disappointing him. He would be furious at his heir's blatant disregard for everything that mattered.

'No, there's nothing I want to tell you,' Glynnis said finally. 'Forgive me, it must be everything's that happened this weekend. There has been so much conflict and unhappiness over your brother's engagement. Your father is clearly displeased by it, yet for the life of me I can't imagine why.'

Alex glanced at her in surprise. 'He doesn't feel that Linette Darling is well born enough to be Peter's bride. She doesn't have the kind of background he was looking for.'

'But she is a beautiful, genteel girl,' Glynnis said. 'More importantly, she loves him and he loves her. Desperately. You have only to see them together to know that.' She turned away, biting her lip. 'Surely that has to count for something.'

Alex stared at her in amazement. He had never heard her talk this way before. Like him, she had always adopted a practical approach to marriage, espousing the benefits of a well-thought-out liaison over sentimentality. He had never heard her speak about love or desire and, like him, had assumed she didn't care about such things, that they weren't part of what she was looking for in a marriage. Could it be he had completely misread her?

'So if my father were to ask you your opinion of Peter and Linette's betrothal,' Alex said slowly, 'you would tell him he should give his approval to the marriage?'

'Of course. Oh, I know it isn't what the earl wishes to hear, but surely when two people are so obviously in love, it would be wrong to stop them from being together. What kind of life would that be condemning them to? I know your father only wants the best for his sons and he is afraid that Peter is making a terrible mistake. But your brother is very much in love with Linette Darling. Everything he's done is proof of that. He's stood by her through every uncomfortable moment. He's faced up to your father and to anyone else who said she wasn't good enough. And even after what happened with Mrs Grand, he refused to abandon her.' Glynnis turned to look at him and he saw an unexpected shimmer of tears in her eyes. 'You see the way they look at each other, Alex,' she said huskily. 'How could I advise your father not to allow them to marry when it is clear they would only spend the rest of their lives pining for each other if they did not? What kind of life would that be?'

'I never knew you felt this way,' he said quietly. 'You've never spoken to me like this before.'

'I know. And I know it isn't the same for you,' Glynnis said. 'You are the heir. You don't have the freedom of choice your brother has. You have always been forced to weigh duty and obligation, as I have. That's why a marriage between the two of us seemed the ideal solution to our parents. I am the type of woman your father expects you to marry and you are the type of man my father wishes me to.'

Alex didn't know what to say. This was a side of Glynnis he'd never seen before. He had never heard her speak so passionately about something she obviously felt so strongly about. And clearly his failure to ask her to marry him was the cause of the sadness he saw in her now.

He suddenly remembered what Towbridge had let slip at dinner—the fact that Glynnis had hired an artist to paint a portrait of her as a gift for him. A portrait that had revealed the depth of her love so clearly that even another man had been able to see it.

And that must be the problem. Glynnis *was* in love with him. She was waiting for him to ask her to marry him, to do what they both knew he should. What everyone expected. And in that moment, Alex knew there was only one thing he could do. 'Lady Glynnis Pettle,' he said softly. 'Glyn. Will you do me the honour of becoming my wife?'

She didn't look at him, but he saw the tears that formed in her eyes and ran silently down her cheek. 'Yes.' Her mouth trembled, but she managed a smile. 'I will marry you.'

He leaned over and kissed her, tasting the saltiness of tears on her lips. But on an emotional level, he felt nothing. The kiss didn't inspire him the way Emma's had. It didn't leave him longing to make love to her, or to hold her as she cried out his name in that moment of passionate awakening. Beyond the fondness he felt for her as a friend, there was nothing.

Drawing back, he raised his hand to gently wipe away her tears. 'Don't cry, Glyn. This is supposed to be a happy moment.'

She laughed, more a gulping sound than anything else. 'Yes, of course. It's just that I'm more…emotional than I expected to be. It isn't every day a lady receives a proposal of marriage.'

He nodded, waiting for her to compose herself. And while he did, he waited for it to come: the feeling of relief that he had done the right thing. The certainty that she was the only woman he was destined to be with. But it did not. The knowledge that she would soon be his wife brought with it no sense of deep and abiding satisfaction. He wasn't looking forward to a future filled with the kind of love he had discovered with Emma because Glynnis *wasn't* Emma. And it was the most tragic thought imaginable that no matter how long he and Glynnis were together, no matter how many children they brought into the world, he would never feel for her after a lifetime of marriage what he did for Emma Darling right now.

The reaction to his announcement that Glynnis had agreed to be his wife was everything Alex expected. Lord and Lady Leyland expressed their heartfelt delight and his own parents left him in no doubt as to their pleasure at hearing that he had finally made up his mind.

'Oh Alex, my dear, I'm so happy for you!' his mother said, crushing him in an unusually affectionate embrace.

'Well done, my boy, well done!' his father said, pumping his hand. 'Damned if I don't feel better already.'

'I'm glad to hear it, Father,' Alex said, relieved that no one seemed to notice his own lack of enthusiasm.

'This calls for a celebration,' the earl said. 'Sarah, you'll start planning something as soon as we get home. An engagement party, followed by a grand ball, and then the wedding itself.'

'I suspect the Leylands will want to take care of that, my dear.'

'Ah, well, you know what's best. But it will be the social event of the Season,' his father went on proudly. 'Only the finest families in attendance. The *crème de la crème* of society.'

'I must go and speak to Glynnis's mother,' Lady Widdicombe said. 'We have so much to talk about and to arrange.'

After she left, Lord Widdicombe walked up to his son and, in an unexpected display of affection, hugged him close. 'Thank you, Alex. You've made me very proud. Lady Glynnis will make you an excellent wife. If you're as happy with her as I've been with your mother, you'll be a lucky man.'

'Thank you, Father, I'm sure I will be.'

'And don't wait too long before starting a family, eh? I'm longing to see grandsons.'

Alex smiled, thinking it typical of his father that he would only consider boys. 'There may be girls.'

'A token one or two,' the earl said with a laugh. 'But only after the boys. Because we all know it's boys that really matter. Especially the first one. The heir!' The earl choked up. 'Like you.'

Uncomfortable with emotion, he turned and left the room.

Alex stood where he was, listening to the ticking of the clock. He had done the right thing. The pride and satisfaction on his father's face was proof of that. He'd never seen him so jubilant. And his mother was delighted. Glyn's parents too. He had made everyone happy by doing what he was supposed to. Everyone but the two people who would suffer for it the most.

'So, you finally did it. Congratulations, brother.'

Alex turned as Peter walked in. 'You heard.'

'I just passed Father on the way out. I don't remember the last time I saw him so elated. Well done.' Peter put out his hand and grasped his brother's. 'At least he's pleased with one of us.'

Alex sighed. 'Give him time, Peter. The more

he comes to know Linette, the more he'll grow to love her.'

'I'd like to think that,' Peter said. 'But who knows? Maybe now that you've finally done the right thing by Lady Glyn, he'll find it in his heart to look more kindly on *my* marriage.'

The pain came out of nowhere, a swift, sharp jab that tore at Alex's insides. Because his brother was marrying the woman he loved—and he was marrying the one he had to. 'Only time will tell,' Alex said, releasing Peter's hand. 'Care to join me for a drink?'

'Why not? It is an auspicious occasion.'

Alex shot him a keen glance as he walked to the credenza. 'So why the note of reserve?'

Peter sighed. 'Perhaps not so much reserve as regret.'

'Regret? What for? Everyone else is ecstatic.'

'Of course, because you are doing what's expected of you. What everyone else considers to be the right thing. I just hope it's the right thing…for you.'

Alex frowned as he poured brandy into two glasses. 'What's that supposed to mean?'

'Oh, come on, Alex. We both know you're not marrying Glynnis for love. Oh, I'm sure you like her well enough, but it's not the same as loving someone, is it? It's not like wanting to be with that woman because you can't imagine being with anyone else.'

Alex replaced the crystal stopper. 'It's all very well

for you, Peter. You have the luxury of being able to follow your heart. I don't. You said it yourself. I have my duty to consider. My obligation to the family name.' He handed his brother a glass, his smile tight. 'You didn't have to take that into account when you asked Linette to marry you.'

The words were harsher than he'd intended, the tone considerably more bitter. But even when he saw the look of hurt surprise on his brother's face, he couldn't bring himself to apologise.

'I meant no offence, Alex. I'm just saying—'

'I know what you're saying, but that's the difference between you and me. Being the first-born means you have responsibilities. I live with them every day of my life. And whether I like it or not, they *do* rule my life.'

'I'm sorry.' Peter's expression grew troubled. 'It was never my intention—'

'I know. It's simply the way it is.'

And just like that, Alex's anger evaporated, leaving him feeling drained and not particularly pleased with himself. His brother hadn't been deserving of the set-down he'd just received, but Alex hadn't been able to stop once he'd started. He finished his drink and set his glass on the desk. 'You should be glad you're not next in line to the title, Peter. There are definitely times when being the heir isn't all it's cracked up to be.'

* * *

Alex waited until both the Leylands and his parents had gone out for a stroll before calling for his horse and heading in the direction of Dove's Hollow. He had to tell Emma straight away. He didn't want her learning of his engagement to Glynnis through the village grapevine. She had to hear it from him. He owed her that much at least.

His thoughts were scattered as he cantered along the road. How would he break the news? Should he do it quickly, hoping it would be less painful, or should he tell her slowly, setting out all his reasons for why he had done what he'd done? Or should he just tell her he was getting married and leave her to work out the rest on her own?

No, that would surely be the most hurtful. God knew it was going to be agony seeing the look on her face when he told her. To live with the knowledge that they would never be together and that their encounters from here on would have to be of the most polite and innocuous kind.

All he wanted to do was hold her in his arms and make love to her.

He closed his eyes, shutting out the images. It was too much to bear. As long as he lived, he would never forget the sweetness of holding Emma in his arms, the incredible softness of her skin beneath his fingers, the blatant sensuality of her body pressed against his.

She was everything he had ever wanted: the woman he hadn't known he was looking for. And now she was lost to him.

Damn.

At Dove's Hollow, he was shown into the parlour where Ridley and Linette were enjoying a quiet game of cards. They looked up in surprise at his entrance. 'Lord Stewart!' Linette said, her eyes darting past him in hopes of seeing his brother.

'Sorry, Linette, Peter's not with me,' he said gently. 'I've come on my own. I need...that is, I'd like to speak to your sister.'

'She's in the garden,' Ridley said. 'Doing battle with the angel.'

Alex smiled, even as Linette frowned, and said, 'What are you talking about, Ridley? How can anyone do battle with an angel?'

Alex shared a knowing glance with Ridley. 'I doubt anyone but your sister could.'

He found her in the garden, her easel positioned about three feet away from the statue. It looked as though she had started a new sketch and that she was drawing the troublesome angel with charcoal first.

He stood for a moment, just allowing himself the pleasure of watching her. How had he ever thought her anything less than magnificent? The roundness of her cheek, the delicate curve of her neck and throat, the smoothness of her complexion. She wasn't wearing her painter's smock today, protecting her dress with a cloth, and had cast aside her shawl. It was a warm afternoon and she was sitting in the shade of a tree so as not to be browned by the sun. He saw the tempting swell of her breasts rising above the lace edging on her gown and the slender whiteness of an ankle where her gown had pulled up.

She was glorious. And she would never be his.

'Emma.'

She turned, her hand poised above the sketch pad. 'Alex!' He saw the pleasure in her eyes, the fleeting moment of joy at seeing him, then watched her smile fade as awareness of their situation came to the fore. 'Lord Stewart.' She put down the piece of charcoal, slowly, as though to give herself time to pull a protective cocoon around her. 'The festivities are over and you've come to say goodbye. When do you leave?'

'I'm not sure. Later this week, I suppose.'

'And Lady Glynnis?'

'Tomorrow, with her parents.'

'I see.' Emma nodded and looked as though she wanted to say more, but in the end she glanced back at the stone angel and said, 'I've started a new sketch. And I'm having more luck with her wing this afternoon.'

'Yes, I see.' Alex cleared his throat, feeling a lump

the size of Gibraltar stuck there. 'Emma, I have to tell you—'

'No, you don't,' she said quietly. 'I already know.' She turned to look at him and her face was as white as the statue's. 'You and Lady Glynnis are engaged.'

Alex wished he knew what to say. When had she found out? The servants couldn't have spread the news that quickly. 'How did you know?'

She tried for a smile, but failed. 'It was a foregone conclusion. When you said she was leaving with her parents in the morning, I knew. It only made sense that you proposed to her before she left.' Slowly, she stood up, her hands pressed against her sides. 'Your father must be very pleased.'

'He is.' The words burned like hot coals against his throat. 'They all are.'

'Of course. Because it is...as it should be. You did what was expected.'

'Emma—'

'No, please, I beg you!' She closed her eyes, her voice thick with emotion. 'It will only make this harder. I wish you...much happiness, Lord Stewart. And Lady Glynnis too.' She slowly opened her eyes. 'I wish I could say I don't like her, but I do. She stood up for Linette at a time when my sister needed it most and I will always think kindly of her for that.' She paused, as if to draw more air into her lungs. 'She is a lady in every sense of the word.'

'Yes, she is.' His own voice was husky, his heart pounding fit to burst. 'But she is not you.'

With that, he turned and walked away. He couldn't bear to spend another moment in her company. If he had, he would have taken her in his arms and made love to her right there, with the damn stone angel looking on. Instead, he clenched his fists at his sides and walked back to where he had left his horse, willing himself to put one foot in front of the other. He knew Emma wouldn't call him back. That wasn't her way. Even if she was hurting as badly as he was, she knew what the realities of their lives were and she would abide by them.

Their worlds were too far apart. And at this moment, they had never been more so.

Chapter Twelve

Because she had no choice, Emma went back to the house and, taking Ridley aside, told him about Lady Glynnis and Lord Stewart. She planned on telling the rest of the family over dinner that evening, but she knew it would be kinder to Ridley if she gave him the information in private. He would need time to come to grips with the information and to compose himself, as she had.

She was not mistaken. He turned pale upon learning of the engagement; Emma saw on his face a reflection of the bleakness she felt within her own heart. 'So, that's it then,' he said in a flat, emotionless voice. 'They are to be married.'

'I'm afraid so.'

'When?'

'He didn't say. I expect they will discuss a date once they are all back in London.'

Ridley nodded woodenly. 'And Glynnis is leaving with her parents tomorrow?'

'That's what Lord Stewart told me.'

'And then life will revert to normal,' Ridley said, his expression bleak. 'All the pieces having fallen into place. All very neat and tidy.'

'Are you going to see her when you return to London?'

'What's the point?' Ridley got up and began to walk around. 'She is now an officially engaged lady. There is no reason for me to call.'

'I'm truly sorry, Ridley,' Emma said softly. 'I know this isn't easy.'

He stopped in front of the window and gazed out. 'No, it isn't. But no one said life was going to be easy. Thank you, Emma. I'd rather have found out like this than at the dinner table, when no doubt everyone will be deliriously happy. You are the only one who understands.'

Yes, she was. But not for the reasons he thought, and it wasn't until her brother left the room that Emma finally allowed herself to cry, sobbing as though her heart would break, aware that nothing anyone could have said would have made the news any the less devastating to hear.

Emma told Linette and her father the news at dinner that evening, and, as expected, they were delighted. Ridley paid diligent attention to his soup and Emma was content to let Linette carry the bulk of the conversation after that. Having discovered a new friend in Alex and a new ally in Lady Glynnis, she was thrilled that the lady was soon to become her sister-in-law.

On a positive note, it did have the effect of easing Linette's despair over Lord Widdicombe's reaction towards her. She had already met with Peter, who had taken pains to assure her their marriage would take place at St David's as planned, and perhaps seeing in Alex's engagement the possibility of the earl's mellowing towards his other son, she was optimistic that everything was going to turn out well.

Having more of an insight into the situation, Emma did not venture an opinion. How it would play out now was completely out of her hands. She was a pawn in Fate's game—and she soon found out that the game could change in an instant, and not for the better.

It was a little after ten o'clock the next morning when she made the unwelcome discovery. She set out on a ride, desperate to get out of the house and be alone with her thoughts. She hadn't wanted to paint or to talk to Linette about the wedding. In fact, if she never heard the word wedding again, she would be just as happy!

Emma wasn't surprised to see that Ridley's chestnut was also gone from the stable. He, too, must have felt a need to get away and be alone with his thoughts. Thank God he didn't know what was going on between her and Alex. There would have been a small degree of comfort in being able to commiserate with one another over the similarity of their situations, but it would have served little purpose beyond that. They had each lost the person they loved to the person the *other* one loved.

Deciding not to follow her usual path up the hill, Emma turned the mare left and headed south. This route was more heavily forested than the one she usually took and unless she wished to incur a lengthy detour by going around the woods, she had no choice but to ride through them. At the best of times, they tended to be dark and gloomy, but this morning they were an exact match for Emma's feelings.

She had ridden in about a mile when she saw Ridley's horse standing in a small copse of trees. The chestnut's reins were tethered to the lowest branch of a tree, but Ridley was nowhere to be seen.

Concerned, Emma drew Bess to a halt and slipped out of the saddle. After securing the mare's reins to the same tree as Chesapeake's, Emma went in search of her brother. Given the state of mind he was in, she worried about him being alone in the woods. She doubted he would intentionally injure himself. Ridley loved life too much for that. But there were definitely times when one's thoughts could turn dark and Ridley was enough of a romantic to fall into an emotional depression.

She moved quietly through the trees, about to call his name, when she came upon the second horse. A very nice-looking mare Emma hadn't seen before. And there, just beyond the mare, in a forest clearing, she saw them.

A man and a woman, locked in each other's arms. The man's jacket and cravat were on the ground, his shirt open at the neck. The lady's bonnet had fallen to the forest floor, as had her shawl.

Suddenly, the lady broke free. The man reached for her, but she pushed him away. She stood with her arms wrapped tightly around her chest as though to hold herself together. She was pleading with him, her voice low and intent, her beautiful face a study in anguish.

And then he spoke. Three words, followed by her name. Then the same three words again.

A shudder rippled through the woman's slender frame. Her eyes closed and a tortured sound slipped past her lips. A battle was raging: the urge to run against the desire to stay.

Emma knew it well. The wisdom of resisting against the pleasures of giving in.

Longing versus duty. Obligation versus love.

Suddenly, the woman reached out her hand, tears streaming down her face, and the next moment they were in each other's arms. Emma watched as the man lowered his mouth to her neck, trailing kisses along the smooth white skin of her throat. He ventured even lower, finally pressing his mouth to the soft swell of her breasts. Wantonly, the lady tipped back her head, a low moan escaping her throat as she drew his head closer, their bodies pressed intimately together in a way that left Emma in no doubt as to their intent.

If nothing happened to prevent it, her brother and Lady Glynnis were about to become lovers.

The decision was agonising, the seconds flying by as she watched the pair sink to the ground. Lady Glynnis's arms were still wrapped around Ridley. He broke away only long enough to spread his jacket over the grass before going back to kissing her, his hand replacing his mouth at her breast.

Emma felt her cheeks flame. She had never seen anything so blatantly erotic in her life. That they were deeply in love she had no doubt, but that they were about to make the biggest mistake of their lives was undeniable.

And yet, what right had she to interfere? It was clearly a consensual arrangement. Neither of them was trying to escape. But if they went ahead and did this, they risked destroying themselves and everything they held dear.

Still, it wasn't her decision to make. Ridley and Lady Glynnis were adults. They knew what they were doing. And if they didn't, God help them when they came to their senses and found out.

Emma stepped back, intending to leave quietly, when her foot landed on a small twig and snapped it in half, the sound echoing through the silence like a gunshot.

In an instant, Ridley was on his feet. He glanced with unerring accuracy in Emma's direction, and as their eyes met she saw his face burn with shame, even as his eyes pleaded with her to understand.

Emma swallowed and backed away. She felt like an intruder, a voyeur into something she had no business witnessing. But they were the ones in the wrong. How could they have been so foolish? So unbelievably careless? What if Alex had been the one to come along and find them rather than she?

Without a word, Emma turned and ran back to her mare. Ridley did not follow. She knew he wouldn't leave Lady Glynnis alone now, but the damage was done, their secret well and truly revealed. Ridley and Lady Glynnis were in love—and Glynnis was engaged to marry Alex.

How on earth could matters ever have gone so completely and so utterly wrong?

Ridley came to her room later that evening. Immediately after dinner, Emma pleaded a headache and went upstairs. Her brother had appeared in the doorway a short time later, begging to speak with her.

Reluctantly, Emma let him in, but she had been harsh in her condemnation of his actions.

'Have you lost your mind, Ridley?' she snapped the moment the door closed behind him. 'Have you any idea of the trouble you're in? She is engaged to marry Lord Stewart!'

'You think I don't know that?' Ridley dragged his hand through his hair. 'Do you think I'm happy about what almost happened this morning?'

'Never mind what *almost* happened,' Emma murmured, her face burning. 'What *did* happen was bad enough!' She looked at her brother and sighed. 'Whatever possessed you to do something so reckless? Asking her to meet you like that?'

'I had no choice. I had to know, Emma, once and for all how she felt about me.'

'But why would she agree to such a meeting? Only yesterday she accepted Lord Stewart's proposal.'

'I know.'

'Then why—?'

'Because she wanted to tell me the truth, too. Before it was too late. The truth that…she loves me,' Ridley whispered happily. 'And that she has ever since the early days of sitting for me.'

Feeling her legs give way, Emma sank down on to the edge of the bed. 'But I thought she was angry

with you for having shown the painting to Mr Towbridge.'

'She was, but you were right, Emma. I painted a
portrait of a woman in *love*,' Ridley said quietly. 'A
woman who'd never felt or looked that way before,
even when she was with Lord Stewart. And Glynnis was afraid Tom would see that when he looked
at it. She was afraid her expression revealed the true
extent of her feelings for *me*.'

'So she *knew* the look of love on her face was
there…because of you.'

Ridley nodded. 'Had it all been on one side or the
other, it might have been all right. But because *she*
was looking at me with love, and I was *seeing* her
that way, there wasn't a hope that our feelings for one
another wouldn't be reflected on the canvas. Glynnis knew that the moment she saw the completed
painting. And when she realised how she really felt
about me and how much she had inadvertently given
away…she panicked. She used my showing the painting to Towbridge as an excuse for being angry with
me. She accused me of betraying her trust, but it was
actually her own feelings she was finding impossible
to deal with.'

'Oh, Ridley,' Emma said with a groan. 'This is
insane! She's in love with you—but she's going to
marry Lord Stewart.'

'She has no choice. Even if she wasn't engaged

to him, she would never be allowed to marry me. Her father cares even more about class distinction than old Widdicombe does. Nothing less than an earl would do for his Glynnis. In fact, he suggested a match with the Marquess of Stahley's son if Stewart didn't make good on his promise.'

'Oh, that's just wonderful,' Emma said. 'But what kind of life do you think she's going to have with Alex now?'

'I don't—Alex?' Ridley frowned. 'When did you start calling him that?'

'Shortly after Linette and Peter became engaged,' Emma said, too distraught to bother making excuses. 'He said that since we were going to be brother and sister-in-law, it made more sense.'

'Well, yes, I suppose it does. Oh, God, and now Glynnis is going to be *my sister-in-law*,' Ridley said. 'I don't think I can bear it. I'm going to *have* to say something to him.'

'Him?'

'Lord Stewart. You're right, Emma,' Ridley said. 'It's madness for Glynnis to marry him when she loves me. She didn't plan on falling in love with me any more than I planned on falling in love with her, but we did and now we *have* to do something about it.' He took a deep breath and said, 'I'm going to ask Lord Stewart to release Glynnis from her promise.'

'Are you mad?' Emma said in horror. 'You'd be

the laughing stock of London. A titled lady can play games if she wishes, but she does *not* back out of a marriage to an earl's son in order to marry an artist. I'm sorry, Ridley, but those are the facts of life!'

'But you just said it's insane that she marry someone else.'

'Of course it is! But going to Alex and expecting him to release her so that she can marry you is equally ludicrous. You just said Lord Leyland is more of a stickler than Alex's father. I guarantee if you go through with this, you *will* find every door in London slammed in your face.'

'Then what would you have me do? Let her go?'

Emma closed her eyes. 'Yes, because you have no other choice. Daughters of earls do *not* marry artists.' *And heirs to earldoms do not marry penniless nonentities.* 'Papa's right. You would have stood a better chance had you stuck it out and become a barrister. At least then you would have been received at Court. You would have had a profession with some degree of respectability.'

'Then I am lost.' Ridley sank down beside Emma on the bed, his expression bleak. 'She will marry Lord Stewart and give him the portrait I painted of her, and I shall never see her again.'

'Unfortunately, you *will* see her.' Emma put her arm around his shoulders. 'At Linette's wedding. At the birth of their first child. And at every family gathering and event that follows. But you will not let on to anyone how devastated you really are because it will gain you nothing. When you go to Linette's wedding—'

'I can't go!'

'When you go to Linette's wedding,' Emma repeated firmly, 'you will greet Lady Glynnis as a friend. Then you will kiss your sister and wish her happy in her new life and only then may you leave. But do not do this other thing, Ridley. You must *not* give Lord Widdicombe any reason to hate you. Because if he finds out about this, he will—and then I doubt very much there will *ever* be a wedding between Linette and Peter.'

The words seemed to shock Ridley awake. 'You think the earl would forbid them from marrying?'

'I'm surprised he didn't do it after the débâcle with Aunt Dorothy. He certainly wouldn't permit it if you were the cause of the break up between his heir and the lady he believes to be perfection in every way.'

The words were as difficult for Emma to say as they were for Ridley to hear, but they were the truth and they both knew it. If Ridley persisted in bringing his relationship with Lady Glynnis out into the open, they would all be ruined.

'Linette would hate me,' Ridley said quietly.

'I don't think Linette is capable of hate, but I know it would break her heart,' Emma said. 'And I think that would bother you far more than if she said she hated you.'

'It would. I can live with my own unhappiness. I couldn't bear knowing I had been the cause of hers.'

'Then it's settled,' Emma said. 'Lady Glynnis will leave with her parents later today and that will be an end of it. She and Al—Lord Stewart will marry. Linette and Mr Taylor will marry. And you and I will make the best of it.'

He glanced at her quizzically. 'You *and* I?'

Emma closed her eyes. 'Yes, Ridley. You *and* I. And if you wish to leave this room with your fingers still capable of holding a paintbrush, I suggest you not ask any more questions.' She sighed. 'There have been more than enough shocking revelations for one day.'

As it turned out, there was still one more shocking revelation in store for Emma. It was just after lunch that the letter was delivered. It was addressed to Emma and the young lad who brought it was told to make sure it was put directly into her hands. Upon breaking the seal, she discovered it was from Lady Glynnis.

Dear Miss Darling,
You will no doubt find the occasion of my writing to you unusual, but given what you witnessed

yesterday morning, I wanted to set matters right between us. I would also beg you to burn this after reading, as what I am about to say could have disastrous consequences if it were to fall into the wrong hands. As it is, I hope you can appreciate the level of trust I place in you by being willing to send such a letter.

It will likely be clear to you now, that your brother and I are in love. I tell you this, because I would hate you to misinterpret what you saw in the forest. You are no doubt aware that I have accepted Lord Stewart's proposal and that we are to be married. I hope you will wish me well, for it was always my intention to marry Alexander. As I told you that day, our friendship goes back a long way and I cannot think of a better or kinder man in all of my acquaintance. But once I met your brother, I realised how shallow my feelings for Alexander were, and how much more there could be between a man and a woman.

My relationship with your brother began soon after I began sitting for him. I found him to be charming, of course, as any woman would, and handsome because it would be silly to call him otherwise. But during our time together I discovered something else about Ridley: a tender and caring side, as well as a compassionate nature that appealed to me very much. And I discovered, for the first time in my life, a side to my own nature that took me completely unawares.

I don't know if you have ever been in love, Miss Darling. Until I met your brother, I had not. I knew attraction and I knew friendship. But I never knew what it was to ache for someone so intensely that to be without them was akin to a physical pain. That came to me over the days and weeks I sat for your brother; perhaps now, looking back, I can safely say that the reason his portrait captured what it did is because I was willing to show that side of myself to him. I doubt the same results would have been achieved had I hired someone else to do the portrait. However, since it was your brother who drew out that side of me, it should have come as no shock to me that the finished painting would reflect what I felt when I was with him. Regrettably it did and I reacted accordingly.

Having said all that, we must also face the reality of our lives. I have accepted Lord Stewart's proposal because it is the right thing to do. My parents expect it. His parents expect it. And Alexander expects it. And knowing how deeply it would hurt him if were I to break it off now, I have no choice but to go through with it. Also, as my father would never permit me to marry a man like Ridley, there would be nothing to be gained by calling it off.

I hope you can understand this, Miss Darling. If wishes were horses, beggars would ride. An old proverb, perhaps, but significant in its message here. I will never forget Ridley, but I also know that there can never be anything between us. The rules that govern our lives are strict, the punishments for flouting them harsh. Please don't misunderstand me when I say that enough heartache has been caused by Mr Taylor's engagement to your sister. I cannot be the cause of further disruption to everyone's lives.

I hope that you and I can remain friends, and that you will keep secret the contents of this letter. There will be occasions when we are required to see one another and, for everyone's sake, I wish it to be civil. But in case you have any doubts, I do like you and your sister very much.

Yours, in friendship,
Glynnis

Emma slowly refolded the letter. It had taken a great deal of courage for Lady Glynnis to write what she had. It was an emotional confession, an outpouring of her soul. And knowing what she risked in sending it, Emma felt a warm glow of affection for the writer because, like she and Ridley, Lady Glynnis had also found love with the wrong person. And because of her awareness of her duties and obligations, she had cast it aside to do what was right.

If wishes were horses, beggars would ride.

Emma tipped back her head and stared at the ceiling. How appropriate the lady's choice of proverb. One needn't be rich to have wishes. Even the most simple of men and women had dreams. Unattainable, perhaps, but dreams none the less. It was what kept people going and gave hope to their lives. It offered something to aspire to. Except in her case, it was a dream that could never be realised.

There wasn't a horse in the world that could carry Emma to the place she so desperately wanted to go.

The day hadn't been much better for Alex. He had hoped, after having offered his proposal to Glynnis, that his life would magically fall into place. That with luck, the confusion he'd felt until this moment would vanish and leave everything remarkably clear. If anything, matters only became darker and more murky. While his head knew he was doing the right thing, his heart screamed that he was not. And as a man who had spent his entire life listening to his head, this sudden, unexpected voice was decidedly unwelcome.

He had gone for a long ride in the afternoon, refusing Peter's offer of companionship as gently as he could. There was no easy way of telling his brother how hard it was to spend time in his company now. Childish as it was, Alex knew himself well enough to know that every time he saw his sibling, he would be faced with the knowledge that while he would get the title and the estate, Peter would live happily with the woman he loved. And the woman Alex loved would likely end up becoming the vicar's wife.

He couldn't bear thinking about that either. Emma deserved so much more than John Tufton. A clergyman needed a woman without goals or opinions of her own. One who was content to live in his shadow and who would mould her life around his. That was what Emma's life would be like married to the clergyman and Alex couldn't think of a worse fate for a woman of her vivacious and creative nature.

Consequently, by the time he got back from his ride, his mood was even blacker than when he'd set out. He walked into the house and stood for a moment in the hall, trying to think what he might do for the rest of the day. Then, deciding a few hours with a book was as good a way as any to pass the time, he turned and headed in the direction of the library.

It was as he was approaching one of the smaller saloons that he heard a conversation taking place between his mother and father. Their voices were raised, and though he would normally have walked on, the anger in his father's voice prompted him to stop. Fearing that something untoward had happened, he paused by the open door to listen.

'—won't have it, Sarah. He should *never* have asked!'

'But why would he not ask, Richard?' his mother said. 'You have always given Peter an allowance. Why should you not increase it now that he is about to be married?'

'Because he is not marrying the woman I wish him to!' his father said peevishly. 'He is determined to marry that Darling chit, and do not think I fail to recognise the idiocy in having to say that! Silly name, Darling,' he muttered.

'You cannot blame the child for her name,' his mother said in a tone of mild reproach. 'She had nothing to do with that.'

'No, but she has everything to do with what's happened since. And if Peter thinks I'm going to increase his allowance in order to provide enough money for the two of them to live in luxury, he's got another thing coming. In fact, it's time I put an end to this once and for all.'

There was a slight, tense pause. 'What do you mean?'

'I mean that, if he insists on going through with this marriage, I will cut him off.'

Alex caught his breath, astonished that his father would even think of such a thing.

It was clear his mother was equally nonplussed. 'Richard, you can't!'

'Yes, I can. The money is mine to do with as I please. If it pleases me to cut my youngest son off without a penny, that is exactly what I shall do.'

'But how will they survive?'

'He can apply to the church for a living. That's respectable enough. They'll provide him with a house and a wage and Linette can become a parson's wife, as her sister no doubt will.'

There was another brief pause. 'You think Emma Darling has hopes of marrying the vicar?'

'Why not? I've seen the way he looks at her,' the earl said in a disparaging tone. 'No doubt he thinks to marry her and to improve *his* lot in life through her sister's connection to us.'

'Oh, Richard, I really think you're taking this too far. If Peter and Linette truly are in love, why not just accept it and let them marry?'

'Because love, my dear, is for peasants and stable boys. Not for those of our class. We marry for the good of our families.'

'I didn't marry you for the good of the family,' his mother pointed out. 'I married you because I fell in love with you.'

'You were the daughter of an earl, like Lady Glynnis,' the earl said, his voice softening. 'I did not flaunt my father's wishes and run off with a dairy maid.'

'Perhaps because you never fell in love with a dairy maid.'

Alex managed a smile at the teasing note in his mother's voice, but it was clear from his father's reply that he was not amused. 'Of course not, because I would never have lowered myself to associate with one. But I've had quite enough of Peter flouting my authority. He should be more like Alex. You don't see him acting like an irresponsible fool. He's marrying as he should, to a woman as noble as himself.'

'But have you ever heard Alex say that he's in love with Glynnis?' his mother asked. 'Do you think he genuinely cares for her?'

'What does it matter if he cares for her? If he decides she's not the one he wants to spend his nights with after they're wed, he can find himself a mistress and take his pleasures there. Once he's secured an heir, they can each go their separate ways, as long as they do it discreetly. But at least Alex is doing what society expects of him. What *I* expect of the man who will one day take my place!'

Standing by the door, Alex felt the beginnings of a slow, simmering anger. His father certainly wasn't painting a very flattering picture of his life with Glynnis, and, given the way his father felt about Glynnis, Alex would have thought him reluctant to see either of them seek out other partners. But it seemed his only concern was that Alex marry well and produce the required number of children. It didn't matter what happened between him and Glynnis once the requisite heir had been birthed. They could each go their own separate ways and take pleasure in the arms of another if that's what they wanted. After all, that was the way society did it.

'—never gave a damn about his obligation to me and this just proves it,' his father was saying. 'Well, we'll see who has the last laugh. When he's living with her and not able to scrape together money enough to buy food, we'll see if he thinks love is worth the trouble. I'll have Sufferton draw up new papers as soon as we get back to London.'

'Oh, Richard! Surely you would not be so cruel!'

'Sometimes it is necessary to be cruel, my dear. A son has to learn obedience to his father. Loyalty to his family name. If he doesn't, how will he ever be able to pass those qualities on to his sons? Who, by the way, will also be shunned by good society through the thoughtlessness of this marriage.'

Alex backed away from the door, having heard more than enough. He couldn't believe his father would go to such lengths. To cut off his own son without a penny just to prove a point was the height of cruel and heartless treatment. No, it wasn't required that a father give an allowance to his second son, but that was always the way it had been done in their family. The earls of Widdicombe were known for their generosity towards their children. Even daughters were permitted liberal inheritances as long as they married men of whom the family approved.

Of course, the sons in the line had always done as their fathers expected as well. But now, one of them had dared to step out of line, and his father had made it very clear that he was *not* the title holder to do that with.

In his room, Alex paced the floor, wondering what he could do. There was no point in trying to persuade his father to change his way of thinking. His mind was clearly made up. Peter's asking for an increase in his allowance to cover the costs of his new life with Linette had obviously been the last straw. But if Peter went ahead with his marriage, he *would* be cut off, and possibly disowned.

At one time, Alex wouldn't have believed his father capable of taking such a hard line, but given what he'd heard today, he knew better. And that left him very little in the way of options. In fact, it left only one. If he could not persuade his father to change his mind, or Peter to break off his engagement, there was only one other avenue he could pursue.

Linette. He would appeal to her sense of fairness and family loyalty, and pray that she would be willing to listen. If she loved Peter as much as Alex believed she did, she would do anything to prevent seeing him cut off from his family. Given that the ties to her own were so strong, she would surely wish to see him remain close in the arms of those who loved him.

And there was only one way that was going to happen. Peter might hate him when he found out what he'd done, but if there was any chance of salvaging his brother's relationship with his father—and possibly his very standing in society—Alex was willing to give it a try. He was doing what he had to for the good of the family.

Hopefully other people would be able to see it that way, and be called upon to do the same.

Emma was just getting up from the dinner table when the letter was delivered.

'What's that, Jenks?' Mr Darling enquired.

'A letter from Ellingsworth, sir. For Miss Linette.'

'No doubt a love letter from her devoted swain,' Ridley remarked without enthusiasm.

'Don't be a tease, Ridley,' Linette said, holding her hand out for it. 'May I be excused, Papa?'

'Of course, my dear. Reading like that is best done away from such mundane matters as family and sustenance.'

Emma smiled as Linette scampered off to read her letter. At least one member of the family was happy. Ridley had been noticeably withdrawn since

Lady Glynnis's departure, and she oft-times found it an effort to smile in response to her father's quips. He had asked her, more than once, if something was amiss, to which she had promptly and emphatically replied that everything was fine.

Fine. Such a pathetic word, Emma thought as she made her way to the drawing room. It was neither descriptive nor emotive and communicated nothing about the way one truly felt. The weather was fine, but did that mean it was excellent or simply not bad? Fine really said nothing at all…and it described her mood perfectly.

Fifteen minutes on, the clock on the mantel chimed the hour. Emma lifted her head from her embroidery and glanced around the room. Strange, her sister hadn't come back downstairs. Linette liked to finish her day with some quiet reading by the fire, but tonight she had taken her letter upstairs and not returned.

Emma set her tambour aside and started for the stairs. She couldn't explain why, but she had a bad feeling that refused to be shaken. It was as though something unpleasant was about to happen. As though something over which she had no control was going to cause serious harm to those she cared the most about.

She reached her sister's room and knocked lightly

on the door. 'Linette, are you coming back downstairs?'

When there was no answer, Emma pressed her ear to the door—and her suspicions were confirmed. The sobs were muffled, but her sister was definitely crying. 'Linette, what's wrong?'

The sobs came to abrupt end. 'Nothing! I'm f-fine.'

'You're not fine, dearest. Can I come in?'

'No. Go away, Emma. Please, just…go away.'

Go away? Linette had never told her to go away before. What could possibly have been in that letter that would make her ask such a thing now? Emma tentatively opened the door and saw her sister sitting on the edge of the bed, the letter lying on the floor at her feet. 'Linette, whatever is the matter?'

Her sister was too upset to speak. Her eyes were red and swollen, her lips compressed as though to keep from bursting into tears again.

Emma closed the door behind her. 'Has this something to do with the letter from Peter?'

'The letter wasn't from…P-Peter,' Linette stuttered. 'It was from…Lord Stewart.'

Alex? Emma glanced at the discarded piece of parchment. Why on earth would Alex be writing to Linette? 'What does it say?'

The younger girl closed her eyes, a shimmer of fresh tears on her lashes. 'Read it. I can't bear to look at it again.'

Quite sure it could contain nothing of a personal nature, Emma picked it up. The writing was bold and slanted, as though written in a hurry. She could almost see his arm sweeping across the page.

Dear Miss Linette,
This letter will not make you happy and I pray you will find it in your heart to forgive me one day, but know that what I am about to say cannot be delayed. You are aware, I'm sure, that my father has not reconciled himself to your marriage to my brother. I had hoped that in doing what was expected of me, he would feel more lenient towards Peter, but it seems that is not the case.

My father has made it very clear that if you and Peter wed, he will cut my brother off without a penny. In short, he will disown him and I think you can understand the consequences of such an action. You will both be denied access to good society and my brother will be forced to vacate Ellingsworth Hall and look for accommodation of a far more humble nature. This will likely lead to his seeking employment within the church, as this manner of occupation does provide somewhere in which to live.

This might be something you could both bear and I have no doubt that the strength of your love would enable you to endure this. But there is another consideration. If my father disowns Peter, he effectively disowns any children resulting from the marriage. Therefore, I am asking you to do what must be done because you are the only one who can.

I am asking you to release my brother from his promise. A harsh request, I know, and one that will cause you deep pain. But I can assure you that nothing else will restore Peter to his father's good graces. A father who, I regret to tell you, is not currently enjoying the best of health…

Emma let the letter fall. There was no need to read on. Everything she needed to know had been said in those four paragraphs. Alex wanted Linette to break off her engagement to Peter. He was asking her to 'do the right thing' by appealing to her sense of goodness and love. It was horrible! After everything they had been through, after everything that had happened, Alex clearly felt no differently about the matter than he had on the day when he had asked her to persuade Linette to break off her engagement. The only difference was that now he had bypassed her and gone directly to Linette in his desire to achieve his goal.

'He wants m-me to b-break it off,' Linette sobbed. 'He says I have to…for the good of our children.

What am I going to d-do, Emma? I love Peter so much! How can I ever let him go?'

Emma had no idea what to say to console the weeping girl. She pulled her sister into her arms and held her close, even as her heart hardened against the men who had done this. Dear Lord, was there no end to the misery that dreadful family was willing to inflict? No pain they would spare? She was beginning to curse the day she'd ever heard of Peter Taylor and certainly rued the day Alex had walked into her life.

Well, it was time to take a stand. No one had the right to meddle in someone else's personal affairs—Alex certainly had no right to meddle in Linette's. Or to shatter the poor girl's dreams. She was the least capable of dealing with emotional heartache. Emma, at least, was older and strong enough to deal with her own disappointment, as was Ridley. But she would *not* allow Alex to destroy the happiness of someone as innocent and trusting as Linette.

Not as long as she had breath enough to say it!

Chapter Thirteen

It was probably just as well the letter had arrived at the end of the day, Emma thought as she prepared to set off the next morning. Had it come earlier, she would probably have marched off to Ellingsworth at once, demanding to see Alex and confronting him without having taken the time to think through what she wanted to say. She would have flown at him like a mother hen at a fox, her only thought being to protect her chick, even though both she and Linette would likely have suffered as a result.

Instead, she had lain awake through the long hours of the night, reviewing everything that had happened and trying to come up with a logical argument. If she did not, she feared she would arrive at the front door of Ellingsworth, angry and emotional, and stumble and stutter her way through her tirade and, in doing so, forget the most important things she needed to say.

She couldn't allow Alex to see her that way. She

had to be cool and rational. She needed him to listen to what she had to say and to present her arguments in such a manner that he would be willing to give some credence to her line of thought, perhaps even be open to working with her to reach some kind of satisfactory conclusion.

She accepted that there would be no resolution to her own problem. Alex was lost to her. There would be no last-minute change of heart. No sudden, unexpected revelation that would allow them to be together. He was engaged to marry Lady Glynnis and nothing was going to change that. All she would ever have was the memory of his kiss.

That would stay with her until the day she died. She would never forget the feeling of his arms holding her close, the tenderness of his mouth as it closed over hers, his lips moving so sensuously over hers. She would cherish that memory for ever, like a jewel in a keepsake box, to be taken out and admired when she was old and alone.

But, hopefully, it wasn't too late for Linette. With luck, Emma would still be able to make Alex see the merit in allowing the marriage to take place. Yes, Peter could apply to the church, if not in Little Moreton, perhaps in a neighbouring parish. Mr Tufton would surely know of something. Or they could live here at Dove's Hollow. Her father would never refuse them a room and then there would be no immediate need for Peter to find employment.

There *were* solutions, Emma told herself as she bent to let her maid set the riding bonnet atop her freshly styled curls. There were ways they could make this work. And by the time she spoke to Alex, she intended to have them memorised and ready to present so that he would find no flaws with her logic.

She took a last look at her reflection in the glass and was satisfied with what she saw. She had decided to ride over to Ellingsworth in her new habit because she knew she looked well in it, and a good appearance gave her confidence. Devoid of excess trimmings, the outfit was elegant simplicity at its best. The jacket was a touch darker than the skirt, both being in her favourite shade of periwinkle blue. Her black, high-brimmed bonnet was trimmed with trailing blue ribbons and sat jauntily on her head.

'Have you been in to see to my sister yet, Jane?'

The little maid shook her head as she picked up the breakfast tray. 'I did, but she was feeling right poorly, miss. Said she was supposed to have gone to see her young man this morning, but given how she was feeling, she had Jenks take a letter over to say she wasn't coming.'

Emma froze. Linette hadn't been planning on going to Ellingsworth this morning. She had been planning to take the trap to visit her friend, Miss Tamblyn.

Linette had told her as much only yesterday afternoon. Then why had she sent a letter to Ellingsworth cancelling an appointment that didn't exist? More importantly, to whom had she sent the letter?

Emma swept up her skirts and headed for her sister's room. 'Linette, may I come in?'

After a moment, she heard a faint voice say, 'Come in, Emma.'

She opened the door to see Linette standing in front of her wardrobe, fully dressed and with her travelling bag lying open on the bed. 'Are you going somewhere?'

'Yes.' Linette did not turn around. 'To London.'

'London?'

'To stay with Aunt Dorothy. She told me I was welcome to come whenever I liked.'

Emma walked in and closed the door behind her. 'But why?'

'Because I cannot stay here a moment longer,' Linette said quietly. 'There is nothing for me now but memories that grow more painful by the minute.'

'Linette, dearest, what are you talking about? Your life is here, with Peter.'

'Not any more. I've…broken it off.'

Emma gasped. 'What?' She flew to her sister's side and turned her around. 'Why ever did you do such a thing?'

'Because I had no choice. Don't you see, Emma?'

Linette whispered, her face crumpling. 'He would have *disowned* him. His own *son*. How could a father do something like that to his child?'

'I fear it is the way of the aristocracy. Obligation and duty mean more to a man like Lord Widdicombe than the love he feels toward his son,' Emma said. 'But that doesn't matter. If Peter still wishes to marry you, his father cannot stop him from doing so.'

'But at what cost?' Linette shook her head. 'I love him so much, Emma. How could I bear to see him reduced to a man with no status? A man forced to give up everything he is entitled to…everything he is used to…because of me. It is more than I would ask of any man, let alone him.'

'Now you listen to me, Linette Darling,' Emma said in a tone that brooked no argument. 'I have been giving this a great deal of thought and there is absolutely no need for you to do anything so drastic. You and Peter can live here at Dove's Hollow after you're married. You know Papa would agree to that. You can have my room and I could use Ridley's. Then Peter could speak to Mr Tufton about employment within the church. He's sure to know how to go about making that happen. And I can give you money—'

'Oh, Emma, it's not the money or the job, don't you see?' Linette interrupted. 'Lord Widdicombe intends to *disown* Peter if we marry. Do you know what that means? It means our children would have no status in the eyes of society. Their own grandfather would not recognise or receive them. How could I do that to them? I can live with the consequences of my own actions, but to know that I would be condemning their lives from the very start is more than I could bear.'

'But you don't *know* he would do such a thing,' Emma said. 'I've yet to see a man who doesn't fall head over heels in love with his grandchild the very first time he sees him or her. Do you really think Lord Widdicombe's heart so hard that he could shut out the sight of his own grandson?'

'I do not know Lord Widdicombe's heart well enough to hazard a guess. But based on what I *do* know of him, yes, I think he would, if only to make a point.' Linette shook her head. 'I could never hurt a child of mine the way he has hurt Peter. Never! But at least now, he won't have to. I sent Peter a note this morning, telling him that I am…releasing him from his promise.'

Emma gasped. 'Oh Linette, you must not—!'

'It's done. And I have asked that he not to come to see me because I am going away. It's over, Emma. Lord Widdicombe has won. I am not going to fight any more. I am going to finish my packing and then get ready to leave.'

'Not if I have anything to say about it.' Emma got up and headed for the door.

Linette spun around. 'Where are you going?'

'To see Lord Stewart. It's time I gave him a piece of my mind. Then we'll just see who's won and who's lost!'

Alex was in the library going over some correspondence when the butler appeared at the door. 'Miss Emma Darling to see you, my lord.'

Alex put down the letter. Emma was here? 'Show her in, Houston.'

Moments later, she appeared in the doorway and it was all Alex could do not to run to her and sweep her up in his arms. She looked lovelier than ever in a deep-blue riding habit, her cheeks dusted with pink, her lips the colour of a newly bloomed rose. But her chin was raised in defiance and her eyes flashed fire. She was upset and deeply so. 'Emma—'

'Are you happy with yourself, Lord Stewart?' she threw at him. 'Are you content now that you have ruined her life?'

Alex stopped. 'I'm not sure I understand—'

'You wrote my sister this letter!' Emma said, waving a piece of parchment in front of his face. 'How could you ask her to break off her engagement? What kind of a man are you?'

At once, the cause of her anger became clear. 'The kind who puts the welfare of his family first. I am sorry to have caused your sister pain, Emma—'

'Miss Darling!'

The coldness of her voice struck him like a blow to the heart. 'Miss Darling. But everything I wrote in that letter is true. My father will disinherit Peter if he marries your sister. I heard it from his own lips. He will cut off Peter's allowance and provide nothing in the way of future income. What do you think that will do to my brother, Miss Darling? How do you think that will make him feel, knowing he would not be able to support his wife and his children?'

'He would not be the first man forced into earning a living,' Emma retorted. 'Your brother is an intelligent man. He can find a living that will provide for all of them. He can approach the church, or teach, as my father did.'

'Oh, yes, the son of the Earl of Widdicombe, tutoring the younger brothers of the boys he went to school with. That's a wonderful thing for a man's pride.'

'Pride be damned!' Emma cried. 'If he loves Linette enough, he will do whatever he has to in order to support her.'

'Yes, he probably would,' Alex said more slowly. '*If* it was only the two of them. But what about their children? Would you have their lives blighted because of a mistake their father made?'

'Your brother has chosen to stay with Linette in spite of everything that's happened,' Emma said, ignoring his use of the word 'mistake'. 'Up until this point, he has stood by her. Now you have gone behind his back and asked the woman he loves to put an end to their engagement. And she has.'

Alex stared at her. 'She broke it off?'

'You didn't know?'

'I haven't seen my brother this morning.'

'Then you should seek him out, Lord Stewart,' Emma said coldly. 'You should ask him how he feels now that his engagement is at an end. Because I can tell you how Linette feels. She is broken hearted! She is going to stay with my aunt in London because she cannot bear to remain here a moment longer. You have ruined her life, my lord. But I don't suppose that matters to you, does it? Now you can go to your father and tell him the good news. Hoorah, Father, your beloved son is not to marry that wretched young lady.'

'Miss Darling—'

'He is free to marry someone from his own class. Someone as stuck up as you—'

'Emma—!'

'Thank God I managed to save him from himself—!'

The rest of the words were cut off. Alex crossed the room in three strides and pulled her into his arms, silencing her with a kiss. It wasn't meant to be gentle. It was meant to punish and it tore his soul apart. He wanted nothing more than to beg her to forgive him, to forget about the duty that had ruled his life from the moment of his birth and to tell her how much he loved and needed her. He wanted to cast off responsibility and lead the life he wanted. A life with Emma.

But he wasn't free to do any of those things. He could no more shrug off his obligations than he could his name and he could no more have Emma Darling than he could the stars in the sky. Both blinded him with their beauty and both were for ever unattainable.

He carefully set her away from him, aware that they were both trembling. Emma's face was white, her lips pink from the bruising force of his kiss. 'Forgive me,' he whispered, the words torn from his heart. 'I had no right...'

'No, you had no right,' Emma said in a voice so low he had to strain to hear it. 'No right to kiss me like that. No right to go to my sister and ask her to break off her engagement. No right to meddle in something that doesn't concern you. I will never forgive you for the pain you have caused Linette, my lord. And though I never thought I would hear myself say this, I pity Lady Glynnis. You think she is marrying you for the benefit of you both, but you're wrong. A woman can say what she likes, but in the deepest recesses of her heart, she will always long for love. Especially when she knows how powerful the emotion can be.'

She left him where he stood. Not moving, scarcely breathing, the pain in his chest threatening to tear him apart. He might have stood there for a minute or an hour, the memory of her voice slicing into his heart. She despised him. And she had every right to do so...

'Alex?'

Peter. Alex hadn't heard his brother come in. But looking up, he asked the question, needing to know if it was true. 'Have you heard from Linette this morning?'

There was no need for his brother to speak. A look of such anguish appeared on his face that Alex knew it would haunt him for the rest of his life. 'You have.'

'She sent me a letter. She has withdrawn her acceptance of my proposal.' There was no inflection in Peter's voice. He could have been an automaton reciting lines. 'She wishes me well and says it is... for the best.'

They stood the length of the room away...and the length of the world apart. 'It *is* for the best, Peter,' Alex said, though even to his own ears the words sounded hollow and trite. 'I overheard Mother and Father talking. He was going to cut you off. To disown you without a penny if you went ahead and married Linette.'

'I know.'

Alex stared. 'You *knew?*'

'Of course. It was the only weapon he had left. He hinted at it when he suggested I make Linette my mistress. He tried to tell me she wouldn't be interested in me if I was nothing but a parish priest, because that's all I would be if I refused to do as he asked. So I told him to go ahead and do it. That I would make the best of it.'

'You *told* him that?'

'What else was I to say?' Peter asked quietly. 'I had no intention of giving Linette up. She was my *life,* Alex. I never knew it could be like that between two people. Never knew how complete a man could feel just by having someone like her by his side. Even when I wasn't with her, I felt…connected to her. The knowledge that she was thinking about me, wherever she was, made me feel whole. I don't expect you to understand. I know your relationship with Lady Glynnis isn't based on love. But mine was. And it truly was the most remarkable thing I have ever experienced. I felt as though I could *do* anything…*be* anything…as long as she was by my side. With her, I could have scaled mountains. Without her, I am… just a man.'

Alex had no idea what to say. What *could* he say to a man who believed he had just lost everything of value in his life? A man whose unhappiness now was as a direct result of his own interference? 'What are you going to do?'

Peter managed a smile, even though he looked close to tears. 'What *can* I do? She has taken the decision

out of my hands. She's told me she has no desire to
see me again. I've lost her, Alex. And there's not a
damn thing I can do about it.'

There was nothing Alex could say. If ever he had
seen a man tortured by emotion, it was Peter. The
life had gone out of his voice and the spirit out of his
heart. His eyes were dead, devoid of the warmth and
humour that had always been there. In one fell swoop,
Alex had destroyed the gentle man his brother was
and alienated Emma—the one woman he had ever
truly loved. The woman who had opened his eyes to
what love was really about and who had made him
feel all the things Peter had just described. Everything he had been willing to give up, all for what he
had believed to be the right reasons. 'Have you told
Father yet?'

Peter shook his head. 'I'll tell him tonight. I'm not
ready to see him gloat. I was on my way to the stables
when I saw Miss Darling leave. What did she want,
by the way?'

Alex grimaced. 'To tear a strip off me for ruining
her sister's life.'

'You didn't ruin it.'

'Yes, Peter, I did.' And with a heavy heart, Alex
told his brother about the conversation he'd overheard
between his mother and father, and about the letter
he had written to Linette as a result.

'I thought I was doing the right thing,' he said,

humbly, at the end. 'But now, I realise I was entirely in the wrong. It wasn't my place to interfere. When I see what it's done to you—'

'You acted the way you did for the right reasons,' Peter said without inflection. 'You were concerned about my future. Maybe I was wrong to say it didn't matter. That I could live without Father's approval. Maybe it would have meant more to me when the invitations stopped coming and Linette and I were turned away from the places I've always been welcome at before. Maybe then I would have believed that he truly had my best interests at heart. But right now, all I can feel is this terrible emptiness. This pain for everything I've lost.' He turned and started towards the door. 'You know, it's funny. Father's approval always meant so much to me. I tried to excel at everything I did so he would be proud of me.'

'He always was,' Alex said.

'Until now.' Peter shrugged again. 'And that's what's funny. I don't care any more. It's as though I'm seeing him clearly for the first time in my life. And for the first time in my life, I'm not sure I like what I see.'

Peter quietly left the room. Alex remained behind, staring at the floor. Emma was right. He had interfered in something he'd had no business interfering in. He had tried to do the best for all concerned; instead, he had just ended up hurting the people he loved most. And for what? His father's happiness? His own sense of having done the right thing? What had he to look forward to for all his efforts? His brother's sad face. His own empty marriage to a woman who probably deserved better.

He thought about what Emma had said. *A woman may say what she likes, but in the deepest recesses of her heart, she will always long for love. Especially when she knows how powerful the emotion can be.*

What had she meant by that? Was she suggesting that Glynnis knew what she was missing and wanted more? Alex had never stopped to consider how Glynnis felt about their marriage. He'd assumed, as most men did, that having several homes to look after and with every comfort at her disposal, she would be happy. But what if she truly wanted more? What if, under the pretence of practicality, she *did* long for love?

He'd never thought about it for himself. Never dreamt he would find anything missing in his relationship with Glynnis—until he'd met Emma and discovered what love was really all about. It was about two people looking out for each other's welfare and happiness. It was his brother being willing to give up his father's approval, his position in society, even his life as a gentleman, in order to be with the woman he loved. It was Linette Darling, willing to set free the man she loved because she feared what it would cost him if he went ahead with the marriage.

And it was Emma Darling. His Emma. Having the courage to stand up to him and tell him he was wrong. To tell him that Glynnis wanted more and deserved better, and that he had a long and empty life ahead of him.

Why? Because he had done what he'd thought right. He had honoured what he had been taught to honour. Respect what had been taught to respect. The traditions that had become the life and breath of his world.

Suddenly, he realised he couldn't have been more wrong.

He found his brother in the stable, waiting for the groom to finish saddling up.

'Ready Thunder as well, would you, Clarke?' he said to the lad tightening the girth on his brother's saddle.

The young lad nodded. 'Right away, m'lord.'

Alex turned and offered Peter a smile. 'Mind if I join you?'

His brother sighed. 'Actually, I'd prefer some time on my own.'

'I understand that. And I'll give you all the time you want...if you'll give me just a few minutes of your time now. There's something I have to say to you, Peter. Something very important. And it can't wait.'

Peter stared down at the stone floor, then slowly nodded. 'All right.'

They set off for the rolling hills behind Ellingsworth. Alex was aware of an incredible sense of freedom, as though on the verge of doing something he had always wanted to do without even having been aware of wanting to do it. But now he knew what needed to be done, and, once having accepted that he was the only one who could do it, it was almost as though it couldn't happen fast enough.

After a vigorous gallop, they reined in their horses and stood admiring the countryside around them. Everywhere he looked, Alex saw new life springing up. Flowers blooming in the hedgerows. Trees budding into leaf over head. The air was warm and sweet with the scent of growing things. London had never looked or smelled like this, he thought wryly.

'Peter,' he said finally. 'I've been giving this situation with you and Linette a great deal of thought. And I've come to the conclusion that I was wrong to suggest to either of you that you break it off.'

Peter's head slowly came up. 'Why?'

'Because you love Linette Darling and she loves you. You were willing to sacrifice our father's respect and approval, and to be disowned without a penny, rather than lose her, and she has released you from your promise, rather than be the one to cause you to lose everything she thinks you hold dear.'

'Yes. So?'

'So, it makes absolutely no sense that the two of you shouldn't be together. That's why I think you should go to her this very minute and beg her to take you back.'

Peter looked stunned. 'Are you serious?'

'Never more so. It's your life, Peter,' Alex said with quiet intensity. 'Not mine. Not Father's. Yours. Even in the short time I've been here, I've seen how happy Linette makes you and how miserable you are now. And I have no reason to doubt that Miss Darling isn't every bit as unhappy. Her sister informed me that she would be leaving for London as soon as it could be arranged.'

'London!'

'Yes. She said she couldn't stay here a moment longer because the memories of you both here were too painful to be borne.'

'But what about Father?'

'Father will have to accept your decision. You're a grown man, Peter,' Alex said. 'And you're not the first-born son and heir. You have the freedom to live your life as you choose and you have a lady out there who loves you to distraction.'

'But you're right about one thing,' Peter said. 'I'll

have no money. How can I support Linette without that? I'll certainly have to let Ellingsworth go.'

'Not necessarily. I've been giving some thought to acquiring a country property and I find I like Ellingsworth very much,' Alex said. 'I could take over the payments on the house and you and Linette could reside there until you found something that would provide you with an income. I'm sure Mr Tufton could be applied to for information. Perhaps he knows of a living that might be available in the area. In the interim, I will pay your expenses and provide for the two of you—'

'No! It is too much, Alex!'

'It is not too much. You are my brother and I love you. Consider it a wedding present, if you like. But I want to do this for you and Linette.'

'But what if Father threatens to disinherit *you*?'

'He can't. I am his legitimate heir. He would hardly disinherit me over my efforts at helping my brother.' He might for the other thing he intended to do, Alex thought narrowly, but he couldn't worry about that yet. 'However, if it makes you feel any better, I will do everything I can to make Father see that this *is* the right thing to do. I know Mother will back me up and hopefully between the two of us we can bring him around.'

'And if you can't?'

'We'll cross that bridge when we come to it. For

now, go and find Linette and tell her the two of you are going to be married. Just don't mention anything to Father yet.'

'But I don't see how——'

'Trust me, Peter,' Alex said. 'I'll be returning to London today as well. There are a few other things I need to take care of. But believe me when I say that I am doing what needs to be done and that, by the time the dust clears, matters will have been settled for the best.'

Chapter Fourteen

Alex had visited the stately home of the Earl and Countess of Leyland and their daughter many times in the past, but never had he expected to be paying a call of this nature. Within minutes of arriving, he was shown into the music room where Glynnis was practising the piano. 'Alex!' She rose immediately to greet him. 'I didn't know you were back in London.'

'I've only just arrived.' He crossed the room to kiss her cheek, then stood back to look at her through the eyes of a man newly awakened to the subtleties of love. She was as beautiful as ever, but for the first time, he saw the shadow across her smile and realised her eyes were curiously flat. 'How have you been?'

'Well. Mama has been keeping me very busy with plans for the wedding.' She bid him sit down. 'Shall I ring for refreshments?'

'No, I won't stay long. I've come to talk to you, Glyn. There's something I have to say.'

Her smile was uncertain. 'It sounds serious.'

'It is. Come, sit down beside me.'

She settled herself on the loveseat by his side and, for a moment, he just looked at her, seeing in her face that of the girl he had grown up with. He remembered laughing with her in the past, the joy in her eyes so apparent, so fresh. He hadn't seen that joy once during their time together at Ellingsworth. Not even when he had asked her to marry him.

How close they had come to making a dreadful mistake by going ahead with a marriage to which neither of them was emotionally committed. 'Glyn, there's something I have to tell you,' he began, 'and it's not going to be easy—'

'Say what you must, Alex,' Glynnis interrupted. 'You and I have always been honest with one another.'

'Have we?'

He knew the question caught her off guard. He saw the blood rush to her cheeks and watched her eyes fall. 'Well, as honest as two people can be, I suppose.'

He shook his head and, reaching over, took hold of both of her hands. 'We haven't been honest at all, Glyn. And I think…no, I know that it's *imperative* that we be honest with each other now. Before we go any further down this road.'

A tiny line appeared between her brows. 'I'm not sure I understand.'

'Glynnis, do you love me?'

Her eyes widened in surprise. 'Surely you know the answer to that.'

'I'm not sure I do. And until this moment, I'm not sure it mattered. But it matters now and I need you to be completely honest with me.' When she still said nothing, Alex sighed. 'Would it make it easier if I told you...I wasn't in love with you?'

It was a harsh thing to say and the last thing he wanted to do was hurt her. But he owed it to both of them to be brutally honest. Especially in light of what he was about to tell her. 'Well?'

Slowly, Glynnis pulled her hands free. She stood up and walked back towards the piano. 'Why are you telling me this now? We are...engaged to be married.'

'Yes, we are. But we aren't married yet. And given the events of the last few weeks—'

'Events?' She glanced at him over her shoulder. 'What events?'

'My brother's engagement to Linette Darling. Our meeting the rest of her family.'

Falling in love with Emma...

Glynnis turned, and for a moment, he saw a flicker of alarm in her eyes. 'What has meeting the rest of her family to do with anything?'

Alex's gaze narrowed. Was it just his imagination or did her reaction to that one remark seem a little out of keeping with the importance of the comment? 'It has a lot to do with everything.' He slowly stood

up and went to stand beside her. 'Because as hard as
it is for me to say this, it's only fair that we both face
the fact that…my brother is not the only one to have
fallen in love with a member of the Darling family.'

Her face went white, her gasp echoing around the
room. 'Oh, Alex, I'm so sorry. I never meant to hurt
you. Truly. I never even meant that you should find
out. It just happened. I was s-sitting for the portrait
and we began talking and—'

'The portrait,' Alex said, grasping hold of something that might explain what she was talking about.
'Towbridge mentioned something about a portrait.'

Her eyes opened wide. 'He did?'

'Yes. He said if ever he'd seen a picture of a woman
in love—'

'Oh God, he said that? Then you've known all
along!' Glynnis said miserably. 'I was stupid to think
word wouldn't get around.'

And then to his astonishment, she burst into tears.

Alex was dumbfounded. He had never seen Glynnis cry before. Except that one time when she had
fallen out of a tree and broken her arm. Other than
that, she had always been one of the most stoic and
controlled women of his acquaintance. And yet here
she was, weeping as though her heart were breaking.
Had he truly misread the situation so badly? Was
she so deeply in love with him that the thought of

losing him to Emma truly had broken her heart...
'Glynnis, I—'

And then just as abruptly, he remembered something else she had said. *I never even meant that you should find out...*

'Glynnis, what *exactly* are you trying to tell me?'

For a moment, she gazed at him, her lips pressed tightly together as though afraid to say the words. Then, shaking her head, she sighed. 'I'm sorry, Alex. I never meant to fall in love with him. But as the days passed and I came to know him better, I realised I had feelings for him that went far beyond anything I should have felt for him, and, well, one thing led to another and before I knew it, it was...too late.'

Alex was very nearly speechless. She had fallen in love...with another man? 'Glynnis, I'm sorry, but I honestly don't know who or what you're talking about.'

'But you just said Tom told you about the painting. And that...you knew I was...in love with a member of the Darling family,' she whispered.

'No. I said *someone* was in love with a member of the Darling family,' Alex said. 'I didn't say or suggest it was you.'

She blanched. 'You didn't?'

'No. I was trying to tell you that it was me. *I* fell in love,' he said quietly. 'With Emma Darling.'

'Emma!' Glynnis whispered. 'You're in love…with Emma Darling?'

'That's what I've been trying to tell you.'

And then, to his astonishment, her expression altered and she actually started to laugh. 'Oh, Alex, this is truly madness! We are both beyond help, do you know that?' She wiped her eyes, took a moment to recover herself, and then said sadly, 'Then you really didn't know.'

'Know what?'

'That I am in love, too. With Ridley Darling.'

Ridley Darling. It took a moment for the words to sink in. 'You're in love…with Emma's *brother?*'

She nodded.

'The painter?'

She nodded again. 'Idiotic, isn't it?'

'I don't know whether to be shocked or relieved,' he said. 'I don't suppose you have any brandy in here.'

'As a matter of fact…' Glynnis started towards a small cabinet in the corner and, opening the door, drew out a decanter and two glasses. She tried to pull out the stopper, but her hand was shaking so badly that Alex had to take over.

'I think you'd best leave that to me. I hate to see even a drop of good brandy wasted.' He filled the two glasses and handed her one. 'But we both need a bit of a bracer. Cheers.'

'Cheers.' They downed the brandy, after which

Glynnis pressed a hand to her heart. 'Goodness! That certainly clears the mind.'

'Excellent shock therapy,' Alex agreed, refilling his glass. He held up the decanter, but Glynnis quickly shook her head.

'Another one of those and I won't have my wits about me. And I think I need to know exactly what we are both saying.'

They were silent, gazing at one another as though seeing each other for the first time. 'You're in love with Emma Darling?' Glynnis said finally. 'Truly?'

'That's what I came here to tell you,' Alex said softly. Then he laughed. 'I thought it was going to be a shattering revelation. As it turns out, it is only one of many.'

Glynnis bit her lip. 'Oh, Alex, I cannot believe this has happened to *us* of all people. You and I have always believed in the sensible approach to marriage. We both agreed that to make such an important decision based on sentiment was the height of stupidity. And yet, look what's happened. We were each promised to the right person, only to fall in love with the wrong one.' She stared at him in bewilderment. 'How could we possibly have been so mistaken?'

'Because we didn't know any better,' Alex said. 'Neither of us ever expected to fall in love.'

'Does she know?'

Alex shook his head. 'I haven't told her in so many

words,' he admitted. 'And given what I did just before I left, it may not matter.' In a few words, he told Glynnis of the letter he had written to Linette, of Linette's reaction to it, and of Emma's response to him as a result.

'But never mind me,' he said. 'What about Ridley Darling? Does he know how you feel about him? More importantly, does he feel the same way about you?' Glynnis blushed, but Alex saw the happiness in her eyes. 'I see that he does.'

'I'm sorry, Alex. I still feel so strange talking to you about this, but…yes, he loves me. I didn't know for certain until the day I was leaving Ellingsworth. We'd had a terrible fight in London. Over the painting. That's why it was so difficult for us when we met at the ball. I'm sure you noticed.'

'I was aware of a certain tension between you,' Alex admitted. 'But we were all a little on edge that night. I put it down to the meeting between Father and Linette.'

'That didn't help,' Glynnis acknowledged, 'but that was entirely separate from what Ridley and I were going through. You see, that was the first time we had seen each other since we parted in London.'

And then she told him what had happened with regard to the painting and to her relationship with Ridley as a result.

'So you thought it was Tom Towbridge who had exposed you.'

'I could think of no other way you would find out. He was the only one who saw the painting and I was sure he recognised the expression of love on my face,' Glynnis said simply. 'Naturally, my guilty conscience led me to believe he would put it down to my feelings for Ridley and tell you the same.'

'He did nothing of the kind,' Alex said. 'He simply said he hoped he would be lucky enough to meet a woman one day who loved him as much as you obviously loved me. So he did recognise the expression on your face, Glynnis. He simply attributed the reason for it being there to me.'

'Oh, Alex. This a fine mess we've landed ourselves in,' Glynnis murmured. 'What *are* we going to do about it?'

'Well, we are going to start by releasing each other from our promises,' Alex said, taking her hand and leading her back to the loveseat. 'And then you are going to tell Ridley Darling that you love him and that he has to marry you. Or he will have me to answer to.'

But Glynnis was already shaking her head. 'There's no point. Father won't allow me to marry Ridley. He's more of a stickler for propriety than your father. He would never allow me to marry so far beneath me. And if I don't marry you, he'll only push me in the direction of someone else with a title as good as or better than yours.'

'But you're in *love* with Ridley,' Alex said softly.

'Yes, and you're in love with Emma. But you haven't said you're going to ride back to Little Moreton and ask her to marry you.'

'I'm not even sure she would have me.'

'You'll never know if you don't ask.'

Alex looked at her and, for the first time, felt a fleeting moment of regret that he hadn't been able to feel more than friendship for her. 'You are a very special lady, Glynnis. Darling's a lucky man.'

She reached out her hand and gently caressed his cheek. 'I think the problem with us, Alex, was that we were always such good friends. You looked out for me and I did my best to protect you from the girls who were after you for all the wrong reasons. Somehow in the midst of all that, we developed feelings for one another that were anything but romantic. You are truly the best of men and I admire you tremendously, but...'

'You don't love me,' Alex finished softly.

She shook her head. 'Not in the way a woman should love the man who would be her husband. I didn't have the courage to tell you that before. And I would have married you, rather than disappoint everyone else. I thought perhaps you did care for me, in that way. But it would have been like marrying my brother.'

He snorted. 'That would have made lovemaking decidedly uncomfortable.'

'Oh, Lord!' Her cheeks flushed crimson, but then she started to laugh. 'Yes, it would, wouldn't it.' And then they laughed together as the truth of the situation hit them both. 'So, what do we do now?' she asked.

Alex got up and said nothing for a moment. He hadn't expected any of this, but now that they had cleared the air, the answers suddenly seemed obvious. 'Glyn, would you consider leaving London if it meant you could be with Ridley Darling?'

She looked up at him with an expression of surprise. 'Probably, but Father would never approve—'

'I didn't say anything about your father approving. I asked if you would be willing to live somewhere other than London if it meant you could be Ridley's wife.'

She gazed at him in silence for a few minutes. Then, slowly, she nodded. 'Yes, I would.'

'Then that is what you must do.' He walked back to where she sat and drew her to her feet. 'You must contact Ridley and tell him that I have released you from your promise and that you and he must make plans to marry as soon as possible.'

'But how—?'

'You are both of age. I will make arrangements for

a special licence and will be present at the marriage to witness that everything is done legally and above board. Then you and Ridley can return to London as man and wife and present yourselves to your parents. Based on what your father says, you will go from there.'

'What if he tells me to get out?' Glynnis asked.

'Then you will have to decide where you want to live,' Alex said. 'You have, I believe, an inheritance from your mother's parents?'

'Yes! I'd almost forgotten. Papa has always been so generous with my allowance, I've never had to draw upon it.'

'And I believe Mr Darling has money of his own. From all I've heard, he is making quite a name for himself as a portraitist; once the scandal of this dies down, he will be in demand again. You, however, may have to reconcile yourself to the fact that you will never be received by good society again, especially if your father chooses not to recognise your marriage. But outside of London, there's no reason why you can't lead a very happy and fulfilled life. Most importantly, you will be with the man you love and I wager your father will eventually come round.'

'I'm not so sure.'

'I am. Your father adores you. He would cut out his heart rather than see you walk out of his life altogether. And I will do all I can to facilitate his acceptance. After all, he will blame me for it happening. Not you.'

'But I do not wish him to have the wrong opinion of you, Alex,' Glynnis said. 'It is only fair that he knows I fell in love with someone else, too.'

'Will that matter to him?'

She slowly began to smile. 'It may not matter to him, but it will to Mama. She turned down a duke's proposal to marry my father, because she loved him and not the duke. She often tells me the story. I think, in her heart, she was always a little sad that you and I weren't marrying for love.'

'Then it sounds as though you're already halfway there,' Alex said. 'Between your mother and myself, I'm sure we'll be able to bring your father around. Especially once he meets Ridley. The man's a charming rogue, but he's likeable all the same.'

Glynnis sighed. 'He is much more than that.'

'Yes, I'm sure he is.' Alex smiled and bent down to kiss the top of her head. 'Or you wouldn't have fallen in love with him.'

'And what about you? How are you going to resolve your situation with Miss Darling? And with your father? He won't be pleased when he learns about this. You saw how he reacted to Peter's engagement to Linette. He will be furious when he hears that his heir has decided to cast aside discretion and follow his heart.'

Yes, he would, Alex acknowledged. But right now, that wasn't his biggest concern. His biggest concern was in finding out if Emma still wanted him. Once he knew the answer to that, there would be plenty of time to decide how he would deal with everything else.

Two days later, Emma sat in front of her easel, trying to muster the enthusiasm to continue with her painting. Ever since Alex had gone back to London, it was as though a light had gone out in her world, immersing her in a Stygian darkness from which there was no escape. She wouldn't have believed it possible to miss a man so much, to feel as though even the effort of living wasn't worth the trouble, but, clearly, that's what losing love was all about.

She gazed at the stone angel in front of her and sighed. 'I would trade places with you if I could,' she murmured, dipping her brush into a pot of paint. 'Stone angels don't have hearts that can be broken.'

'Are you sure?' a man said quietly. 'Have you ever considered that someone did break her heart and maybe that's why she's not smiling?'

Emma stiffened. *It couldn't be.* He had no reason to come back to Dove's Hollow. And why had he come back now? This was the *worst* possible time for him to be here. She wasn't strong enough to see him. She couldn't talk to him rationally when it was as much as she could do just to breathe.

She stretched out her arm and carefully touched the flat side of the brush to the canvas. 'Angels don't fall in love. They live in heaven where all is bliss and harmony. Love is part of this world. Or of hell.'

'It doesn't have to be.'

'Sadly, it is. At least for this family,' Emma said, feeling the onset of unwelcome tears. Oh, yes, that was perfect. Now she was crying. Why couldn't he have just stayed in London and left her alone? 'What do you want, Alex? I thought you had gone back to London for good.'

'No.' She heard the crunch of his boots on the gravel path. 'I went back to London because there was something I had to do. Someone I had to see.'

He stepped into her peripheral vision. Emma turned her face away so he wouldn't be able to see her tears. 'Am I supposed to know who you're talking about or are you going to make me guess?'

'You probably already know.'

'Lady Glynnis.'

'Yes.'

Emma stabbed paint against the angel's wing. 'Have you set a date for the wedding?'

'There isn't going to be a wedding,' he said, forcing her to draw back her arm as he moved to stand between her and the canvas. 'At least, not between Lady Glynnis and myself.'

Emma's gaze flew up to his. 'But...you are engaged!'

'Not any more. We talked about it when I was in London and we both agreed it wasn't going to work.'

Wasn't going to work? Emma thought her heart had been pounding before. It was close to exploding now. 'I don't understand. You asked her...to marry you. She said yes. It was a long-standing arrangement.'

'Yes, it was. But I asked her *before* I knew she was in love with another man. But you knew that, didn't you, Emma?' he said gently. 'You knew all about the relationship between Glynnis and your brother.'

Emma jumped up, knocking over the water jar. 'How did you find out?'

'Glynnis told me. Why didn't you?'

'Because it wasn't my place to say anything,' Emma said, flustered. 'It wasn't my secret to reveal.'

'Maybe not, but surely I deserved to know that the woman I was marrying was in love with someone else.'

'Of course you did, but Glynnis asked me not to say anything. She asked that it be our secret.'

'How fortunate for all of us then, that it isn't a secret any more.'

Emma looked at him. Was he furious—or devastated? He didn't appear to be either, but a man like

Alex was good at hiding what he was truly feeling. He only let a person see what he wanted them to. 'You don't seem overly upset,' she said cautiously.

'That's because I'm not upset. I am *delighted* to know she is going to marry the man she loves.'

'Marry!" Emma gasped. 'Lady Glynnis is going to *marry* Ridley?'

'That was her intention when I left London.'

'But…what will her parents say? What will society say? He is an artist. She is the daughter of an earl!'

'Yes, but she is also a woman in love. And now that she is free to be with the man she loves, nothing is going to stand in her way. Very determined is Lady Glynnis when she sets her mind to something.'

'She must be,' Emma said in bewilderment. Because she would be going against the tide of popular opinion; doing something frowned upon by society and likely by everyone else she knew. All because she wasn't willing to live without the man she loved.

And then, an even more daunting thought occurred to Emma. 'What is your father going to say when he hears about this? He adores Lady Glynnis.'

'Yes, he does. And I hope that when he realises how much she loves Ridley, he will be able to find it in his heart to wish her well and to forgive me.'

Emma bit her lip. 'What do you think the chances of that are?'

'Realistically? Not good,' Alex admitted with

a shrug. 'But he will have no choice. Unless your brother changes his mind, he and Glynnis *are* going to be married. They probably won't end up living in London, but I don't think either of them cares about that. Ridley will find work elsewhere and, knowing society the way I do, this notoriety will only add to his cachet and people will seek him out even more. Glynnis's only concern is that they be together.'

Emma looked up at him, struggling to grasp everything he was saying. 'Is this what you came to tell me?'

'One of the things.'

'There's more?' she squeaked.

'Yes. The other reason I went to London was to tell Glynnis I could not marry her.'

'Yes, I know. Because she was in love with Ridley.'

'But I didn't know that when I went there, did I?'

'Then why…?'

His smile had a slightly wicked edge…and suddenly, there wasn't enough air in Emma's lungs to finish the sentence. Her mouth opened, but the words didn't come.

Alex just smiled. 'I did a lot of thinking after our last conversation, Emma. And I realised you were right. I had no right to interfere in Peter and Linette's relationship. Your sister is a sweet, gentle woman and she is marrying my brother because she loves him. And he loves her. I don't think I realised how much until I saw his face after he received her letter breaking off their engagement.'

'But they aren't getting married,' Emma whispered. 'Linette is in London with Aunt Dorothy.'

'Yes, I know. I thought Peter would have gone to see Linette before she left, but apparently he went to see Mr Tufton instead to ask him about employment within the church. But Peter is in London now, intent on trying to change your sister's mind.'

'*What?* But you said they should not—'

'I know what I said and I was wrong. I told Peter as much, too,' Alex said. 'I told him to go after Linette and beg her to marry him because I couldn't bear knowing that I was the one who had caused those two dear people so much heartache.'

Emma had no idea what to say. She was hard pressed to believe what Alex was telling her; though she was delighted for her sister and Peter, she couldn't believe that Alex would change his mind so completely, even to allowing Ridley and Lady Glynnis to marry.

If only…

No, that was asking too much. Cupid had only so many arrows in his quiver and he had already expended more on her siblings than any one family had a right to expect.

'To say I'm happy would be putting it mildly,' she said finally. 'I never thought it possible that matters would turn out like this. I had hoped Linette and your brother might have an opportunity at finding happiness together, but I never dreamt there was a chance for Ridley and Lady Glynnis as well.'

'We don't ask to fall in love with the people we do, Emma,' Alex said quietly. 'Sometimes it's the last person in the world we expect to fall in love with; sometimes it is the last person we *should* fall in love with. But none of that matters because when you find that person and when you know it's right, you'll move heaven and earth to try to be with them. You will defy your family and fly in the face of society because all that really matters is being with that person.

'Sometimes, it doesn't work out,' he said. 'Sometimes, no matter how hard we try, the odds are too great and the sacrifices too high. But I have come to believe that if the love between two people is strong enough, they *will* find a way. A piece of iron only becomes stronger the more time it rests in the fire. I think that's true for relationships. When put to the test, love either gets stronger or melts away entirely.'

Emma nodded blindly. Tears were filling her eyes as fresh pain welled in her heart. She had never loved this man more than she did at this moment. He had done everything he could to facilitate the relationships between Linette and Peter, and Ridley and Lady Glynnis. He had swept aside duty and obligation to help them be with the people they loved and he had done so without thought or consideration for himself. She had no doubt he would receive a chilly reception from his father and from society for the part he had played in bringing those two couples together.

'And what will you do now, my lord?' Emma asked softly. 'You will find things very difficult in London for a time, I think.'

'Perhaps, but it has been on my mind to leave London for a bit,' Alex said. 'I told Peter I would take over the lease of Ellingsworth Hall, and that he and Linette could live there until they are able to make arrangements for a place of their own.'

'You would do that for them?'

'Of course. He is my brother. I would do all that I could.'

'But…what will your father say?'

'I don't know, but, whatever it is, he will have to resign himself to the situation. I dare say when he sees his first grandchild, those resentments will fall away, as they should.'

'What about the state of his health? This might be more than he can tolerate.'

Alex smiled. 'I am convinced he will outlast us all. I told Mother as much and I stand by my claim. But I'll speak to the doctor once I return to London and find out exactly how things stand.'

'Then, you will be living here. In the area,' Emma said, wondering how she would bear it.

'Yes. I find I rather like Little Moreton. It has a charm I didn't expect, but then I suspect that has much to do with the people who live here. Especially with the Darling family, who seem to have made such a lasting impression on every member of my family. By the way, I never did tell you what I wanted you to paint for me.'

The abrupt change of subject left Emma frowning. 'I was hoping you had forgotten all about it.'

'I haven't. Fortunately, the picture is almost completed, so you can finish it for me now.'

'Finish it?' Emma said. 'I haven't even started it.'

'Yes, you have. It's right there in front of you.'

Emma stared wide-eyed at the painting. 'The stone angel?'

'Yes. I've grown rather fond of this particular angel,' Alex said, looking down at the canvas. 'But there is one thing I would like you to add. One word. But only the right word will do. Otherwise, I don't want it.'

Emma gazed at him in bewilderment. 'You want me to paint a word. On this painting.'

'That's right.'

'Why would you want a painting with writing on it?'

'As a memento of the day.'

'Why? Is today special?'

'I'm hoping it will turn out to be, yes.'

'And what is the word?'

'You will have to be the one to tell *me* that, Miss Darling.'

'I cannot read your mind, my lord.'

'You won't have to. Now, if you wouldn't mind sitting down again.'

Emma frowned, but resumed her seat in front of the easel. Alex picked up her brush, dipped it in a bright blue blob of paint and handed it to her. 'Now, somewhere on the painting, I would like you to write the answer to a question.'

'I still don't understand.'

'You haven't heard the question yet.'

'Oh, very well.' Emma turned to look at the painting. 'What is your question?'

'Just this. Emma Darling.' He slowly dropped to one knee on the ground beside her and said, 'Darling Emma, will you marry me?'

She dropped the brush.

Patiently, he picked it up, wiped the gravel off the bristles and, dipping it in the blue paint again, handed it back to her. 'Would you like me to repeat the question?'

'No...yes, that is, I heard the question. I just don't understand—'

'I shall explain later. Just paint your answer.'

Emma faced the canvas. This was impossible. It couldn't be happening. He wasn't really asking her to marry him, was he? She turned back to look at him, but he sat without moving. Waiting.

She glanced back to the canvas. He *was* asking her to marry him. He was waiting for her to write her answer, yes or no, on the painting of the angel. He wasn't teasing her. He was very serious.

And ever so slowly, Emma began to smile. She smiled until she thought her face would split. So, this was how it felt. This was how you knew when it was right. When the world seemed a brighter place and no problem seemed insurmountable. This was how you knew you were in love.

She took a long, deep breath and slowly pressed her brush to the canvas. He had given her paint enough for one short word. And there, right where the stone angel's heart would be, she carefully, and lovingly, painted the word *'yes'*.

Beside her, Alex made a sound. It might have been a murmur of joy, or relief, or a combination of the two. But whatever it was, Emma knew she had given him the answer he wanted.

'I love you, Emma.' He slowly got to his feet and drew her up with him. 'You know that, don't you?'

'I do now.' Aware that she was still holding on to the brush, she set it down, and then looked up into the face of the man with whom she would be spending the rest of her life and whispered, 'I love you too, Alex. With all my heart.'

His mouth covered hers hungrily, demanding a response, and willingly Emma gave it to him. She held nothing back, kissing him with a passion that surprised her and a depth of sincerity that could leave him in no doubt as to her feelings. A passion that was echoed deep within her soul.

Yes, there would be challenges. Their life together would not be as easy as some. But as long as Alex loved her, Emma knew she would be able to face whatever came her way.

'There might be one small problem,' Alex said when he finally, reluctantly set her away.

'Other than your father and most of society, you mean?'

'Yes. Do you think your Mr Tufton will agree to marry us?'

Emma blushed and laughed softly. 'He is not *my* Mr Tufton.'

'Of course he is! He's besotted with you.'

'Really? Then why did he ask Miss Cynthia Brown to marry him last Tuesday?'

'He did?'

'So Mrs Connelly informed us. And if Mrs Connelly says it's true, it must be.'

Alex smiled. 'Perhaps he did that because he knew you were mine.'

'You did a very good of keeping *that* a secret, my lord.'

'Only from you. I'm sure Mr Tufton knew exactly how I felt. But it is just as well. At least now I won't feel the need to glare at him as he pronounces us husband and wife.'

Emma tutted. 'There would never have been the need for that. You are the *only* man I have ever cared about, Alex. You must have known I was falling in love with you?'

Alex bent his head to kiss her one more time. 'I didn't. But I shall never get tired of hearing you say it. Now, shall we go and tell your father the good news?'

Emma nodded and, with Alex's arm tucked around her waist and the other holding his newly acquired painting, they walked back to Dove's Hollow as the real stone angel smiled her crooked smile and the warm spring rain gently began to fall.

Epilogue

Ellingsworth Hall—September, five years on...

It was a happy crowd that gathered to celebrate the fourth birthday of Michael Richard Percy Taylor, son and heir of Lord and Lady Stewart, and grandson of the Earl and Countess of Widdicombe. Peter and Linette arrived first, bringing with them their three-and-a-half-year-old daughter, Mary, followed by Ridley and Lady Glynnis, the latter suffering through the early stages of her pregnancy, but joyous nonetheless.

Next came the grandparents: Lord and Lady Widdicombe, the Earl and Countess of Leyland, and Emma's father, who had become even closer to Emma during the weeks and months following Michael's birth. Only the two aunts were missing, Aunt Dorothy having written to say that she and Augusta were travelling in Switzerland as they had reconciled in the weeks following Augusta's separation from her husband.

A tent had been set up on the grounds of Ellingsworth Hall to offer protection in case of rain, but as the day had dawned clear and bright, no one sought to use it—except to procure refreshments from the magnificently laden tables set out within. Emma fondly watched her husband prepare a meal for her, smiling when she saw him place an extra piece of chicken on an already heaping plate.

'I shall not fit into any of my gowns if you keep on feeding me like that,' she complained good naturedly.

'Ah, but you're eating for two again, my love,' Alex said, adding a spoonful of potatoes, a helping of roast parsnips and a generous portion of Cook's excellent bread stuffing. 'And I would not wish to see my lady go hungry.'

Emma sighed as she eyed the plate, knowing that despite her protestations, she would most likely finish off every delicious bite. 'I wasn't this hungry when I was carrying Michael. I must be having twins.'

'Or a girl. Remember how ravenous Linette was when she was carrying Mary? I swear Peter had to bring her food at all hours of the day and night. Made it devilishly hard for him to finish his sermons.'

Emma laughed. Oh, yes, she remembered well her tiny sister's unusual preoccupation with food. Once she had recovered from her initial bout of morning illness, Linette had gained a very healthy appetite and six months later had been delivered of a beautiful baby girl: a pink-and-white angel who charmed everyone she met, including, and most particularly, her two doting grandfathers.

'Would you mind if this baby was a girl, Alex?' Emma asked as they left the tent and strolled out into the golden autumn sunshine.

'I would be delighted if it was a girl, but would be equally pleased if it were another boy.' He glanced down at her, his eyes darkening as they lingered on the lush fullness of her breasts. 'Knowing how much you want a daughter would give me an excuse to keep on making love to you.'

Emma blushed at his blatantly sensual tone. 'You hardly need an excuse for that, my lord. Given the frequency of our lovemaking, I'm surprised it took as long as it did for me to conceive again. It took so little with Michael.'

'Ah, yes, but I had all those weeks of pent-up longing and frustration to get out of my system.' Alex leaned over to nuzzle a kiss into his wife's neck. 'The first time we made love was *very* powerful.'

Emma felt the familiar sense of urgency, aware that the memory of their first night together still had the power to move her. The intensity of their passion had caught both of them unawares and Emma still blushed when she thought about all they had done and how wantonly she had responded to her new husband's caresses.

She blushed even more when, upon approaching the group seated on chairs in the shade of the big elm tree, she caught Linette watching her and saw her begin to smile.

'I swear Linette had developed the ability to read minds since becoming a mother,' Emma murmured. 'She always starts to smile whenever I'm thinking about you.'

'Then she must be smiling all the time.'

'Odious man. Are you insinuating you are all I think about?'

'Of course.' He stopped and drew her against him, mindful of the well-laden plate he was still carrying. 'God knows, you are all *I* ever think about.'

'All right, you two,' Ridley drawled. 'Need I remind you that there *are* others present, including two young and highly impressionable children.'

'You need remind me of nothing, brother-in-law.' Alex kissed his wife soundly on the lips, then turned to grin at Ridley. 'I just wanted to make sure no one questioned the depth of my love for this woman.'

'I doubt there's *ever* been any question on that score,' Lord Widdicombe said drily. He was bouncing his granddaughter on his knee, but turned to glance fondly at his younger son. 'Or on your brother's.'

Peter smiled, looking completely relaxed and at

ease as he stood behind Linette's chair, gently rubbing her shoulders. He was now the vicar of St Anne's
in the neighbouring parish and it was clear from the
look on his face that church life suited him. He and
Mr Tufton had become fast friends and Linette had
taken to her role as a clergyman's wife like a duck
to water. They had set up housekeeping in the old
manse, a lovely stone house reminiscent of Dove's
Hollow, and were already well loved by their parishioners.

'Thank you, Father,' Peter said now. 'I am the first
to admit that I've never been happier and that it is all
due to Linette being my wife.'

'And what more could a father ask than to see both
of his sons so happy?' Lady Widdicombe commented
with a smile.

'I venture to say your sons' choices have made you
a happy man as well, Widdicombe,' Lord Leyland
observed. 'You're in far better health than you were
when they met and not nearly as cantankerous. You
haven't stopped grinning since the day Michael was
born.'

'Don't forget that Mary has him wrapped around
her pretty little finger,' Lady Widdicombe added.

'Guilty as charged,' the earl said. 'But wait until
it's your turn, Leyland. You have no idea what holding your first grandchild in your arms is going to do
to you. I certainly didn't.'

'Well, I'm definitely looking forward to finding out,' Lady Glynnis said weakly. 'Given the way I'm feeling today, it cannot come soon enough.'

'Never mind, dearest,' her mother murmured. 'Like you, I suffered dreadfully in the early days of my pregnancies, but it does eventually pass. It just means everything is proceeding as it should.'

Emma's heart went out to her sister-in-law. Glynnis and Ridley had been forced to endure much more in the early days of their marriage than either she and Alex or Linette and Peter had, and when Glynnis had miscarried in the early weeks of her first pregnancy, no one had been overly surprised. So when Ridley made the announcement a little over four months ago that his wife was pregnant again, the news had been received with great joy and quiet prayers that all would be well. Emma knew how anxious they were to start a family.

'Uncle Ridley,' Michael said, abruptly getting to his feet after obviously having had enough of adult conversation. 'Have you brought me a present?'

'Michael!' Emma gasped. 'It's not polite to ask people if they've brought you something.'

'Why not? I did it all the time,' Ridley said, ruffling his nephew's blonde curls. 'And of course I've brought you something. In fact, if you ask your grandfathers nicely, they might just take you down to the stables and show it to you.'

'The stables!' The little boy gasped. 'You bought me a *pony?*'

'I didn't say that.'

'But you said my gift was in the stables! That must mean it's a pony!'

Mr Darling got to his feet and reached for his grandson's hand. 'Well then, young man, I suppose we had best take a walk down there and see if you're right.'

'You come too, Grandfather Widdy,' Michael said. 'And you, Mary.'

Lord Widdicombe, who seemed not to mind that his revered name had been shortened in such an unseemly fashion, gently set Mary on her feet and then stood up to take her hand. 'Come along, my dears. Let's go see what all the excitement is about.'

As the two men and their grandchildren started in the direction of the stables, Emma glanced at her brother with an expression of mingled affection and annoyance. 'Have you really bought him a pony, Ridley?'

'I have. In fact, I've bought ponies for *each* of them.'

'What?' Linette squeaked. 'For Mary as well?'

'Well, I wasn't here for her birthday in April and when I was down at Tat's and saw these two little gems, I knew they would be perfect. And I did clear it with your respective husbands first.'

'That doesn't justify your continuing to spoil them,' Emma said.

'Of course it does. Spoiling is the prerogative of uncles and grandparents,' Ridley said. 'Besides, given that I'm such a rich and successful artist now, I can well afford it.'

That was another unexpectedly happy conclusion to a situation about which Emma had harboured serious doubts. After Ridley and Lady Glynnis's secret marriage in the neighbouring parish, one arranged by special licence and witnessed by Alex and Emma, the pair had returned to London, only to be met by the stony disapproval of Glynnis's father. Alex had done his best to try to smooth things over, but the earl had been intractable, refusing to acknowledge the marriage or even to receive the pair in his house.

It had been a heart-wrenching time for all of them and a situation for which Emma had seen no hope of a happy resolution.

Until Lady Leyland had taken the matter into her own hands. Daughter of a marchioness, she had refused to be denied access to her own daughter and, secretly delighting in the news that Glynnis had married for love, she had set about re-establishing the pair in society. She had called together several of her closest friends, all of whom were very highly placed and all of whom had married for love, and told them the truth of Glynnis and Ridley's situation by also telling them of Alex and Emma's.

She had explained that it was Alex who had released Glynnis from her promise because he was in love with another woman, only to discover that *she* was in love with another man. The countess had also stressed that no improprieties had taken place and that surely four such good-natured and well-intentioned people should not be cut off from the company of others, simply because they had chosen to follow their hearts and marry for love rather than obligation.

Her strategy had worked. Doors that had been closed in the newlyweds' faces slowly began to open and the invitations had started arriving again. At that point, the countess had turned her attention to her husband, knowing that his approval mattered far more to Glynnis than society's ever could. And using every stratagem she could think of, the countess had slowly begun to chip away at his anger.

Naturally, there had been resistance. Even when society had begun to welcome Glynnis and Ridley back, the earl had refused to back down. But when his wife had gone to him with the tragic news of Glynnis's miscarriage, concern for his daughter had driven all other thoughts from the earl's mind and he had immediately gone to see her. In the following days, all had been forgiven, the marriage had been accepted and, as a result, Ridley's popularity as an artist had soared.

'Speaking of gifts, there's something in the house for you, Emma,' Ridley said casually. 'You might like to take a look at it before the grand unveiling after dinner this evening.'

'Before the *what?*'

Emma looked to her husband for an explanation, but he only smiled and drew her up out of her chair. 'I think that's an excellent idea, Ridley. You don't mind if we leave all of you for a few minutes, I trust.'

'Not at all. Just don't forget to come back,' Ridley warned. 'I don't want to be the one to explain to Michael why you're not here when he gets back from his visit to the stables. Or for some time after that!'

Her gift was hanging on the drawing room wall. It was a large canvas, beautifully framed, and the moment Emma saw it she knew how special it was. 'Oh, Alex!'

It was her stone angel, even to the smudge of blue over her heart. But it was a painting within a painting. Arranged around the stone angel was a portrait of her new family. Alex standing tall and proud, dressed as he had been on their wedding day and gazing at her with so much love that anyone looking at the painting would have to be able to see it. Emma was standing next to him, wearing the gown she'd worn the night the two of them had met, and she was holding Alex's hand. And there in front of them was Michael, his bright blonde curls reflecting the warmth of a late afternoon sun. It was an incredibly moving portrait of a family bound together by love.

'Oh, Alex, it's beautiful!' Emma whispered, touched beyond words by what her brother had done.

'Happy birthday, darling,' Alex said, drawing her into the circle of his arms. 'I knew you would like it.'

She looked at him in wonder. Her *birthday?* But of course! In all the preparations for Michael's birthday, including the week-long visit of Ridley and Glynnis and all the grandparents, Emma had completely forgotten that it was her birthday as well. She turned back to stare at the painting in wonder. 'You asked Ridley to do this for me?'

'Yes. He's been working on it for quite some time.'

'He must have been.' Emma moved closer to the painting, lightly touching the canvas. It was truly remarkable the way Ridley had combined her painting into his so that it was almost impossible to see where one canvas had ended and the other began. 'I don't know how he did this,' she murmured, 'but I can see why he's gained such a reputation for brilliance. He has managed to incorporate my painting of the stone angel perfectly into his own.'

'Yes, because the painting wouldn't have meant

nearly as much to either of us if Ridley had painted a new angel. It would have been…imperfect.'

'Imperfect?' Emma glanced back at the painting. 'Ridley would have painted the statue a hundred times better than I ever could.'

'Exactly. Your flawed stone angel means more to me than…than a flock of perfectly painted angels ever could. And you know why.'

She turned her head to meet his gaze and felt the familiar longing begin. 'Yes, I know.' Her voice grew husky as she stepped back into the warmth of his arms. 'Because only our angel knows how much we went through to be together.'

The kiss was slow and thoughtful and when at last Alex raised his head, his eyes were dark with desire. 'I love you, Emma. You know that, don't you?'

'Yes, and I love you. But…I'm not sure you can refer to a group of angels as a flock, my lord,' she whispered against his throat. 'It makes them sound like sheep. Or pigeons.'

'Then what do you call a gathering of angels, beautiful lady?'

'Perfection.' Emma closed her eyes and felt the thrum of desire as his lips brushed over hers again. 'Exactly like my life here with you.'

* * * * *

HISTORICAL

Large Print

THE LADY GAMBLES
Carole Mortimer

Incognito at a fashionable gambling club, Lady Copeland is drawn to a rakish gentleman, whose burning gaze renders her quite distracted! She can't risk letting anyone close enough to expose her secret—though her body craves to give in…

LADY ROSABELLA'S RUSE
Ann Lethbridge

Lady Rosabella must pose as a widow to find the inheritance she and her sisters so desperately need! Baron Garth Evernden is known for his generosity and is so *very* handsome…surely becoming mistress to this rake would bring definite advantages?

THE VISCOUNT'S SCANDALOUS RETURN
Anne Ashley

Wrongly accused of murder, Viscount Blackwood left home disgraced. Now he has returned, and, along with the astute Miss Isabel Mortimer, he hunts the real culprit—while battling an ever-growing attraction to his beautiful companion …

THE VIKING'S TOUCH
Joanna Fulford

Courageous widow Lady Anwyn requires the protection of Wulfgar Ragnarsson, a legendary mercenary and Viking warrior. Anwyn learns from Wulfgar that not all men are monsters— but can they melt each other's frozen hearts?

MILLS & BOON

Mills & Boon®
Large Print Historical

THE LADY FORFEITS
Carole Mortimer

Lady Diana Copeland is determined to reject the outrageous marriage demands of Lord Faulkner! But on meeting him, she finds she must fight not to get lost in his intoxicating gaze… Or to make the worst forfeit of all and become his Countess!

VALIANT SOLDIER, BEAUTIFUL ENEMY
Diane Gaston

Rejecting Captain Gabriel Deane broke Emmaline Mableau's heart. She wears his ring around her neck: a reminder of the love she lost. Two years later, however, Emmaline has a proposal for him… but will *he* say yes?

WINNING THE WAR HERO'S HEART
Mary Nichols

The last thing war hero Viscount Cavenham needs is more conflict, but that is exactly what he gets when he comes up against rebellious Helen Wayland. As their animosity turns to attraction, he finds he no longer wants an enemy—he desires a wife!

HOSTAGE BRIDE
Anne Herries

Lady Rosamunde Meldreth is the prey of a dangerous man. As much as Raphael wants to walk away, he's forced to keep Rosamunde locked away in his castle—but then she discovers the dark knight wants a bride…

THE LADY CONFESSES
Carole Mortimer

Having run away from home, Lady Elizabeth Copeland must keep her drab disguise as a lady's companion at all times. Even when she's called upon to nurse the lady's nephew—who happens to be the handsomest man Elizabeth's ever seen…

THE DANGEROUS LORD DARRINGTON
Sarah Mallory

Lord Darrington may be an earl, but his bad reputation precedes him! Now the wicked Lord has found out the dark secret Beth Forrester will do *anything* to protect. How to buy a rake's silence? There is only one way—with her body!

THE UNCONVENTIONAL MAIDEN
June Francis

Headstrong Beth Llewellyn is put under the guardianship of Sir Gawain Raventon after her father's murder. Working with him to solve the mystery of her father's death, Beth begins to think perhaps marriage isn't such a terrible thing after all…

HER BATTLE-SCARRED KNIGHT
Meriel Fuller

It is only Count Giseux de St-Loup's code of chivalry that sees him escorting a sharp-tongued woman on a quest to help her injured brother. The Lady Brianna is fiercely independent and finds his powerful presence disturbing… but strangely enticing!

Mills & Boon®
Large Print Historical

THE DISAPPEARING DUCHESS
Anne Herries

New bride to the Duke of Avonlea, shy Lucinda felt her harrowing past was finally over—until word from her enemy forces her to flee. Lucinda leaves in order to save her husband Justin from scandal… But will he give her up so easily?

IMPROPER MISS DARLING
Gail Whitiker

When Alexander Stewart protests his brother's engagement to her younger sister, Emma Darling is furious at his effrontery—but her attraction to him is worse still! For if their siblings' match is unsuitable, a relationship between them is unthinkable…

BEAUTY AND THE SCARRED HERO
Emily May

Major Nicholas Reynolds returned from Waterloo a hero, but his battle-scarred face exiles him from high society. Lady Isabella Knox is intrigued by the man…but can she let herself lose her heart to the most notorious gentleman of the *ton*?

BUTTERFLY SWORDS
Jeannie Lin

During China's infamous Tang Dynasty, betrayed Princess Ai Li flees before her wedding. With only her delicate butterfly swords for a defence, she enlists the protection of Ryam, a blue-eyed warrior who finds it hard to resist her…

Mills & Boon®
Large Print Historical

THE MYSTERIOUS LORD MARLOWE
Anne Herries

The kidnappers of Jane Lanchester soon realise they have underestimated her. She escapes, helped by one of her captors! Fleeing for their lives, Jane and her mysterious gentleman form an attachment—now she can't bear the thought of losing him...

MARRYING THE ROYAL MARINE
Carla Kelly

Illegitimate Polly Brandon knows that Lieutenant Colonel Hugh Philippe Junot would never usually look at her, though having his protection for her journey to Portugal is a great comfort. But can she trust the growing desire she sees in Hugh's eyes?

A MOST UNLADYLIKE ADVENTURE
Elizabeth Beacon

When Captain Darke mistakenly presumes Lady Louisa Alstone to be her brother's mistress, she is shocked! But could the confusion be Louisa's chance to cast off the dictates of life as a Lady? The devilishly handsome Captain is *certainly* tempting ...

SEDUCED BY HER HIGHLAND WARRIOR
Michelle Willingham

Alex MacKinloch may have united the people of his clan, but can't breach the void between him and his wife. The pleasures of the marital bed seem long forgotten to Laren—yet lately, her husband has been gazing at her with an unmistakable hunger...

HIST0712 LP